the

pillow boy

of the

lady onogoro

Also by Alison Fell

the

pillow boy

of the

lady onogoro

ALISON FELL

Harcourt Brace & Company

NEW YORK   SAN DIEGO   LONDON

Requests for permission to make copies of any part of the work should be
mailed to: Permissions Department, Harcourt Brace & Company,
6277 Sea Harbor Drive, Orlando, Florida 32887-6777.

Library of Congress Cataloging-in-Publication Data
Fell, Alison.
The pillow boy of the Lady Onogoro/translated by Arye Blower:
with an introduction by Sir Geoffrey Montague-Pollock:
edited by Alison Fell.
p.   cm.
ISBN 0-15-100186-3
I. Title.
PR6056.E43P55   1996
823'.914—dc20   95-13169

First U.S. edition

A B C D E

Introduction

The Pillow Boy of the Lady Onogoro was written during the great mid-Heian flowering of the late tenth to early eleventh centuries, in a period which produced not only the world's first psychological novel in Lady Murasaki's *Tale of Genji*, but which saw Court poets like Izumi Shikibu and diarists such as Sei Shōnagon raise the feminine vernacular to a zenith of poetic expressiveness in works which, some scholars argue, form the cornerstone of classical Japanese literature. Into the brilliant circle at the Heian Court, then, came the poet Onogoro of the title, of whose real life we know little, except that she soared across the literary firmament in the first decades of the eleventh century and vanished thereafter into obscurity, bequeathing to Japanese literature some two hundred poems in which conciseness, clarity of image and philosophical reflection find their most eloquent and plangent expression.

The original manuscript of *The Pillow Boy* disappeared well before the end of the Heian era, and we can only guess at the magnitude – as well as the potential pitfalls – of the task faced by Professor Arye Blower and his collaborator, the poet and novelist Alison Fell, in assembling this version of the great prose romance from the six fragmentary variants discovered in the Kamakura period. Except in the unlikely event that a Heian manuscript is discovered, we shall never be sure which version of *The Pillow Boy* is closest to the original, but we must nevertheless admire the combination of scholarly rigour and literary flair which have imposed such an elegant order on what is virtually a literary jigsaw puzzle, thus bringing us the most authoritative version to date.

Ever since the attribution of *The Pillow Boy* to the poet Onogoro herself was first contested – in my opinion rightly – in the *Harvard Journal of Asiatic Studies* in the spring of 1963, a lively debate has raged around the question of authorship. Some scholars have ascribed the text to Sei Shōnagon, pointing to compelling similarities of tone between *The Pillow Boy* and her own *Pillow Book*, and suggesting that a rivalrous impulse on the part of the diarist might well have inspired this picaresque, not to say slanderous rendering of the life of the poet. Still others have argued with some persuasiveness that the lascivious fantasies contained in *The Pillow Boy* could only have stemmed from the overheated pen of a sexually and socially frustrated celibate – a young *bonze*, perhaps, in some provincial cloister. Indeed, much of the erotic material of the period – for example the *shunga*, or poem-picture scrolls, with their explicit depictions of sexual congress – did issue from a religious fraternity eager to supplement an income all too dependent on the shifting alliances of the noble clans who were their patrons. Of this overly psychological approach, however, let it merely be noted in passing that there are obvious dangers inherent in appraising the cultural products of ancient societies with the analytical eye of the post-Freudian.

In her wide-ranging book *Sexual/Textual Marginalisation and the Myth of the Great Author*, the respected feminist scholar Herta Baxter-Jones makes a case, albeit an idiosyncratic one, for joint authorship, pointing to the talented circle of women at the heart of mid-Heian literary activity and arguing that the erotic stories which are such a striking feature of the novel were intended explicitly to amuse and even to titillate an exclusively female *salon*. In my opinion, however, this approach, for all its militant modernism, runs the risk of belittling the sheer overarching stature of the work.

An hypothesis no less iconoclastic but more difficult to refute is put forward by the brilliant American classicist J. Dwight Ferguson, who proposes that the work may well be a deliberate parody of the predominant feminine genres of the Heian, executed by a talented but obscure scribe of middle rank. Certainly the combination of earthy vigour, emotional *chiaroscuro*, and formal innovation which distinguishes *The Pillow Boy* from the *zuihitsu* genre of the time and obliges us to set it at the very least on a level with the *Tale of Genji*, makes this an attractive if unorthodox argument.

The latter part of the Heian period saw the breakdown of the manorial system, the fall of the hegemonic Fujiwara house, rivalry between the Court nobles and the newly rising military class, and finally, in the twelfth century, the growth of a feudal society based on the authority of this military class. At the end of the twelfth century the Shōgunate, a system of government by military leaders, was established at Kamakura, replacing the old Imperial city with a new capital far away to the east. Civil war and social confusion left their mark on literature and the arts generally, and the great epics of war, such as the *Heike Monogatari*, took the place of the diaries and novels of the Court ladies. Whether the broader canvas employed by the writers of the Kamakura period represents a more mature stage in Japanese literature is of course arguable. But about the beauty and evocative power of the language of *The Pillow Boy* Japanese readers have always agreed since the first appearance of the book in the early eleventh century, and it is to Professor Blower and Alison Fell, that English-speaking readers are now indebted for affording them, a thousand years later, the same pleasure.

Geoffrey Montague-Pollock
St Antony's College, 1993

the

pillow boy

of the

lady onogoro

For Dave Cook, with love

It would console me
to see your face,
even fleetingly, between
lightning flashes at dusk

Izumi Shikibu (c. 976–1030)

Let me tell you, then, what I have heard of the one whose real name we never knew but who went under the title of the Lady Onogoro. Onogoro: the self-curdling one. It has a ring of hubris, as if she wished above all to disown her parents and create herself anew, rise from the foam like her namesake, that very first island of Japan which, legend tells us, curdled itself from the brine dripping from the Heavenly Jewelled Spear of the god Izanagi.

To be quite honest, none of us was entirely sure how the Lady came to the Imperial Court in the first place. It could have been that her father the Tax Inspector was owed a favour by someone of influence in the Capital, or perhaps word of her poetic talents had reached the ear of the *Dainagon* himself; whatever the truth of it, Palace records tell us only that the so-called Lady Onogoro arrived in the City of Peace and Tranquillity in the sixth month of the Year of the Hare in the reign of Emperor Ichijō II, during the Regency of Fujiwara Yorimichi, son of the great Michinaga.

We can't be certain which gate she entered by, or whether she came by bullock-cart or gilded litter; we can imagine, though, that she was fatigued by the long journey from her father's manor in the Eastland, and that she clutched her inkstone and brushes – her only collateral, as it were – anxiously to her breast, and perhaps, as she passed under the carved and lacquered arch which marks the entrance to the Imperial Enclosure, that she lowered her arrogant brows and for one apprehensive moment frowned at herself for her cheap slippers and her unwomanly ambition.

Without delay, then, the lady would have been installed in one of the apartments reserved for Ladies-in-Waiting, dressed by maidservants in underwear of scarlet lawn and outerwear of layered silk embroidered with almond blossom and peacocks, and presented with all due ceremony to her mistress the Princess Saishō, although God knows the Princess was still at the age for dolls and could hardly have been expected to show much interest in a provincial poet twice her age.

With what occupations, then, would such a newcomer have busied herself in the ensuing months?

She wrote, of course; she attended the poetry contests that coincide with our seasonal festivals – the Chrysanthemum Festival, the Festival of First Fruits, and the like; she became acquainted not only with the interminable regulations of the Court but also with the protocol surrounding the composition of poetry.

For instance, our lady learned that Chinese characters, being so very difficult to execute, are considered inappropriate as a medium for female poets, and are reserved for masculine use. But if feminine stubbornness dictated that she apply herself, therefore, to the study of the proscribed language, our Onogoro rapidly came to the opinion that Chinese was an unwieldy instrument which was ill-suited to convey subtle imagery and tended, furthermore, to foster the most archaic forms of expression, and accordingly she decided that she would far rather be fluent in her own tongue than clumsy and pretentious in another.

There were other duties besides poetry to claim her attention, however. Onogoro was also required to preside regularly at the table of the young Princess Saishō, to instruct her in calligraphy, and, with the other Ladies-in-Waiting, to attend her in the bedchamber.

Sometimes she was obliged to attend the gatherings in the Daigoku-den which marked the anniversaries of the Emperor, his Imperial Consorts, and their children, the many half-brothers and sisters of the Princess Saishō, and although her father wrote from the Eastland that this was high honour indeed, Onogoro, observing the studied manners of the Emperor's entourage with dislike, decided that she could not think of anything more hateful than to be yet another filly in the Imperial stable. (Some have suggested, in fact, that Onogoro's father expressly intended that his daughter should catch the eye of Emperor Ichijō and attain the elevated position of Imperial Concubine, and if this never came to pass it would certainly be fair to conclude that the Lady Onogoro's temperament, being somewhat standoffish, militated against it.)

The lady was not without suitors, however, being courted, if not by the Emperor himself, then by courtiers of fairly high rank. In keeping with the libertarian practices of the Court, she entered eventually into a liaison with His Excellency the General Taira no Motosuke, about whom, being inexperienced for her age, she conceived many fantasies.

For instance, she wished that her lover the General would build her a moon-viewing terrace on the roof of her apartments, so that she could see clear across the roofs of the Capital to Lake Biwa and the starry mountains beyond. Dreaming of this, her heart would swell with happiness and her body would mysteriously take on the configurations of the night landscape – dark, slumberous, bamboo-thicketed, a landscape dotted with pines shaped like parasols and cleft by gleaming rivers where herons bent their necks to fish.

Better still, if the General would build her a house of her own, in the Third Ward, perhaps, outside the Imperial Enclosure, where she could come and go freely. Here at Court she was cloistered, observed, constrained by rules. It is exactly like living with one's mother, she decided. Whenever discontent surges up in me, there is someone at hand to tell me not to complain! Whereas on a high terrace, she thought longingly, one could speak to the moon in all her phases, one could sleep sweetly under her protection while the landscape, bathed in pale rays, took on the configurations of a woman's body; one could stir at midnight, startled into happy wakefulness by her good and brooding light.

Daylight separates us all too often from our dreams, however, and the General Taira no Motosuke was a married man who visited his mistress only at those times when he could properly extricate himself from his responsibilities. And although it is far from uncommon for a nobleman to move a prized mistress into the domestic abode, or for a concubine to supplant a wife entirely, the love affair had already lasted several months and Onogoro – who was impatient in love as in all other matters – found herself still in the irksome position of playing second fiddle.

Now, when hopes and dreams, however childish, are continually frustrated, one can be sure that rage, in one guise or another, will preside like an unwelcome guest at the banquet of lovemaking. And so by and by it happened that the Lady Onogoro found herself facing a certain obdurate problem which she could not bring herself to confess to her lover but rather – since the passionate pessimism of her nature was offset by a cool ingenuity of mind – contrived to solve in her own way. We speak here, of course, of that satisfied desire which must be the aim of all lovers, and which adverse circumstance or unruly emotion may delay to a degree incompatible with conjugal pleasure and dignity.

Tongues of Silver

~

When you visit me in winter,
Don't be deterred by the curtain
Of icicles over the door:
Just bring your sharpest sword.

'Oyu! Oyu!'

From her vantage point on the balcony Onogoro once again sent her voice fluttering out across the Almond Blossom Garden to the walled stableyard beyond. Obtaining no answer, she turned back to the interior and cried for her serving maid, who hovered behind the inner screen door. 'Tokiden! Where is that boy?'

Her mistress's anxiety had quite communicated itself to the phlegmatic girl, and Tokiden's voice trembled a little as she whispered urgently: 'My Lady, His Excellency is in the entrance hall!'

'Well tell him to wait,' Onogoro ordered. 'Show him to the anteroom and fetch rice cakes and wine.' Shrugging helplessly, she touched two lacquered fingernails to that point between the eyebrows where tears gather and, if unshed, form unsightly wrinkles, rather in the way that a fever unbled by leeches will live on in the circulatory system and congeal in crystalline deposits around the vital organs. She allowed the tears to flow for a few moments during which the painted cranes on the *tsuitate* screen behind the bed dais swam and dissolved agreeably, but the respite was short-lived. For the General was in the antechamber, the General was at the door, and the Lady Onogoro was dry as a black bean in a winter larder. Not that this would have mattered with her previous lovers, who had been neither numerous nor sophisticated; General Motosuke, on the other hand, was both experienced and discerning, and the boy Oyu was nowhere to be found.

Just then three soft knocks on the screen door announced the young man himself.

Oyu was a tall, stooping young fellow, more wiry than strapping in build, with a reserved demeanour which, rather as the leaden skies of early spring are pierced by sudden teasing shafts of sun, gave way from time to time to a sweetly slanting smile all the more tantalising for the sheer scarcity of its appearance. Their acquaintance was too recent, however, to dispense with the protocol demanded by Onogoro's superior rank and so, standing before her in the plain indigo robe which replaced his stableboy's apron on those occasions, Oyu bowed scrupulously and listened without expression to the lady's whispered instructions.

With some relief, then, our self-curdling lady sets about preparing for her General. First she draws down the blinds, shutting out the distant haze of the river and its red dots of sampans. Next she reverses the *tsuitate* screen so that the innocent painted cranes on the outside disappear, and the inner screen unfolds to reveal the hidden *shunga* – an elegantly executed design of a coupling which, though precise enough in its detail to arouse the General, had unfortunately ceased to have any effect whatsoever on Onogoro. Men, Onogoro's mother had reminded her in the course of their chilly farewells, require constant novelty, and it is therefore not only impolitic but fruitless to upbraid them for their infidelities. As the Lady Onogoro loosened her *obi* and disposed her limbs on the bed the memory of this unwelcome wisdom filled her mind with mutinous thoughts. What women require, she brooded resentfully – for, as we shall see, she was much given to brooding – is never an issue!

His Excellency Taira no Motosuke divested himself of his sword and quiver, his eyes absorbing the low table by the balcony screen on which lay Onogoro's writing box, its lid open to reveal a paraphernalia of inkstone, untidily strewn brushes, and half-finished scrolls. In the brief periods that he allotted to reflection, the General had decided that his most recent mistress was admirable, if enigmatic. In truth he did not know what excited him most – her coolness, the elegance of her verse, or her capacity for unpredictable outbursts of passion and weeping.

Onogoro reclined on the bed, looking quite ravishing, he thought, in her wistaria-coloured kimono with its *mon* of a peacock with spread tail. Bowing low, he paid his respects with a poem composed laboriously – for the General lacked a facility – over several days:

> Do not imagine that I am as patient
> As the woodsman in the old fable,
> Who waited so long that leaves sprouted
> From the handle of his axe.

Onogoro inclined her head in acknowledgement, allowing Motosuke to glimpse the contrast between the bluish sheen of her hair and the soft whiteness of her nape.

Holding out her hands to display the ink stains left by the afternoon's labours, she responded with the well-known poem from the Eastland:

> I pound the rice
> And my hands are chapped.
> Tonight my young prince
> Will take them and sigh.

Hiding her agitation, Onogoro drew the General down beside her and allowed him to loosen the folds of her robe. What else she would allow him to loosen, however, was a matter in the face of which soothsayers, herbalists, and astrologers had confessed themselves helpless – not, after all, often being required to answer queries on a subject which is generally considered to be satisfactorily addressed, if not by the man's technique, then by the numerous *shunga* which he may employ to excite desire in his mistress.

Not, it must be stressed, that the Lady Onogoro was deficient in desire itself, but rather in the certain achievement of its sweet and explosive culmination. So what harm would it do to His Excellency, she thought, if a lady had in her head a cornucopia of stories to arouse her past the point of no return? And what harm could it do if the stories issued not from her own imagination but from the imagination of another – from a book, as it were? And if the tales issued not from a book – their author being, by no fault of his own, illiterate – but from a warm-blooded body? And if that body were to conceal itself behind the *tsuitate* screen at the head of the lady's bed – a living book, if you like, blowing the warm breath of its stories directly from human mouth to human ear – well then, what possible harm could it do?

On the *tsuitate* screen, from her vantage point behind a spray of cherry blossom, the tiny *voyeuse* spied interminably on the conjugation of veined penis and whorled labia. She had long ago given up envying these painted companions of hers, and with the demise of her jealousy her desire also had faded. It was as if her creator, the lowly painter Ko-Iyu, had transmitted through his passionate brushstrokes his agonised desire for God knows which courtesan or Lady of the Bedchamber; as if, decades ago, he had fired the minuscule body of the *voyeuse* with his own quivering lust, but as time passed and the ink faded upon the yellowing screen, all verve had gone out of her, and her bright little eye had dulled, and her spying had become as half-hearted as Ko-Iyu's cooling passion.

Silver-tongued Oyu, as it happens, would gladly have sacrificed the entirety of his story-telling talent in exchange for that jaded little eye – had he only known about it, which of course he did not. Blind as he was, Oyu could not see the *tsuitate* screen at the head of the bed, nor the thumb-sized *voyeuse*, nor the coupling that bored her so. Nor, more importantly, could he see the bed itself, and upon it the Lady Onogoro, and, between her thighs, the greying, noble, industrious head of the General Taira no Motosuke.

Chameleon Fritters

'In ancient times there once reigned at Nara an Emperor of such cruel lusts that the Gods punished him by causing to grow on the back of his head a protuberance not unlike the new spring horn of a deer. This misfortune befell him in his fiftieth year, but did not deter him from his lustful pursuits, for which he neglected not only the Lady Empress, his Second and Third wives, and several mistresses and their offspring, but also the affairs of State. These last he delegated to the Minister Li an Sho, who devised a tax-gathering machinery which so inflamed the masses that the Empire was rocked to its foundations. But that, however, is another story.

'In the Emperor's Northern Palace in Shinano lived a Lady-in-Waiting whose daughter Akido, although only fifteen, grew daily in beauty, liveliness and intelligence. Not only was she a skilled performer on the zithern, and adept at Chinese characters, but she also had a flair for naturalism, and nothing delighted her more than to wander the summer mountains observing the many species of butterflies which sported among the gorse and azalea flowers of the high pastures. With her inkstone and brush she would dazzlingly record the flicker of a wing in mid air or the poignant second of a coupling – for the virginal Akido was too pure to see anything in nature that was not innocent, a fact which both touched and excited the Emperor, accustomed as he was to jaded courtesans and their over-expert attentions. But his loins, as ever, took precedence over any gentle empathy in his heart, and he resolved to lay before the girl visions that would shatter her childish attitudes and awaken in her the knowledge of evil, not to mention the capacity for desire.

'As summer turned to autumn the Emperor was obliged to return to the Capital, but the girl Akido was never far from his thoughts. At the first possible opportunity he summoned his retinue and set out through the reddening maples to the Northern province of mists and rainbows. As the ox-carts drew near to the mountains of Shinano, snow whitened the rutted road, growing deeper as they toiled up the steep pass which led to the Palace.

'At the head of the pass the Emperor paused a while beneath a pine tree to meditate on the melancholy beauty of the scene spread out below – the snow-covered roofs of the Palace poised above scarlet pillars and emerald-tiled eaves, the bare black branches of the cherry trees in the ornamental gardens, and the steam which rose from the bath-house on the shores of the ice-bound lake.

'Having already established that tomorrow was Akido's sixteenth birthday, he had brought with him an inordinate number of gifts of bright silk stuffs, finely worked ivory fans, *netsuke* of enamelled porcelain, and tortoiseshell combs inlaid with gold *hiramaki* lacquer, all to be presented to her at the celebration feast. But the best gift of all, the gift which held pride of place in the Emperor's cruel wooing, would be saved until last, and savoured till then in secret.

'On the following evening Akido received her anniversary gifts with all the modesty and poise of her well-bred young womanhood. The Emperor watched the birdlike movements of her fingers on the strings of the *samisen* which was her mother's gift, and his senses were aroused. Akido lowered her eyes shyly when the Emperor's gifts were presented, but as the silks were unfolded and the precious combs admired, the Emperor's thoughts were on his last and final offering, and he could hardly contain his impatience.

'So many and various were the delicacies the Emperor refused at the banquet that his Ministers and Bodyguard feared he had succumbed to a fever. From the delicious jellied soup of the region to the succulent roast duck, from the ptarmigan to the sweet fritters of chameleon, everything was offered humbly and everything was refused.

'At last the Hour of the Bull struck, and the assembled company, red-cheeked and merry from rice wine, were instructed to move to the balcony.

17

'Over the mountains a cold moon was setting as into the courtyard below was led the Emperor's final gift, to the accompaniment of wild applause. A proud black stallion stood before the revellers, and at his side a chestnut filly on the elegant threshold of maturity. On the balcony Akido, her modest demeanour quite overtaken by enthusiasm, clapped her hands in delight at this combination of power and grace. Tethered to a rail, the filly stood docile and lovely while the stallion, bridled by a servant, showed a fine mettle.

'Meanwhile the Emperor had been spying on Akido with sidelong glances, and now, with a nod at the servant, he indicated that the animal should be unbridled and loosed. Whereupon the beast, rolling a gleaming eye at the tethered filly, reared up on her tender flanks and exhibited a member such as had never been seen by the oldest crone in the company, let alone by the sheltered Akido.

'Springing forward at some risk to his skull, the manservant anointed both the vast rod and the defenceless rump of the filly with pig's grease, abetting the entrance of one into the other without miss or mistake. The hapless filly let out a great whinny of pain at this invasion of her immature orifice, but still the rod stretched and the stallion plunged, and on the balcony the Emperor smiled into his sumptuous sleeve and watched Akido for signs of reaction. Surely the lustful thrusts of the stallion would arouse a quiver in her, if not the piteous cries of the ravished filly? On the balcony one of the Ladies-in-Waiting uttered a shriek and fainted clean away, but Akido's lovely profile remained grave, and although she did not avert her eyes from the beastly performance in the yard, nor did she betray by any slight moistening of the lips or quickening of the breath other than a scholarly and scientific interest.

'The Emperor's unsatisfied lust kept him sleepless until

the dawn of the next day when, hearing that Akido and her maids were to journey to the temple of K. to make offerings on behalf of her late grandmother, he leapt from his tousled couch and ordered his drivers to convey him to the Hanging Cloud Bridge which spanned the Hyo gorge, and over which Akido's party must assuredly pass. Before setting out, however, he instructed his Bodyguard to procure a donkey from the stables and tether it behind his carriage.

'When the Emperor's party came in sight of the airy bridge a howl of wolves sounded from the dark pine forest on the mountain slopes, and the donkey, whose back was laden with a thick coat of new snow, brayed with distress. With a smile of anticipation the Emperor ordered a fresh loin of pork to be strapped under the beast's quivering belly, and in this way, swaddled by the dripping meat, and tethered to the rail of the narrow bridge, the donkey awaited its fate, while the Emperor, concealing himself in a pine grove beside the road, awaited the arrival of Akido.

'Before long the hungry howls of the wolves grew louder, and first one silvery shape and then another slunk out of the purple-shadowed snows of the forest and, pointing their sharp snouts to Heaven, bayed their thanks for the breakfast that had been prepared for them.

'With a tinkle of harness bells and the high clear sound of feminine laughter, Akido's party came into view and started across the bridge. The sight that met them was a chilling one, and even the stolid oxen stamped and snorted in horror. For as the first wolf sprang at the pork meat on the donkey's belly, the second sank its teeth in his throat, and the poor beast let out a terrible shriek and went down.

'Akido and her ladies sat frozen on the cart, while the Emperor spied from the pine grove, once again hoping to discern some sign of excitation on the young woman's lovely features. By now the wolf pack had grown and the pork loin was strewn in red slivers across the snow. When the teeth tore into the belly of the donkey Akido let out a cry and buried her face in her sleeve, so that the Emperor was denied the satisfaction of observing her response to the sight of the burrowing heads and urgent paws which dragged out the donkey's entrails and drew them steaming across the bloody snow. So frustrated was he, in fact, and so inflamed by the spectacle, that he dragged the cook's daughter from her father's ox-cart and, throwing her garments over her head, had her without ceremony on a frozen carpet of pine needles.

'There was little sleep for the Emperor on the nights that followed, and on the day of Akido's expected return he found himself, thick-headed and sullen as a thief, prowling through her apartments in the west wing of the Palace.

'Dismissing the elderly attendant who remained there, he entered Akido's bedchamber and saw in the centre of the room a cage woven of palm-leaf slivers, in which poised, perched, and fluttered butterflies of all the colours of the rainbow.

'The Emperor brooded on the delicate cage and its frail occupants until his heart thundered in the cage of his body. Unable to bear this dumb unaccustomed drumbeat a moment longer, he threw back his garments and produced a more familiar organ. In a fit of vengeful fury the Emperor opened the door of the cage and thrust his member inside, hoping perhaps to crush the senseless beauty of the wings, hoping to put an end to something.

'But as he thrust angrily he felt the first touch of a wing against his erect flesh, and then another, and then the hovering feet as light as whispers, until his member was no longer a bare rod but a veritable baton of butterflies, which caressed it with such graceful generosity that had the Emperor been a man of imagination he would have given thanks, and wept, and adopted the rough habit of the monastery. But being an Emperor with a heart hard as horn and two protuberances to prove it, he could accept the exquisite sensations no longer. To stand there swooning like a Fool at the Flower Feast was an affront to dignity, rank, and manhood, and, thrusting mercilessly once again, the Emperor reached his Imperial climax stickily in the butterfly cage, and raged out of the bedchamber.

'When Akido returned that afternoon she saw the open door of the cage and, within, the midden of crushed butterflies, and she knew that if she were to escape the Emperor's cruel attentions she must flee the Palace immediately. Her maidservants, who understandably feared for their own lives more than for their mistress's honour, begged her pardon but urged her to consider accepting His Highness. After all, as a valued concubine she would be granted riches and manors and her children would attain the highest positions in the Empire. But Akido shook her head, and pointed to the ravished cage, and, weeping, released them from her service. She would escape alone, she told them sadly, so that no hint of blame could fall on their heads.

'By this time the Emperor, maddened by the insistent memory of the gentle wings, decided that he had dallied long enough. In his darkest moments he was certain that even the lowest serving-man was whispering behind his sleeve about this foolish wooing, and that he was fast becoming a laughing-stock.

'As the Emperor brooded on his balcony his Bodyguard approached in haste and bowed low. One of Akido's sewing-women, fearing His Highness's wrath should he discover that her mistress had slipped away, had sent word that the flight would take place that very evening. Would His Highness give the order to apprehend the Lady Akido? the Bodyguard enquired. Thanking the man, the Emperor ordered a phalanx of bowmen dispatched to the girl's apartments without delay; then, with the image of the butterflies still nagging in his mind, he commanded the sewing-woman to be brought before him.

'That afternoon the Palace resounded with scandal and rumour. The Emperor had abducted Akido; the Emperor had arrested Akido; the Emperor held Akido under armed guard in his Imperial apartments.

'In the evening a messenger set out from the Northern Palace at a gallop, with orders not to pause for sleep or refreshment until he had reached the distant town of N., and procured there, from a certain street vendor, a cage of the many-hued butterflies of the mountain pastures.

'Next day came, and the next, and still Akido awaited her fate. In the meantime the messenger had returned, and the sewing-woman, cursing the craven impulse which had led her to betray her mistress, was employed night and day upon a task which pierced her heart and stung her eyes with bitter tears.

'That night snow fell thickly on the roofs of the Palace. On his balcony the Emperor inhaled the frosty air and, laughing, quoted Princess Nunakawa's famous reply to Prince Ōkuninushi of the Eight Thousand Spears:

> Although now I may be
> a free, selfish bird of my own,
> later I shall be yours,
> a bird ready to submit to your will.

There was no pleasure, he reflected, greater than that of anticipation.

'At last he ordered Akido to be brought before him. What an enchanting picture she made, he thought, with her eyes downcast and her face half-hidden behind a flower-patterned fan! With a cruel smile he took her hand

and led her to the couch, where he bade her sit and be comfortable.

'The sewing-woman, summoned to attend, entered the room with a woeful face. In her hands she held a scarlet lacquered box, and this she presented to the Emperor. "My dear girl," he said, beaming at Akido. "Let it never be said that I am not lavish with my gifts."

'First the Emperor knelt down and removed Akido's sandals. Then he took off her white slipper-socks. And then, opening the lacquered box, he brought forth a pair of shoes which made Akido's face turn alabaster white, and her eyes roll upwards in their sockets.

'For the shoes were fashioned from several hundreds of butterflies: orange and black Red Admirals made up the soles, Silver Fritillary the uppers, and the ankles boasted three contrasting trims of Tortoiseshell, and Swallowtail, and Cabbage White. And all the lovely wings fluttered in a helpless unison of pain, for the sewing-woman had been under strict instructions that every one of the creatures which made up the vile shoes should remain alive.

'The Emperor took Akido's right foot in his hands, and inserted it into the right shoe. Then he took her left foot and inserted it into the left shoe. Then he drew her roughly to her feet and, grasping her arm, commanded her to walk.

'The poor girl wept and shrieked at such a fate, but the Emperor, triumphant, brooked no resistance. Under her soles she felt the delicate framework of the wings crack and crumble, and the dying bodies crushed to a soft and horrible mire until her blameless feet were steeped in crime, for every move she made was a murder.

'Forcing her on, the Emperor watched her tremors with an awful relish. For with each step she took, and each frail back she broke, he felt her resistance break a little more. As the tremors mounted up her slender calves to reach her thighs, the Emperor put his hand on her virgin breast and felt a burning heat rise to his fingers, and saw with joy the brutal shame which flowered scarlet on her cheeks.

'And when the whole wide room was crossed and the last butterfly limp and broken, the Emperor thrust his hand into Akido's nether garments, where his fingers encountered a pleasure-point already slicked with the first meltwaters of spring. Hearing the fledgling cries rise up in her throat, he loosed his bursting member from the folds of his robe and scooped her on to the bed dais in the triumphant knowledge that, despite herself, the Lady Akido wished for nothing more cruelly and more keenly than to surrender herself utterly to her own pleasure.'

The Lady Onogoro, who had been poised on the brink for so long that His Excellency's tongue was quite limp with fatigue, rose up like a phoenix towards the sun and expired with a series of birdlike shrieks, her spread wings aflame with incandescent pleasure.

Hearing her cries of gratification, Oyu too was gratified, for his nature, as befitted his modest station in life, tended to the worshipful, and if the restrictions of his role caused him undue suffering, he could console himself with the thought that the General might in this instance be the craftsman of love, but he who addressed the deeper complexities of the heart was most certainly the artist.

As for those sceptics who refuse to believe that Onogoro's lover was oblivious to the heady whispers of the story-teller, let them merely search their experience, for there they will surely find more than one fellow whose brain, ruling him like a tyrant, entirely suppresses the intelli-gence his five senses might otherwise afford him. In this way, as we shall see, by censoring from his awareness all that does not accord with will, decision, and reason, a powerful man may persuade himself that he is in full command of his destiny.

Cloves on the Wind

~≈

Some days after the Festival of Red Leaves a storm blew up on Lake Biwa and moved south across the Capital, whipping the Great North Gate with hailstones and sending gales through the galleried corridors of the Imperial Enclosure, so that all the Ladies-in-Waiting fastened their screen doors tightly and watched from the Plum Blossom Chamber or the Wistaria Chamber as the trees which gave the pavilions their names lashed to and fro, and the tall poplars beyond the garden walls swayed dangerously.

From the window of the Almond Blossom Pavilion the Lady Onogoro watched the perilous rooks' nests in the topmost branches, so rickety that the sky appeared to blow right through them. Taking out her inkstone and brushes, she wrote swiftly:

> Clouds scratch the tree-tops.
> When you are gone the sky
> Sweeps through the sparse twigs
> Of my empty nest.

Now on a gloomy day in late autumn a lady might be better employed in drinking tea with her acquaintances, mixing perfumes, or replenishing her winter wardrobe than in brooding on the imaginary losses sustained in the game of love. But, like all poets and solitaries, Onogoro pursued her morose moods with tenacity, hoping thus to hunt down the cause of her unease and remove its claws, but contriving as often to lose sight of her elusive quarry and merely entangle herself more deeply in the undergrowth.

Determinedly, then, Onogoro waited for her mood of melancholy to curdle into thoughts, and as usual a vision of the General's wife rose up to torment her. In the Lady Ochibu's chamber the braziers always glowed, and the vases, lit and quiet, contained delightful flowers, and the Lady's silk-clad belly swelled with its legitimate fruit, and the General, all unarmoured, murmured love-words to her in the lap of the firelight.

This was the theatre of earthly delights at which Onogoro was a mere spectator, but now the voice of her mother nagged from the wings, and its first brusque utterance was, Think yourself lucky, my girl. Think yourself honoured indeed that His Excellency treats you with consideration, visits you whenever his commitments allow, and is not one of those libertines who keeps three wives and six concubines, and deceives all of them by embarking on secret intrigues! Furthermore, the voice enjoined, for the daughter of a District Tax Inspector of the Tenth Rank to rise to the station of Court Poet and Lady-in-Waiting is almost without precedent. The voice continued its reproachful litany, reminding Onogoro that her mother had married beneath her, and that the lot of a country tax inspector's wife could hardly be compared to the radiant elegance of life at the Imperial Court. Be grateful, it warned, for the General's protection, and banish absolutely any jealous ill-wishing of his wife, or things will surely go badly for you.

Remorse gripped Onogoro, for if any harm should come to the Lady Ochibu during her confinement, the responsibility would certainly be seen to lie with her rival. Drawing to her a scroll of heavy cream-coloured paper scented with cloves, she dashed off a hasty note in the form of a poem.

> Not all the raging storms
> Of autumn
> Can mar the beauty
> Of the ripening moon
> Or taint its light.

Tying the scroll with a spray of almond blossom cunningly rendered in shaded silks, she dispatched Tokiden to the house of the Lady Ochibu. Tokiden hurried through the moated streets with her mantle clasped tightly around her and her head tucked in like a turtle's against the butting wind. On arrival at the house, however, she found the servants in disarray.

'The Soothsayers are here,' said a young maid of her acquaintance. 'Last night My Lady had a dream of black crows, and now she's all on tenterhooks about the child. Between you and me, it'll take more than dream-interpreters to soothe her!'

Tokiden pressed her mistress's gift on the girl, who persuaded her to linger in the servants' quarters until the storm had abated. The maid, whose aunt was midwife not only to the Lady Ochibu but also to many noblewomen of the Capital, was much given to lugubrious gossip, and entertained Tokiden with reports of recent Bad Omens. For instance, only yesterday the Lady S. had given birth to a boy child with one natural brown eye and the other blue as the emerald tiles on the roof of the Daigoku-den. Common rumour had it that the father was a bandit-priest who had sought shelter in the lady's house after escaping the custody of the Palace Guard; on inspecting the child, however, the Soothsayers had declared a Possession, and mediums were at this very moment attempting to drive the evil spirit from the unlucky infant . . . The girl related this and other tales with relish, and would probably have gone on all afternoon if Tokiden, refusing the steamed rice pressed upon her, had not reminded her that the Lady Onogoro's letter remained to be delivered.

In the Lady Ochibu's chamber incense burned in the four corners of the room, and wind and rain battered at the closed shutters. Concealed behind her curtains-of-state, Ochibu submitted to the Soothsayers' interrogation.

'If My Lady could only remember whether the crows came from the north or west, and whether they flew high or low, and whether they uttered human cries or barked like dogs, and, most importantly, what colour were their eyes . . .'

'Red!' cried the Lady Ochibu, starting up from her couch. 'Red like the eyes of Hachimon the war god.'

The Soothsayers were much disturbed, and retired to the far side of the room to consult in whispers. An ill-wishing or a possession was one thing, they agreed, but a Portent of the First Class must be recorded at the Bureau of Divination without delay, and a copy of the report passed to the Regent himself. Particularly since this Portent issued from the wife of a noble of the great Taira family, which in recent years had extended its fiefdoms to include some eight northern provinces, and which, like the Minamoto family before it, could ultimately threaten the power of the Fujiwara. If it came to open conflict, which way the General's allegiance might swing was a moot question.

But this was not, they reminded themselves thankfully, a question for them, rather one to be dealt with by the highest echelons of the Council of State. And so they prudently checked their thoughts, which otherwise might have spiralled as wildly as leaves in the storm wind, and agreed to say nothing to the Lady Ochibu, but instead to pass the matter on to the appropriate authority.

A timid knock on the door announced the Lady Ochibu's maid, who carried in the elegant scroll with its ribbon of silk blossoms, and also a draught of wind which disturbed the curtains-of-state around the couch and bore the heavy scent of cloves to the lady who reclined there, so that even before she extended her hand to receive the letter, Ochibu sensed the powerful and exotic presence of her rival, the poet Onogoro.

In her delicate condition the Lady Ochibu was already prey to a host of worries and alarms, and the sight of the letter whipped those to a frenzy. For although the position of the First Wife is secured by both law and custom, she had succeeded only in taming the jealous feelings occasioned by her husband's secondary liaison, not in banishing them. She knew, of course, that a nobleman who cleaves only to one wife offends propriety, and will be considered no man at all if the position continues for too long. But although Ochibu had bowed her head before convention – jealousy being, after all, one of the seven grounds for divorce – she could not help resenting the passing of those sweet years when she had had no rival. Her one consolation was that, after the first few days of fervent protest, she had not betrayed her feelings by word or deed, but had kept them not only from her husband but even from her closest intimates. None but her own conscience could have known the bitterness she felt towards Onogoro. Now, however, as she held the letter in her hand, her fury threatened to fly out into the room for all to see and all to judge. How she must hate me! Ochibu told herself. What harm she must wish me!

Trembling, the gentle Ochibu forced herself to open the scroll and read. But as she scanned the poem urgently her eyes filled with tears, for she could discern no ill will in the perfectly formed characters, only the most generous of good wishes. All the same, she took the precaution of cupping a protective hand over the child which nestled in her belly. When the birth was due, she decided, she would have ten Ladies-in-Waiting, rather than the usual six, to lie on the west side of the couch and lure the evil spirits away from the precious infant!

In the Almond Blossom Chamber Onogoro once again bent over her writing table. In two days time the Princess Saishō would undergo the Ceremony of Initiation, and the Putting on of the Skirt required a celebratory poem from all the Court poets. Try as she might, however, inspiration eluded her, and her brushstrokes produced only characters rickety as the perched crows' nests, a lattice of black twigs through which the white paper ached like empty sky.

Hidden on the inner side of the *tsuitate* screen the tiny *voyeuse*, who knew everything there was to know about the pains of envy, and who had heard a multitude of courtiers chide their jealous concubines, laughed grimly to herself. Little wonder, she mused, that the crow was a bird which was never depicted: never painted by artists, nor enamelled by potters, nor sung of by poets. The mandarin duck, the crane, the cormorant – all those had their place. But of all the birds, none but the exiled crow could speak of the empty nest which jealousy left in the heart. Meanwhile, beyond the wall of the Great Enclosure, the poplars tossed their heads like angry women, and inside their apartments the noble ladies burned incense at their corner shrines and humbly begged forgiveness for their wicked and rivalrous thoughts.

Fallen Arrows

On the steps of the Hall of Military Virtue His Excellency Taira no Motosuke watched the archers of the Bodyguard of the Right draw back their bows in unison. There was a satisfactory twang as the arrows were released, and then a high-pitched song as they arched across the courtyard, but in the buffeting wind few found their targets, and instead fell impotently among the blown leaves at the far end of the Riding Ground.

It was hardly a day for archery contests, brooded the General, who was irked by Yorimichi's absence. His Excellency the Regent was indisposed, the Bodyguard had told him. A slight fever. Physicians in attendance. A fine excuse, he suspected, for Yorimichi to slip away for a few hours at the House of the Flower Fan – as if the man didn't already have three consorts and the pick of the Palace concubines!

Shrouded in his ceremonial armour, the General fumed unseen. If Yorimichi had charged him with the responsibility for imposing discipline on the ranks of the Imperial Guard – a thankless task, and one which he would not have sought of his own accord – then the least the Regent could do was attend this sorry display!

Rain pitted the yellow dust of the compound as the second rank of archers shuffled forward, ungainly in their hinged iron leg-guards and bearskin-trimmed boots, weighed down by their canopied skirts and breastplates of stencilled leather. The General noted the raggedness of the line with a mixture of scorn and dismay. Once the glory of the Capital, the Guard were by now as useless as their armour was archaic – yet from this raggle-taggle crew he must forge a fighting garrison!

More and more Yorimichi's absence smacked of half-heartedness. But then, he reflected, the Fujiwara had always been slow to recognise the need for force, and when civil unrest obliged them to, they were happy enough to call upon the military families to defend their interests. When the priests' mercenaries had swarmed down from Hiei-zan to threaten the City of Peace and Tranquillity, the General himself had summoned the Taira armies from their northern domains and routed the invasion. Statesmen the Fujiwara might be, and skilled as snakes in diplomacy and intrigue, but what they failed to recognise was that in the world beyond the confines of the Capital land mattered more than honours, and force was more effective than law. And Yorimichi could scatter Ministerial Honours and tax immunities like morning-glory petals at the Flower Feast, but ultimately it was the military power of the Minamoto and the Taira on which the stability of the country depended.

Not for nothing, then, did the Fujiwara marry its sons and daughters into the ranks of these great families, as well as into the Imperial clan itself. His own wife, the Lady Ochibu, was one of the many offspring of Yorimichi's brother Motostune – although his marriage, he reminded himself, had been a love-match, at least in the first years, before childbirth and three miscarriages had taken their toll of the Lady Ochibu's slender figure and physical vitality. He had to admit, however, that she remained a woman of sterling qualities. Indeed, her docility and tact were so renowned at Court that even those ladies who in the past had been his concubines were drawn to her as friend and confidante. In short, apart from a few regrettable scenes when he had first begun to visit the Lady Onogoro, Ochibu's temperament was a blessing, and one much envied by his less fortunate acquaintances, who considered that the General had settled on the perfect type of wife: a woman without a hysterical bone in her body, a veritable treasure in the house.

Thinking this, the General's gloom lifted, and his mood changed to one of satisfaction. As soon as the tedious competition was over, he decided, he would send his serving-man to order a nest of thirty sandalwood boxes containing nursing-robes for Ochibu and swaddling cloths for the new child. He would also instruct the monks of the Kiyomizudera to recite *sutras* every day until the birth. Then, his affairs in good order, he would pay a call on the lovely and troubling Onogoro.

The Zig-zag Bridge

While the General congratulated himself on his good fortune his mistress, who had failed to summon the tender patience with which the muse must be wooed, and had mistakenly tried to bully her instead, gave vent to her temper. First she ripped the draft of her poem for Princess Saishō in two, in four. How can one celebrate the coming of maturity, she seethed, when one knows too well the unhappy lot of woman? She tore the four pieces into tiny scraps and, going to the window, hurled them out into the storm. And the three-score pieces that made up the south-west quarter turned into a pack of chattering monkeys, and those of the south-east quarter were transformed into delicate wind-dragons; as for the scraps which comprised the north-west, they became a litter of tiger-cubs, while the north-eastern fragments were transformed into cockerels and raised the dead with their crowing.

Then Onogoro picked up her lacquered sandals and tossed them after the shreds of the poem, and they ran of their own accord to the house of the crippled aunt of the flute-player, and such was their redemptive power that when the old woman put them on she rose up straight-legged as a crane and walked as gracefully.

Then Onogoro unwound her *obi* and, taking it in her teeth, tore it asunder, and the one half became a yellow iris on the marshy shore of Lake Biwa, and the other a golden sail to speed a sampan's journey. But still the lady's rage, like the zig-zag bridge at Yatsuhashi, could find no straight path to its goal. And perhaps in this matter the rage was wiser than she, for it is a known fact, is it not, that hate kills, and a hate that misses its mark can produce neither corpses nor lawsuits.

Round and round went the rage, like lead in a spinning drum, and Onogoro spun with it, until the tortoiseshell combs which the General had given her snapped into two, and her hair fell down unseemly and lashed at her face, and her robe wound tight as swaddling clothes around her body until at last, compressed and small, she curled up on the *tatami* mat and wept bitter tears.

Purple-black as the wet trunks of the almond trees, her hair hung around her. As if in a vision, she saw how exceedingly small she was, and above her towered a great silk screen on which was inscribed the vast and saturnine face of her lover, sleeping and Buddha-like. And across the cliff of the cheek, moving inexorably towards the cavern of the eye socket, marched a small army of termites.

<pre>
            the armies of my rage   Why did they ~~stop~~
I marshalled ~~my armies~~   go no further
and set them marching   than
~~Northwards~~   ~~at~~ the Great
How come they never   North Gate
left   North Gate   of the Capital?
~~passed~~ the ~~Lion Gate~~
~~of the Capital~~
</pre>

Behind the darkness of her closed lids characters began to assemble. To the accompaniment, we can be sure, of the muse's laughter, Onogoro's attention withdrew from her turbulent unhappiness and began to focus on the poem that was forming itself – an unsuitable, a scandalous poem, a poem which would be met, she was certain, by a shocked silence.

Tokiden's knock interrupted her forebodings. The maid had brought tea, and a message from His Excellency, with a poem enclosed.

> As the arrows sighed overhead
> I heard only your laughter on the wind.
> Is it any wonder that I speed
> To your chamber?

The General would arrive within the hour. Hurriedly concealing her work Onogoro penned a reply-poem and dispatched it with Tokiden.

> Bamboo-canes rattle
> In the rain-driven wind.
> I stir the embers of the brazier,
> Already I can smell
> The wet rabbit-fur of your cloak.

Then she sent Shune the kitchen servant to fetch Oyu from the stables.

Pickled Cucumber

The pale horse grunted with pleasure as Oyu stroked the curry-brush across the ripple of her flank. Leaning close he crooned into her plaited mane: 'Izanami, goddess among mares; Izanami, whose step is light as a dragonfly; Izanami, repository of secrets.'

Like an infant tranced by a lullaby the horse stilled and listened, and all of Oyu's secrets, of which there were many and none of them told to any human, shone in the intelligence of her eye and limned her muscles with power. And where the mare went, so did they: fleet, proud, bounding, she carried them with her to war, hunt and parade, to the misty provinces of the north and the luminous islands of the south, so that they experienced much, and returned to him richer in wisdom. Or so Oyu imagined, being a dreamy young man, and somewhat passive, as are all those who have been torn from a loved mother too young, and it pleased him to fancy how the faculties of his soul might merge with those of the great mare and, allied with her benign power, might act forcefully upon an intractable world.

'Oyu! Oyu!'

Hearing the rasping voice of Shune the kitchen servant, Oyu laid the brush on the grooming stool.

'You're wanted at the Pavilion again. Her ladyship says I'm to wait while you change and fetch you over.' Shune let out a ribald laugh. 'So go to it, boy!'

'You've got the wrong end of the stick, I assure you,' said Oyu bashfully, moving behind the curtain that screened off the washing alcove.

'Story-telling indeed!' cried Shune. 'A handsome lad like you? I know all about these randy court ladies. I wasn't always this decrepit, you know, and as long as there was still something in the old watering-can they'd be after it.'

Shune launched into a long and bawdy account of his seduction in the kitchen stores by an Imperial concubine whose craving for pickled cucumber was only exceeded by her appetite for lovemaking, and not for the first time Oyu had occasion to wonder if the description the old servant had supplied of the Lady Onogoro was as capricious as his memory. A lady midway between twenty and thirty, Shune had said; not in the first bloom of youth, but lovely nonetheless. To this scant picture Oyu had added his own embellishments – her doe eyes, her mouth red and plump as a tamarind, her oyster-shell complexion – and if this image of her was entirely of his own making, then at least it was one which none could challenge, or alter, or otherwise alienate from him. For, to the besotted Oyu, stripped to his undershirt and hurling water at his armpits, the Onogoro of his mind's eye was nothing less than perfect. Holding this happy thought in the very centre of his heart, he dressed hastily and allowed Shune to guide him across the gardens to the Almond Blossom Pavilion.

Always it was Onogoro's scent which met him first and flared his ardent nostrils: a scent of cloves, mingled with night jasmine and a sharp hint of aloes. Then her cool hand grasped his hot one and led him to the bed, then she pulled the wings of the *tsuitate* screen around him, leaving a jug of cold rice wine within his reach. At a pre-arranged signal – the lady would toss her head so that the long snakes of her hair lashed against the taut silk of the screen or even (most precious memory) slithered underneath to brush against his fingers – Oyu would begin his tale. Lately, however, the signal was becoming all but superfluous, for Oyu seemed to sense exactly when his services were required. It is almost as if I, not the General, am making love to her, thought Oyu, while Onogoro, who had noticed this uncanny sensitivity, had cause to wonder whether she had not employed some kind of magician.

From his hiding place Oyu heard the clanks and grunts which signified that the General was divesting himself of his accoutrements. Jade cups clinked as the couple drank a little wine, and then the bed dais creaked as the General, Oyu assumed, gathered Onogoro in his arms and deposited her on top of the quilted covers. He listened for the first fervid noises which signalled that the General had entered and was plying away heartily, and then for the whispered consultation which indicated that like any well-bred lover His Excellency, putting his mistress's pleasure before his own, would now remove his head and tongue to an efficacious position between the lady's thighs. By and by Onogoro's sighs would start, and then her lashing hair was black as the dark behind his eyes, her hair was scented, her hair licked like flame at his fingers . . . Wetting his dry lips with wine, Oyu began his tale.

Bamboo Shoots

'Once in the reign of Emperor Reizei there lived at Court a Minister of the Third Rank who was much in demand with the ladies of the Palace, despite his high-handed ways and his constant breaches of etiquette. In the matter of sexual relations, in fact, he was positively unscrupulous. While he would instantly break off with any courtesan whom he suspected of having another lover, he showed neither patience nor consideration for the finer feelings of his three concubines, nor attempted in any way to mediate between the rivalrous women. Advice was pressed upon him from all quarters, and even the Emperor himself – a man not immune from these problems – took the Minister aside and explained how ill feeling could be minimised by means of firmness, courtesy, and a strict division of attentions.

'At last the Minister, irritated by such well-intentioned meddling and exasperated by the complaints, tantrums, and coldness of his three concubines, resolved to take matters into his own hands. Far too much was made of the sensibilities of aristocratic women, in his opinion, and indulging them was no fit occupation for a man with affairs of State on his mind.

'One evening, arriving at the apartments of his first concubine, the Minister dismissed the lady's servants and dispatched a messenger to the houses of his second and third concubines with orders that they must present themselves before him immediately.

'The Minister's first concubine, whom we shall call Y., was a tall and handsome lady of some thirty years, with an unusual brownish glint to her abundant hair and more wit than the Minister could readily deal with. On hearing his orders, the Lady Y. bowed low, but there was an angry gleam in her eye as, servantless, she unrolled the sleeping mats on the dais, unfolded the *tsuitate* screen, and otherwise obeyed the Minister's instructions.

'The second concubine arrived soon afterwards in a rush-roofed carriage with gilded wheels, and suffered the same indignity of seeing her maid summarily dismissed. I intend to wait on the ladies myself, the Minister told the astonished girl, who fled back to her mistress's house and lost no time spreading the scandal. The second concubine, whom we shall call K., was a young noblewoman whose family, fallen on hard times, had been obliged to place their daughter in circumstances they would otherwise never have considered.

'If the Minister had retained any doubts about his plan, one glance at the snobbishly flared nostrils of the prideful K. would surely have banished them. Restraining his temper, he bade the Lady K. sit on the couch next to her rival Y., and thus they awaited the last and youngest concubine, the Lady S., a mettlesome girl of sixteen with the loveliest nape in the Capital.

'This lady was not bidden to sit on the couch with her rivals, but instead was ordered to serve them with rice wine and water chestnuts from the kitchens. That done – and it was done with frostily averted eyes – the Minister made a short but eloquent speech, telling his mistresses that their jealousy and pettiness was not only insufferable, but sprang also from a deep immodesty of character – a fact which he intended to prove by enacting in reality the contents of their fevered and lascivious imaginations.

A woman's mind, he told the three, should not stray beyond the confines of her apartments, and what her lord sees fit to do outside her chamber for his comfort or distraction was never, and will never be, a proper concern of hers. But since your wretched jealousy betrays your desire to spy on me, he continued, I have granted your wish, and by bringing you all together only mean to make it easier for you to indulge it.

'At this the Lady K. stood up and would have stormed out of the chamber, but the Minister easily restrained her. For your disobedience, he told her, you will be the last to receive my attentions, for I intend to take you one by one.

'With this the Minister fetched from the antechamber a low swordstand of lacquered wood inlaid with mother of pearl, on which lay two swords in their ornamental scabbards. Taking the Lady Y. by the hand, he loosened her garments and made her bend over the swordstand like a schoolboy awaiting chastisement.

'The Lady K. and the Lady S. hid their faces in mortification, seeing how white were the limbs of the Lady Y., all bared now to their gaze, and how red-glinting the tendrils of hair which peeped out between those limbs, and how perfect the tender openings which revealed themselves, curled like chrysanthemum petals and coloured in all tints from dewy rose to burnished crimson. And they did not know whom they hated more – the Minister whose practised fingers, moistened with almond oil, gently tested first one tender cleft and then the other, to the evident humiliation of his mistress; or the Lady Y. herself, who must surely be (they thought wretchedly) the most desirable woman in the Capital: more skilled, more seductive, more passionate than they could ever hope to be . . .

'The Minister now drew aside his robe and, taking his member in one hand, slipped it first into one opening, then the other. His fingers, meanwhile, continued their skilful manipulations, and the horrified onlookers saw the Lady Y.'s sinuous response begin, heard her moans of pleasure, saw the flush which spread across her thighs. And all the time the Minister whispered to her shoulders, to her sleek hair, to her narrow back, words of utmost vulgarity and tenderness, so that despite themselves the ladies craned and strained to hear, and under their robes they grew hot and furious with desire. Steadily the Minister was ploughing now, while the Lady Y. bucked under him, her white back rippling, until at last her groans merged into one long wavering shout, and the Minister with a blush of sweat on his countenance cried out sharply and subsided in spasms.

'Without so much as a pause to savour the aftermath of pleasure, the Minister sprang up and led the subordinated and trembling lady back to the couch. The Lady S. could not help but notice that the Lady Y. was heavy-lidded, her face slumberous with gratification, but the Lady K., quite unable to deal with the turmoil inside her, stared straight ahead, and forced herself to think of the chilly skies of her father's northern province, and the icicles which bearded the maple trees, and willed herself to feel nothing.

'With a bow the Minister took the Lady S. by the hand. Eschewing the swordstand, he led his youngest mistress to the dais where the sleeping mats were unrolled and, propping her against the wall, spread open her robe so that the other ladies could enjoy this view of her ample and youthful charms.

The Lady Y. gazed at the girl with an admiration in which envy might well have played a part had she not been quite exhausted by her recent pleasure. The shoulders were snowy, the breasts perfect pomegranates, the belly rounded, the skin of the thighs undimpled and glowing with health. Surely the Lady S. must be the most beautiful, the most desirable concubine in the Capital!

'The Lady K. kept her eyes averted, and therefore did not see the Lady S. displayed on the dais, but heard instead the merry and mischievous laugh which had echoed in her jealous ears through many long nights when she lay alone on her couch.

'For unlike her companions the Lady S. had accepted the rice wine, and the Minister, prone between her thighs, had flicked too enthusiastically with his tongue, and the incorrigible girl, whose entire temperament was ticklish, let out a giggle of protest.

'The Lady K. and the Lady Y. looked at each other, and the Lady Y., conscious that her own cries of pleasure had betrayed her as surely as this girlish laughter, curled up her toes in her slipper-socks and hid her face in her sleeve. Still, she could not resist peeking through her fingers at the pearly plumpness of the Lady S., and at the small white teeth now visible between her parted lips as the Minister sat up and took her on his lap. Turning the girl round so that the ladies could continue to enjoy the spectacle, he inserted his member from below. The Minister placed her fingers on her rosy nipples, but the Lady S. needed no such instruction, and began to squeeze and pull them with alacrity, wriggling with puppyish pleasure, while the Minister's insistent finger started its work among her swelling folds. All this was in full view of her rivals, who could not help but feel that with her unsophisticated enthusiasm the Lady S. was altogether more seductive than the most chic and elegant courtesan of the Capital.

'Quite rapidly the Lady S. expired in giggling bursts and, with an appreciative slap on the thigh from her lover, was conducted back to the couch, where she guilt-ily tried to compose her face into a sisterly gravity.

'The Lady K. was outraged. It's all very well for callow

youth, she thought. When sensation is all-important higher values can easily be dispensed with! She stiffened herself as the Minister stretched out his hand to lead her to the dais, and fixed her eye on the corner shrine in which sat a statue of Fudo with rope in one hand and sword in the other, for binding and killing wickedness.

'When the Minister bade her loosen her *obi* and drew aside the folds of her robe, the Lady K. icily refused. And so the Minister himself unwound her sash and tied her two hands with it; then, stretching out on the sleeping mat and propping his head upon a glazed ceramic headrest, he drew the lady down on him in one swift motion. In her confusion the Lady K. could no longer decide which was the major object of her anger – her rivals, who sat before her meek and gratified, yet eager, she was sure, to judge her womanhood – or the Minister, with whom she had believed she was in love. Her will tensed against all three as the Minister's questing finger prepared her for the powerful member which, slicked with almond oil, was soon to follow.

'The room darkened and the air grew clammy, for outside a thunderstorm had begun to gather. The Lady K.'s face grew scarlet with the effort of resistance, for the Minister had entered her with art and adroitness, and the turbulence that ensued threatened to transport her beyond pride. The inner voice that was her womanhood enjoined her to co-operate with heart and body, and thus outstrip her rivals, but her stern will was stronger.

'The Lady S. looked on with astonishment as the Minister laboured mightily with fingers and member, and as the minutes stretched into hours she and the Lady Y. decided that they had never before seen such evidence of excitement, such swollen lips, such slippery molten folds, such pulsing ridges.

'Yet still the conflict raged within the Lady K., and still she would not give in. The room was greenish-dark now, the first thunderclap echoed over the Capital. Under her the Lady K. sensed a hesitation in the exhausted Minister, a faltering which told her that the stronger will had triumphed. The Lady K. was filled with a fierce gladness, and for a moment relaxed her tight hold on her senses.

'But in that unwary moment a greedy female demon seemed to take possession of her, a demon that was both hungry and angry. Lightning flashed and rain lashed violently at the balcony screens as the demon in the Lady K., vowing to steal her pleasure before the Minister's potency subsided, rose up with the wild and virile movements of a rutting stag, and with many terrifying grunts and cries, took revenge upon the fading Minister.

'The Minister grew pale with fright as this *tengu* thundered above him. His member, however, which had its own life and its own intention, breasted the wave of his terror and submitted to the devastations of a pleasure he had never dreamed of. The room echoed with the beastly sounds of the lovers, and the dais on which they wrestled lurched and shuddered, until at last the combat ended in an attenuated, conjugal, deathlike scream.

'On the couch the other ladies clung together, hiding their faces in alarm and stopping their ears against this cacophony of thunder-gods and humans.

'Let them now judge who is the winner, thought the Lady K. with secret satisfaction, but although her senses were gratified her rage had not abated. The Minister lay below her with the rosy countenance of a trustful babe, for, like most of his fellows, he lacked the imagination to see that there were transgressions which satiety could not atone for, and discontents that would not be so easily compensated.

'Rousing himself with difficulty, the Minister untied the lady's hands and prevailed upon the Lady Y. to bring refreshments. The storm had by now abated, and the ladies who had observed the unnatural congress were torn between envy of the Lady K.'s thunderous performance and relief that they themselves had not exhibited such unwomanly rage to their protector.

'When the delicacies were spread out on aloe-wood trays before them, and the wine poured into jade cups, the Minister leaned back on the couch and began to revive. The ladies, meanwhile, had tidied themselves, and knelt in a semicircle on the *tatami* at his feet. With eyes lowered, they toyed with the warm spiced cheese, the mussel soup with dumplings, and the lotus-seed tarts, each absorbed in her private reverie.

'The Minister chaffed them. Why so silent? he demanded. Would they not tell him honestly, what were their feelings now? Did they not agree with him that jealousy was a base emotion fit only for scullery maids?

'The ladies did not reply, and the Minister laughed angrily. So what am I to do with you? Tell me that! Rummaging in the folds of his robe he brought out his member, which for once lolled sleepily in his hand. Then, kneeling on the mat between his concubines, he laid it on the aloe-wood tray beside the other sweetmeats. You see, there is only one of him, and three of you, so what on earth is His Excellency to do?, he said, pointing with self-satisfaction to the incongruous delicacy.

'To this the Lady K. replied in tones so uncommonly obedient that the other ladies stared at her in surprise: Your Excellency, concubines must learn to share and share alike.

'Indeed! cried the Minister. At last here's a woman who has seen sense! And, calling for his mantle and his sword, he declared the matter settled.

'The three ladies bowed their heads submissively, as was fitting. The Lady Y. brought the Minister's sable mantle, and the Lady K. fetched his great curved sword from the stand. The Lady S., meanwhile, slipped the Minister's feet tenderly into his sandals.

'But then, in the twinkling of an eye, the sword was unsheathed, and the shining blade bore down once, twice, three times on the insolently bared member of the Minister, and sliced through it as easily as if it had been a young bamboo shoot.

'Amid the shrieks of the hapless Minister, the Lady K. gave one slice to the Lady S., and one to the Lady Y., and, tucking the last slice into her voluminous sleeve, said calmly: Now what could be a fairer apportionment than that?'

At this Onogoro, already quite overheated by the tales of beastly congress, could contain herself no longer, and rose up in an ecstasy of rage, and the General cried out in delight as she whipped to and fro in her culminating pleasure.

The Snow Boat

On the eve of the New Year the Lady Ochibu gave birth to a healthy boy, and the General's household breathed a sigh of relief. Receiving the good news at her writing table, Onogoro fell to her knees and wept thankful tears.

After the New Year's festivities were past, snow fell thickly on the roofs of the Capital. Out on the slushy streets everyone was red-nosed and ill-tempered, but inside the Imperial Enclosure the snow was pristine, crisp, delectable. Careless of her new status as young lady, the Princess Saishō romped with Onogoro and the other Ladies-in-Waiting in the gardens of the Palace.

'Build me a white swan with spread wings!' she cried.

'Build me a snow boat!' Onogoro and Tokiden, fur-booted, skirts tucked up, waded in the thigh-deep snow, digging a path for the tiny Princess, who might otherwise have disappeared entirely in the drifts. Helped by the other ladies they fashioned great bricks from the snow-balls which left tracks of bare earth in their wake, pummelling them flat with spades. Then they sculpted the packed snow into a curved prow with a swan's neck and head, a winged belly with snow seats in it, and a graceful, pointed, tail-like stern.

'We must have a sail,' cried Saishō, clambering aboard. 'We must have oarsmen! Fetch cotton stuffs, Nyo, fetch bamboo cane!' While Nyo ran to the stores, Onogoro and Tokiden sat with the Princess on the snow benches. Stretching out their legs they leant back, pretending the heaviness of oars, and rocked back and forth with many grunts of travail, until the Princess, quite overcome with excitement, shrieked: 'We're moving, we're moving!'

Onogoro glanced up at the dazzling sky and tears ran from her squinting eyes, blurring the edges of things – the ornamental pines, the bare almond trees, the wall which backed on to the stableyard where Oyu the teller of forbidden tales forked hay into mangers and polished the golden bosses of bridles. For a moment she too could have sworn that they were moving, that the distance between them and the stables had decreased, and that the swan boat might detach itself at any moment from the ground and fly over the wall, glittering with its load of laughing girls.

Like all those of morbid temperament for whom delight is never simple but always comes accompanied by its superstitious shadow, Onogoro felt an ache in her soul for the fact that Oyu would never see the snow boat and its light-hearted cargo. How terrible, she thought, and her tears of joy became tears of pity. A nobler self rose up before her and enjoined her to enter the lack and make it good. Her mind flew high and, yearning, filled with grace. I must write a poem for him, she decided. In that way I will give him this swan, this boat, the brilliance of this blue day. Yes, I will write a poem for Oyu.

But here comes Nyo now with a length of red lawn from the stores, red the colour of women's undergarments, red which makes the Princess scold her maid with frowns and giggles. And the sail is strung up on the bamboo cane, and Onogoro is laughing harder than she has since childhood, and in the stableyard Oyu stands in the warm steam of the horse Izanami, in the deep rhythms of its piss and shit and sumptuous breathing, and hears the higher, fleeting, fragile note of her laughter. Meanwhile, on the balcony of the Plum Blossom Pavilion, the poet-genius Izumi Shikibu leans on the arm of her lover Tame-taka and smiles with pleasure at the girlish antics in the boat with the scarlet sail, the snow boat trying to fly.

In the milder days that followed Onogoro saw the contours of the boat melt and blur into a slug-shape, and its swan's-neck prow shrink to a mere memory. But the red sail still flew as gaily from the bamboo cane, and each time she looked up from her writing table and saw it she felt the same airy relief she had felt on hearing of the safe delivery of the General's child.

For in the period leading up to the birth Onogoro had suffered much guilt on account of her jealous thoughts, and each night had brought trial and punishment. In her dreams she was beaten with bamboo cudgels, branded on the forehead with characters detailing her crimes, and finally, bolted into a wooden collar, was led away to

exile in a far-off frontier station. But now that there was
no crime and therefore no criminal, relief, like the snow,
made her biddable and gay, and she twirled the tip of
her sheep's wool brush to a fine point and bent happily
over her writing. And all the time the part of her mind
that was not employed in poetry chattered to itself in
cheerful gratitude. I won't ask so much of the General,
it said. I'll be quite content with what I'm given!

Onogoro hummed and felt perfectly good as the poems
flew out of her, she knew they would fly out of her as
long as the snow lay white and perfect on the ground, and
they filled first the whole room, and then the corridors, all
on ochre paper faintly scented with cloves, and in a few
days they reached the far end of the Palace, where they
piled in drifts at the doors of the Plum Blossom Chamber,
behind which lived, dreamed, scribbled and dallied the
poet-genius Izumi Shikibu.

> Cold snowballs fly from the fists
> Of the garden girls.
> Tell me, is your face flushed
> From the stable's heat
> Or from those blizzards of laughter?

In high humour, Onogoro went to the stables to read her
poem to Oyu. The boy stood before her with bent head
and hands clasped across his leather apron. 'The honour
is too great,' he murmured politely into the darkness, as
her eyes unfairly stripped him, as her advantaged eyes
gouged into him. It was a poem slight as a snowflake,
thought the humiliated Oyu, and teasing as the spring
sun. The sort of thing one might dash off for a favourite
godchild. He bowed deeply, but his heart was dull with
anger, for what the sighted constantly fail to see is that
the blind too have their pride.

Meanwhile the Lady Izumi raised her magnifying glass and, allowing the bowl of green tea Ben had brought to cool on the table beside her, read the poems a second time.

'Who is she?' she enquired of her maid. 'This Onogoro woman.'

'You saw her in the snow,' Ben replied. 'Remember, with the young Princess Saishō.'

Shikibu recalled a pretty blur, a blue robe, a certain slender haughtiness. 'Ah yes,' she said. 'The lanky one.'

Outside the windows the snow was melting from the gardens and the first buds were already beginning to open on the plum trees. Shikibu felt stirred, irritated, disturbed. However rash the sentiments they contained, the poems showed a definite flair. A young woman like Onogoro, she mused, could benefit from some sound advice, from the kind of guidance that she herself had lacked in her first confusing years at the Court. And who better to give counsel than one who had fought long and hard with similar demons? Shikibu made her decision with typical speed. She would ask the girl to call at the Plum Blossom Pavilion; other poets would also attend; they would make an evening of it. A young woman of Onogoro's calibre, to be sure, deserved a helping hand to set her on the path to happiness.

Taking advantage of her buoyant mood, Onogoro wrote to her father in Echigo, who was gratified to receive the following good news.

My dear father (he read)
My duties keep me so busy these days I'm utterly in a spin. Yesterday, for instance, was the sixteenth of the month, and poems and songs in honour of the

New Year were recited in front of the Emperor to the accompaniment of dancing by 40 Ladies-in-Waiting. The judges spoke highly of my offering – although I was not entirely satisfied with it myself – and the Second Empress (the First Empress has removed to the Seiryō Palace to await the birth of her child) came up and offered her congratulations in the shyest and most charming manner imaginable. I write this knowing the pleasure it will give you and, of course, my mother. Please forgive me, however, if I confess that what pleased me even more greatly was making the acquaintance of the poet Lady Izumi, whom I have long admired. I believe that she likes my work, and wishes me to attend a gathering of poets at her establishment. As you may imagine, I am wild with gratitude at having attracted her good offices, but I must admit that I am a little apprehensive about how I may fare in such an exalted circle. For any hare-brained courtier can recite his feeble pomposities at the Ceremony of the Poetry Dances, whereas Izumi Shikibu, I am assured, carries the strict rod of the true poet and does not stint her criticism.

Your affectionate daughter
Onogoro

The Hexagram of the Army

Yorimichi threw aside the report on the Lady Ochibu's dream and cursed at his clumsy manservant. 'I told you to trim my toenails, not my toes!' he exclaimed, kicking over the bowl of rosewater in which his feet had been soaking. Seeing the old servant's crestfallen face, the

Regent was immediately remorseful. Osamu's hands did tremble, it was true, and his eyesight was not what it had been, but he had attended Yorimichi's father, and his father before him, and so some allowances had to be made.

The real cause of his unfortunate outburst, he had to admit, was not the tweak at his small toe, but the worm of worry planted in his mind by the Soothsayers' report – a document which he would certainly have consigned to the waste basket if Prince Atsumichi had not insisted that it required his urgent consideration. 'For goodness' sake don't fret, Osamu,' he entreated. 'Just clean up the mess and see that His Excellency Prince Atsumichi is summoned at once.'

When Atsumichi arrived the Regent waved the document at him. ' "Beware marriages between warlords in the north-east," ' he quoted, in a sneering tone intended to conceal his concern. 'If these pronouncements are so urgent, perhaps you will translate them for me?'

Atsumichi bowed suavely. 'The Bureau of Divination notes, Your Highness, that intermarriages between previously warring branches of the Taira family are on the increase. They draw your attention to the resulting possibility of an expansion of Taira lands not only in the provinces of Dewa and Mutsu, but also in Hitachi and Shimosa, and urge that you reconsider the matter of the defences of the Capital.'

'And the Minamoto are more honourable?' The Regent regarded the Prince through narrowed eyes. As a member of his father's administration, Atsumichi had schemed determinedly to promote the interests of the Minamoto. Whereas, as anyone knew who could see beyond his own nose, the first task of statesmanship was to maintain a balance between the great military families. By appointing key figures like General Taira to posts in the Capital, one not only secured their allegiance, but kept them well away from the expansionist temptations offered by the lawless outlying provinces. And if the Minamoto had had their heyday during Michinaga's Regency, well, it would not hurt if their wings were clipped a little under his son's.

'Bearing in mind that the dream-portent came from your own brother's first-born, the Lady Ochibu,' Atsumichi persisted, 'the Diviners believe you should regard it as a matter of the utmost gravity.'

'I'm well aware that the wife of General Taira no Moto-suke is my niece,' said Yorimichi impatiently. 'I'm also aware of your prejudice against her husband.' As Major Counsellor, Atsumichi had always opposed the appointment of the General as Head of Military Affairs, arguing that a man whose prime interest lay in the furtherance of family power could not be trusted to take command of the Imperial Guard and bring them to order. Would it not be in the General's interests, rather, to preside over a decaying and impotent force, knowing that when the time was ripe his armed and powerful clan could swoop down from the North and end the rule of the Fujiwara? Thus the Prince had argued, whereas it was the Minamoto brothers, the Regent reflected, who had allowed the Guard to fall into disarray in the first place, while using the threat of the Taira to build up their own military might. Yorimichi sighed. Atsumichi was one elder statesman he would rather not have inherited from his father. 'I might draw your attention to the fact that the Lady Ochibu is also a Fujiwara,' he ended irritably.

'The Diviners merely indicate a worrying trend, Your Excellency,' said Atsumichi in the mildest of tones.

'Good!' said Yorimichi. 'Now we know where we are.'

Atsumichi cleared his throat. 'However,' he continued, shuffling through the papers, 'if I may draw Your Excellency's attention to the following predictions gained by the Chinese Method: "At the throwing of the 49 yarrow stalks the Hexagram of the Army was obtained, with a six in the third place which cautions as follows –

> Perchance the Army
> carries corpses in its wagon.
> Misfortune." '

Atsumichi was gratified to see that the Regent's cheeks had lost some of their colour. He read on: ' "Since at burials and sacrifices to the dead it is customary in China for the deceased to whom the sacrifice is made to be represented by a boy of the family who sits in the dead man's place and is honoured as his representative, on the basis of this custom the text is interpreted as meaning that a 'corpse-boy' is sitting in the wagon; in other words, that authority is not being exercised by the proper leaders but is being usurped by others." '

Shaken, Yorimichi sat in silence, brooding on the mounting evidence against the General, a man whom he rather liked and who had, as far as he could see, carried out his duties towards Emperor and State with a stolid and unfaltering loyalty.

'Shall I go on?' asked Atsumichi, and the Regent nodded resignedly. ' "A reading of His Excellency's horoscope produced supplementary reasons for extreme caution, since an inauspicious alignment of P'o Chūn, the Broken-

Army Star, with Ursa Major, signified ill luck in the Life/
Fate Palace during the Fifth Month." '

'So what do you propose, Atsumichi,' the Regent
demanded, 'if you seriously think I'm at risk?'

'I suggest that the General be placed under arrest,' said
Atsumichi immediately.

Yorimichi winced at the Prince's impetuosity. 'No
arrest,' he insisted. 'I forbid it.'

Atsumichi bowed in acquiescence. 'If Your Excellency
considers arrest precipitant, I urge that the General at
least be placed under surveillance. I have only Your
Excellency's safety at heart.'

'Surveillance,' mused the Regent, somewhat mollified.
Well, it could do no harm, since any conspiracy could be
nipped in the bud immediately, and if the General turned
out to be innocent he need never even know that he had
been under suspicion. 'Very well, Atsumichi. Put a watch
on him day and night. But get someone who knows his
business. What I mean is, make sure the man's absolutely
discreet. I don't want any embarrassment.'

*

> On mornings when you leave
> At dawn,
> I stretch my limbs languorously
> Like that crane
> At the misty edge of the lake.

When the General sent word that he was once again
free to visit the Almond Blossom Pavilion, Onogoro was
overjoyed. The General greeted her with warmth and
received her congratulations on the birth of his son with
proper gravity, thereby contriving – with impeccable tact
– to conceal his great happiness. For her part, Onogoro
was at pains to conduct herself with dignity and affection,

56

and if mean or hungry thoughts threatened once or twice to overthrow her equanimity, a glance at the lush harvest of poems on her writing table served to assure her that she was no beggar, but bountiful, and could therefore well afford to distribute her blessings, and sacrifice some of the childish greed of passion to the requirements of a more generous and adult love.

Time wore on, meanwhile, and, conscious of Oyu's long wait behind the screen, Onogoro hurried the General through spiced chestnut cakes and tea flavoured with pine-kernels and led him at last to the bed dais. Her lover, however, wore the wary look of one who, while pleasantly surprised by the cordiality of his reception, nevertheless still expects recriminations. This diffidence seemed to extend even to his member itself, which required a surplus of caresses before it could regain its typical opulence, so that Onogoro had cause to wonder whether fretful feminine tears might not have aroused her lover far more effectively than her current mood of benevolent high-mindedness.

Peony Flowers

❧

'Once in Hitachi province there was a Prince who had a cold wife and a passionate mistress. His wife, the Princess Tsunebo, had a wardrobe composed entirely of garments the colour of pearl, whereas his mistress Osaku dressed exclusively in red and in her splendour was surpassed only by the famous peony fields of Shimosa.

'It so happened that when the Lady Osaku became pregnant the Prince moved her into his apartments in the Palace, an event greeted by his wife with a cool civility which quite disarmed him. Soon after her arrival, however, Osaku began to complain of fatigue, and eventually succumbed to a fever which carried her off in the first days of the Third Month, when the cherry blossom was at its height.

'The Prince was so distraught that he eschewed the dark *shiishiba* mourning dress, and instead wrapped himself in peony-coloured robes and paced the Palace corridors, quite unable to believe that such a passionate spirit could be so rapidly erased from this earthly life. Indeed, so intemperate was his mourning that even after the Forty-Nine Days were over the spirit of the Lady Osaku could not detach itself from its worldly bonds and take flight towards the resting place in the Western Paradise, but instead was held back by pity for her bereaved lover.

'All this time the Princess Tsunebo remained in seclusion in her apartments, for she was sorely afraid that she would be accused of ill-wishing the Lady Osaku, and thus having brought about her death.

'When, after many weeks, the Prince at last returned to his wife's bedchamber, hoping at least for the consolation that years of marriage might afford, he found Tsunebo deep in meditation on the Scriptures. Raising a pale and penitent face to him, she told him that she had instructed the priests of the Hasedera to recite the Lotus *Sutra* on behalf of the Lady Osaku, and was herself considering taking holy orders. Her remorse was so palpable that the Prince's heart was touched and, weeping, he begged her to set aside her misplaced guilt and postpone all plans to enter a nunnery. Surely she did not want him to be doubly bereft, he pleaded. At the thought of the loneliness that would be his lot the Prince wept even more profusely, until Tsunebo's pity overcame her piety, and she took him in her awkward arms and rained cool little kisses on his brow. Through his copious tears the Prince became aware that his wife, although thin and rather ethereal, looked exceedingly attractive in her pearl-coloured robe with its dove-coloured lining, and for the first time in several months he felt his passion stir.

'Once under the bedcovers, however, the Prince embraced the apprehensive body of his wife and was stricken by a terrible yearning for the vibrant flesh and energetic appetites of his late departed mistress. Meanwhile, like a busy mother who feels a tweak at her sleeve and for some moments does not realise that it is her own child demanding her attention, the captive spirit of the Lady Osaku felt the tug of her lover's longing. Turning absent-mindedly to attend to it, she was dragged pell-mell down through the ether and forced to enter the very bedchamber where the Prince was attempting to make love to his wife, with sighs of grief which were quite heart-rending to hear.

'The generous and passionate spirit of the Lady Osaku was utterly beguiled by her lover's worldly need. In the clear knowledge that she was transgressing the divine rule, and would in all probability never reach the shores of Jōdō, Osaku breathed a hasty prayer and slithered like a whisper into the narrow nostrils of the Princess Tsunebo, thus gaining entrance to her body.

'To the unhappy Prince the transformation was as resounding as the shudder of the earth during an earthquake. It was as if, inside the pearly shell of his wife's body, lava had begun to boil. Heat radiated from her belly and her dark-tipped breasts, and moans issued from her open mouth. The Princess, astonished, fought the alien spirit which had taken up residence in her body, but the struggle only heightened the waves of willing pleasure which surged from her oyster-shell toes to her white-powdered temples. To her chagrin her hand reached out to clasp her husband's eager member, and her back arched, and she plunged her body greedily upon it and flew up and down to the accompaniment of the

59

grunting and slapping sounds which accompany the animal in its search for gratification.

'Thunderstruck, the Prince opened his eyes to see that it was indeed his wife Tsunebo whose untrammelled lust was driving him to such extremes of pleasure, and not, as he would have sworn, his mistress Osaku. Thanking the gods for his good fortune, he closed his eyes again, and thus the two shuddered towards their culminating ecstasy, which for the Princess was all the more voluptuous for being so stubbornly resisted, and made her utter such shrieks that the Prince felt obliged to stop her mouth with his hand in case the servants should come running to her aid.

'With a final expiring cry the Lady Osaku wholeheartedly relinquished the passion of her nature and bequeathed it in perpetuity to her rival the Princess. The departing spirit of the lady set a draught of wind funnelling through the chamber, so that the peonies in the vase by the bed shed their petals in a brilliant shower, and some of the petals scampered across the Princess Tsunebo's hair, and others spiralled down on the Prince's sated body.

'Had he been watching, the Prince might also have glimpsed the scrap of crimson which floated up to the roof-beams and escaped like a sigh through the slatted window-shutters. For Our Lord Amida of Boundless Light, having seen the flushed and happy faces of the Prince and his wife, was touched by Osaku's generosity, and had not only forgiven her transgression, but indeed had granted her full and final release from all the coils of this world.'

Such a vast red sun rose next morning that from the moment Onogoro opened her bleary eyes she felt the longings of her soul expand unbearably to meet it, and she knew that all her good resolutions must collapse as surely as wooden temples which, thrown up in haste, succumb to the first earthquake. Try as she might, she could not cultivate the temperament of a concubine, the wheedling and cajoling and the false obsequious gratitude. It was as if the General wanted to keep her in a pretty box like one of those pet locusts in the marketplace which, with a string tied to one leg, are paraded on festival days and then locked away until the next time. She clenched her fist to her cheek and sighed mutinously. For there was the sun, round and fruitful in the dawn sky, and here was Onogoro, with her excellent belly and the bushels of poems she gave birth to. And in the Hall of Military Virtue was her lover the General, advising engineers on the disposition of stockades and moats to modernise the Capital's defences, and quite impervious to her unhappiness. The truth was that the General wanted no more than a sliver of her, a mere taste of her succulence. And all the rest, thought Onogoro with furious self-pity – seeing her lover now as a positive villain – all her desires, her intense and complicated candour, her showers of words, could rot, as far as he was concerned, like melon seeds in the midden.

The Origin of Love-Stories

I marshalled the armies of my rage
And set them marching:
How come they never left
The Great North Gate
Of the Capital?

Onogoro gazed round the company assembled in the

Plum Blossom Chamber. 'But is it not true,' she appealed, 'that men have the power to use and abuse us, while we women have none?' Izumi Shikibu laid the *samisen* aside and took Onogoro's hand in hers. The girl was hasty, the girl was haughty, the girl would break herself like a lotus blossom washed up against the rocks of Ise if something was not done. She must learn to expect less from men, Shikibu reflected; she must learn to place less value on that pompous Taira fellow. Or else let her break her heart on him and harden: soon she would realise that when it comes to the opposite sex, the less affection bestowed means the more commanded.

Izumi Shikibu was approaching forty, suffered from short-sightedness, was plumpish, lovely, and blessed not only with a supreme self-confidence but also with a hard-won and fine-honed sense of irony. Now, however, hearing this unmannerly, yet oddly enthralling poem by the young Onogoro, she could not help recalling her own youthful rages at the sclerosis of the Court, and wondered for an anxious moment whether she had not in fact become cynical. But did not all animals adapt in order to survive, and was not survival itself an honourable aim, even if it required compromise? In childhood games one could play Emperor, could abolish ranks, turn hierarchies on their heads. One could dispense justice and equality to one's populations of dolls, and neither ministries nor patriarchs could stop one. Real life, however, was too short to be frittered away in fruitless rebellion, and if the rules of the game were not susceptible to change, then surely the only sensible strategy was to exploit them to one's best advantage. At the same time Shikibu could not avoid feeling a certain admiration for Onogoro's excesses. The girl, she decided, positively takes one's breath away.

Squeezing Onogoro's hand sympathetically, she returned to the intimate topics which had inspired the liveliest debate of the evening. 'But my dear,' she urged, 'have you considered taking other lovers? A girl of your accomplishments need not look far, I assure you.'

'As it happens,' Sei Shōnagon interjected with a flirtatious toss of the head, 'so many Ministers of the Third Rank have been making enquiries about you I was quite convulsed with jealousy! See how I've decked myself out for combat!' Parting her over-robe to reveal a sumptuous underdress of apricot silk embroidered with kingfisher motifs, Shōnagon smiled so disarmingly that Onogoro, who felt far less assured than her outward appearance suggested, wanted to weep for sheer gratitude. How kind they are, she thought, marvelling at the reception afforded her by these distinguished ladies. She had anticipated hauteur and reserve, and had bargained neither for such frank exuberance nor for the attention they lavished on her – although certainly she had longed for it. Now that the desired attention had arrived, however, it had the perverse effect of making the fortunate recipient feel both diffident and undeserving.

(This curious reversal will be easier to comprehend if we recall that, for those in whom desires seethe all the more strongly for having been constantly frowned upon and damped, rejection is a habit of mind that the mere advent of more benign conditions will not immediately alter, for it will always prefer to hark back to the familiar, and go on battering at the door of acceptance rather than acknowledge that the door has been flung open.)

Casting around blindly for the cause of her discomfiture, Onogoro remembered the dream which had wakened her that morning to the sight of the great dawn orb of the sun. A vast lonely sea had surrounded her, a sea quite empty of islands. On its blank surface she had bobbed in a clam-shell boat, scooping sour pith from a bamboo cane out of which – on her mother's orders – she was fruitlessly attempting to carve a zither. It was this sad dream, no doubt, which had put her out of sorts, this unlucky dream which, by reviving the memory of child-hood wounds, had stirred unhappy sediments and caused her to reflect now, with a recognising jolt of the heart, that she had never had the faintest idea how to make her mother love her, had always been, yes, entirely at sea about that.

'It's either that or the nunnery, believe you me!' said Shōnagon's opinionated cousin, startling Onogoro out of her self-absorption. Onogoro had learned in the course of the evening that this stylish young woman, although barely past the age of the Putting on of the Skirt, had already embarked on three love affairs and was confi-dently intent on acquiring a reputation as a poet. Nor did she hesitate to blow her own trumpet – a characteristic Onogoro was inclined to forgive on account of the girl's youth, for it would hardly have been dignified to envy mere precocity.

If, like all provincials who have set their hearts upon the Capital, Onogoro viewed the world through the blinkers of self-doubt and, seeing sophistication everywhere, met it either with excessive condemnation or with an equally disproportionate adulation, it was the latter sentiment that possessed her as she turned once more to Shikibu, her eyes downcast, her mind buzzing with a hundred questions which she felt unable to ask for fear of being considered gauche and girlish. Shikibu, she thought, would know how to bring a lover into line, how to make him faithful or cut him off like a rotten branch; she would know when to be obdurate and when yielding, when to confess her feelings and when to keep her counsel – she would know, in fact, everything an adult woman needed to know . . .

But now Shōnagon wagged a mischievous finger at Onogoro. 'Whatever you do, don't turn into a prig like the Lady Murasaki! You'll bore us all to tears.'

'Tsk, Shōnagon,' Shikibu chided. 'Murasaki may not know how to live but she writes with the wisdom of the gods. You, on the other hand, live too knowingly and write like the charming courtesan you are.'

'Oh! Oh!' laughed Shōnagon, flapping the long sleeve of her robe at Shikibu, 'but I'm much more *fun* than she is!'

'It's true, dear Shōnagon, that I'll shed more tears at your funeral . . .' With sudden comic abandon, Shikibu drummed her fists on the table so that the *Go* counters leapt off the board and scattered over the floor. 'But it's so *unfair*,' she cried, 'the woman's a genius!'

Onogoro quickly concurred, for how could anyone fail to admire the author of the sparkling *Genji*? But Shōnagon's young cousin, who had moved to the window to watch the moonrise and who stood listening now with her arm round the waist of her friend Yomiko, interjected. 'Pity she eats like a carp!' she cried, pursing her lips in an insolent parody. Such vulgarity made Onogoro quite uncomfortable, and inclined her to feel protective towards the unknown Murasaki and her uncouth habits. If I were Shikibu, she thought angrily, I'd box that young woman's ears! But her good-humoured hostess merely laughed and, bidding Onogoro to take no notice of 'these terrible girls', turned her attention once more to her new protégée.

'But do you love this Taira fellow?' Lowering her voice, Shikibu added, 'I mean, does he please you?'

'Yes,' said Onogoro at once, but her cheeks flushed scarlet. In her mind's eye she saw Oyu behind the *tsuitate* screen, and the General at his lowly labours, all unsuspecting. She could not bring herself to tell Shikibu that it took two men to please her, although not for the first time it occurred to her that there was a certain symmetry in this, since the General himself seemed to require both wife and mistress for his satisfaction. It also struck her that she could be accused of using the boy Oyu, however many bolts of stuff and casks of tea she made sure to dispatch to his grandmother in the Eastern Mountains. And although she suspected that her companions were as likely to applaud her ingenuity as to scorn her for her deficiency in passion, when she imagined the gossip Shōnagon's impudent cousin might disseminate humiliation flooded through her. No, she decided, I simply cannot risk it. Once again Onogoro found herself at sea, for while she had no desire to lay herself open to ridicule, neither did she want these worldly women to think that she had no weapons in her armoury.

Life in the provinces, as we can see, had not prepared the unfortunate Onogoro for admission to such an exalted circle: a circle, moreover, made up entirely of women who could talk in the same breath of love and literature, of sculpture and architecture and history. The tutors in her father's house had been countrified and hangdog, men she had on the whole felt superior to, but she had not been aware until now just how grievously unschooled they had left her in all but the basics of the arts and sciences, not to mention the refined and mysterious art of pursuing happiness – a concept, her mother had impressed on her, which had little place in a woman's life. Yet however fiercely Onogoro had resisted this gloomy augury, she could not help thinking that Shikibu and her companions took matters to the other extreme and treated life with rather too much levity. Was it not possible, she mused, that the love affairs they juggled so dexterously were little more than bulwarks against experiencing the deeper emotions – not all of them pleasant – which were surely part of the human condition? If we women are to turn our backs on the nadirs and zeniths of feeling, thought Onogoro with increasing severity, will we not then become as shallow and meretricious as men?

She gazed in confusion at the clever and lovely face of her hostess. How priggish, on the other hand, to be seen to preach suffering over pleasure, and the torments of passion over equanimity! Onogoro's mind raced to and fro like a snipe in a net. Most of all she would have liked to lay her head on Shikibu's womanly breast and escape entirely from the world of men, to melt into the arms of her new mentor and be cosseted and redeemed there. But these hungry longings seemed to Onogoro so childish, so mawkish, even, that shame barricaded her heart against them, and, turning away to take a gulp from her cup of wine, she laughed a brazen laugh and heard herself declare: 'And if he doesn't please me, I can always resort to my stories!'

Shikibu's puzzled face regarded her. Suppressing her misgivings, Onogoro went on: 'Stories I tell myself. To . . . well, you know.'

Shikibu's black eyes sparkled. 'To arouse you?' Onogoro

lowered her lids and shrugged modestly, offering up a silent plea for forgiveness. The lie had not even made her blush.

'During lovemaking?' Shōnagon clapped her hands in delight. 'Darlings, come and listen to this.'

'A woman's own *shunga*,' mused Shikibu, flashing her wickedest smile. 'I'm sure Shōnagon wishes she had thought of it first! But won't you tell us one of these stories of yours?' she begged, as the other ladies gathered round them curiously. 'I'm sure we are not such paragons that we could not make good use of them.'

Panic seized Onogoro, for she had not foreseen that such a request might follow on the heels of her braggadocio, and she was suddenly unable to recall a single word of Oyu's repertoire. 'Surely everyone is too tired,' she protested. But Shikibu would insist that the brazier be restoked and the wine reheated, and everyone swore that they were so eager to hear Onogoro's 'love-stories', as they called them, that they would stay up till dawn if need be, and eventually the hapless Onogoro saw that she had no choice other than to begin.

Meanwhile the Lady Omoto sidled into the room, placed a delicate paw on Onogoro's knee, and eased herself into her lap, where she sat with head held high, as befitted her rank, and her ears poised, listening. This fine animal was a direct descendant of the first Emperor Ichijō's cat, the Lady Myōbu, and was entitled to wear the same head-dress of nobility bestowed upon her legendary great-great-grandmother. Omoto was a steel-blue colour, golden-eyed, broad of forehead and narrow of muzzle, with legs slender as a crane's and an immensely skinny tail which she held straight up in the air even when seated, as she was at the moment, with all the ladies' faces turned towards her like chrysanthemums.

What the cat saw, from deep in her dazzling Chinese brain, was the colours of the women, their underdresses of violet and iris-blue and plum, their paler cloaks with cherry- or peach-coloured lining, their *obi*s of mustard or primrose. There was a good lady-smell in the room, a sumptuous fishy smell of lovemaking and blood, a smell of mothers' milk and freshly-killed sparrows. Lady Omoto's eyes narrowed to golden slits and a languid love-purr thrummed in her chest, a hymn in memory of childhood and the fragrant slippery straw of the first litter, a hymn to the clumsy nuzzling and the first membrane licked away and the first eye-opening on the first round white moon of her life.

The one whose lap the Lady Omoto occupied, and whose voice vibrated a foot above her head, and whose fingers gently caressed her ears, went on telling her tale, and the bright-hued ladies, becoming excited, loosened their *obi*s and the underdresses of silk stuff that rustled and gave off tiny brilliant sparks, so that here and there the Lady Omoto could glimpse the scarlet lawn of underwear. Then the liquid smell grew overpoweringly musky and sweet, and the fans of the ladies came out of their loose sleeves, and their hands moved in the air like humming-birds.

The Lady Omoto was swooning with pleasure now, as she savoured this happy stew of memory and warm laps and moistening, and she stretched her claws out quite unconsciously and kneaded the silken knee of Onogoro. And if her high-strung hostess squealed and tipped her off on to the *tatami* mat, the promiscuous Lady Omoto, who dined on larks' tongues and turtle meat and had never encountered scarcity, knew that in this litter of ladies there were six other laps every bit as sleek and six other pairs of hands as soft to stroke her steel-blue fur and tug at her steel-blue ears.

The Way of Yü Hsüan-chi

'There was once in Ch'ang An Province in China a poet called Yü Hsüan-chi, who became the concubine of a minor official. Since the ways of China are harsher than ours, the official's wife, jealous of her husband's new mistress, tortured her and forced her from the house. The homeless Yü Hsüan-chi wandered far and wide through the province, and all she had to comfort her were these lines of Li Po, which she recited to herself over and over again:

> Journeying is hard
> Journeying is hard
> There are many turnings
> Which am I to follow?
> I will mount a long wind some day
> And break the heavy waves.

'Eventually the girl came to a monastery high on a red-ochre rock, where the monks, had she but known it, were renowned for their licentiousness. As she climbed the steep rock steps she saw them above her, leaning over the parapet and giggling at her progress. When Yü knocked at the carved gate a hatch was drawn back and two merry identical faces peered out at her. Brother Li and Brother Hu were twins, and it was to them that she was presently to owe her initiation, not only into the Taoist Scriptures, but also into less devout practices.

'The Brothers conducted Yü to a clean bare cell, and brought washing water, food, and a hempen robe to replace her soiled and tattered garments. Then they left her alone to fall into the blissful sleep of exhaustion.

'In the morning the resilience of her youth reasserted itself, and Yü sprang up, eager to explore this sanctuary in which, the Brothers had reassured her, she could remain as long as she pleased. That there was a price to be paid for her lodging Yü did not discover until later that day.

'By afternoon, since the Brothers had to attend to their devotions, she had wandered the cool stone corridors and sat in the peaceful gardens relishing the sharp smell of the cypresses, and she was eager to meet her new friends again and ply them with questions about the Way of Life of Lao-Tzu.

'During the evening meal in the refectory Yü was obliged to suffer many curious stares and whispers, but after it was over the Brothers knocked shyly on the door of her cell. There were a few formalities to be observed, they told her: initiation rites which must be carried out before a woman could be admitted as a novice. So saying, the congenial twins brought in a jug of water, a sharp blade, and a red-ochre inkstone and brushes.

'Yü sat calmly on her pallet and bent her neck, since she fully expected her head to be shaved and was perfectly willing to sacrifice her long lustrous hair should this be required.

'However, with a blush that enveloped his tonsured pate, Brother Li shook his head and nudged his more forthright twin Hu, who informed Yü that the nether hair only was to be shaved, and if she would be so good as to uncover the parts, his brother would carry out the purification without delay.

71

'Yü was surprised, but the request was put with such delicacy that she obediently opened her hempen robe and spread her thighs so that Brother Li could shave her *hisho*. This the young *bonze* did with great artistry, leaving not a single hair and tweaking not at all, and although he murmured simple words of appreciation as the small pink bud emerged, never once did he utter an immodest or irreligious one.

'When Li had completed his task his twin Hu, with many gentle encouragements, instructed Yü to kneel on the *tatami* mat and place her hands on the floor before her. Trustingly Yü complied, turning her head to watch Brother Hu as he mixed a red-ochre ink and wetted a brush fastidiously with the tip of his tongue, and if she had thought Brother Li an artist with the razor, she was to find that his twin surpassed him a hundredfold with the brush.

'Kneeling behind her, Hu parted her plump cheeks to reveal her whorled orifice, while Brother Li stroked her hair soothingly and murmured words of encouragement. If Yü found the ministrations to her nether regions somewhat shocking, the teasing sensations of the brush and the coolness of the red-ochre were far from unpleasant. Gravely Brother Hu licked his brush and carried on with his work, until he had painted a perfect circle of red-ochre around the now-expanding orifice. Then he bowed deeply to Yü and asked her if she was now ready for the final rites of initiation.

'So mischievously did he ask, and so meekly did his brother echo the question, that Yü would have thought herself mean indeed to refuse, so deep was her urge to follow the Way of her new friends. Indeed, if all the rites were as pleasurable as what had gone before, she could not imagine why anyone ever chose to leave the priesthood!

'By all means, she replied, and Brother Hu left the

room to return a few moments later with two other monks as sweet-faced as himself, and several vials of the aromatic oils for which the monastery was famed throughout the province.

'Opening one of the vials Brother Hu poured a little oil of thyme first into Yü's palm, and then on to the outstretched hands of the other monks. Yü bent her head and sniffed devoutly, but this was not, Li explained, what orthodoxy dictated.

'At a sign from Brother Hu, Li and the other monks, Brother Chen and Brother Yung, knelt down and drew back their cassocks to reveal their erect members, and Brother Hu indicated that Yü should anoint each one with scented oil. As Yü stood before them, she was anointed in her turn, both the shaven anterior orifice and the perfect painted O of her nether opening, while the kneeling priests chanted an arcane *sutra* in reverent voices.

'Brother Hu, whose personality was suited to leadership, motioned his twin to lie down on the pallet, and guided the by now sweet-smelling Yü into a posture astride him. Despite the ineptitude of her one and only previous lover, Yü understood quite quickly what was required. Sliding her orifice on to Brother Li's blushing and well-slicked member, she began to move her hips with some enthusiasm, until halted by a command from Brother Hu.

'Putting his hands round Yü's slender waist, Hu lifted her up until the head of his twin's member barely touched the entrance of her budded cleft. Meanwhile he inserted an oil-anointed finger into the inviting red circle of her nether opening until it flowered out, and in its whole-hearted blooming easily admitted his questing member, which burrowed eagerly as a bee into the moist interior. Once snugly rooted between Yü's cheeks Brother Hu slowly withdrew, so that his fortunate twin below could once more reclaim the honeyed depths of Yü's anterior cleft, and so they thrust in perfect tandem, one twin withdrawing while the other dove deep, and vice versa, in a harmonious seesaw motion which all but ravished Yü's inexperienced senses.

'As if this were not enough, Brother Chen and Brother Yung approached with pious faces. Straddling the torso of the recumbent Li, Brother Chen offered his member to the panting Yü, who gobbled at this sweetmeat with a greedy abandon only intensified by the intervention of Brother Yung who, with eyes devoutly averted, laid his head on Li's belly and proceeded to ply his tongue with unerring flicks across Yü's pulsating bud, which burgeoned and thrust forward now as never before, until she felt herself draw near to Heaven.

'And God said to her in a sonorous voice, "One who has a man's wings and a woman's also is in himself a womb of the world, and being a womb of the world, continually, endlessly gives birth."

'Hearing this, Yü surrendered to the holiness of all things, and when, heavy with sweet delight, she returned at last to this earth, it was to hear the voice of Brother Hu offering thanks in the immortal words of Lao-Tzu himself:

> These are the four amphitheatres of the
> universe
> And a fit man is one of them:
> Man rounding the way of earth
> Earth rounding the way of heaven
> Heaven rounding the way of life
> Till the circle is full.

'And this is how the poet Yü Hsüan-chi took her first and faltering steps on the Way to enlightenment.'

Unsuitable Things

When the applause and laughter had died down it was already the Third Quarter of the Watch of the Tiger and therefore an inauspicious hour to bring the proceedings to a close, and so more refreshments were called for, and Shōnagon was prevailed upon to read from her infamous book, although not before Shikibu had secured an undertaking from the glowing Onogoro to provide another instalment of Yü Hsüan-chi's adventures at the next soirée.

Shōnagon's piece was evidently an old favourite with the ladies, and so Onogoro listened attentively, eager to gauge whether her borrowed tale or the 'Unsuitable Things' of the acclaimed diarist gained the warmer response.

'Hollyhock worn in frizzled hair,' read Shōnagon, to a chorus of giggles and groans.

'Snow on the houses of the common people,' she continued. 'This is especially regrettable when the moon shines down on it.'

'A woman who, though well past her youth, is pregnant and walks along panting. It is unpleasant to see a woman of a certain age with a young husband; and it is most unsuitable when she becomes jealous because he has gone to visit someone else.'

Here all except Shikibu nodded their heads and flapped their fans in a consensus of disgust, but although Onogoro was obliged to admire the verve of Shōnagon's delivery, she could not subscribe to the vanity of the sentiments. How snobbish, she thought. I really cannot see how snow on the meanest thatch should be any less lovely than snow on the roof of the great Daigoku-den! And as for ageing women, what else is Shikibu, not to mention Shōnagon herself? In the chatter that followed, Onogoro berated herself a great deal. In succumbing to light-mindedness, surely she had not only treated the loyal Oyu deceitfully, but had also – for the sake of a fleeting notoriety – betrayed herself as a poet? For if the applause which had greeted the Chinese tale was quite equal to the applause commanded by Shōnagon, had not her poems, by comparison, received from all but Shikibu a lukewarm response? Hunger for approbation had tempted her to make a show of sophistication, and rivalry had pushed her forward ... so ran the thoughts of unhappy Onogoro, until self-blame usurped the throne that gratification had earlier occupied. Meanwhile the vivacious Shōnagon – who, we can be sure, would never have wasted time on such heart-searchings – moved on by popular request to a rendering of her 'Hateful Things'.

'A lover who is leaving at dawn announces that he has to find his fan and his paper. "I know I put them some-where last night," he says. Since it is pitch dark he gropes about the room, bumping into the furniture and mutter-ing, "Strange! Where on earth can they be?" Finally he discovers the objects. He thrusts the papers into the breast of his robe with a great rustling sound; then he snaps open his fan and busily fans away with it – only now is he ready to take his leave. What charmless behaviour! "Hateful" is an understatement ...'

'Indeed, one's attachment to a man depends largely on the elegance of his leave-taking. When he jumps out of bed, scurries about the room, tightly fastens his trouser-sash, rolls up the sleeves of his Court cloak, over-robe, or hunting costume, stuffs his belongings into the breast of his robe and then briskly secures the outer sash – one really begins to hate him.'

Concluding, Shōnagon's face was so droll that even in the midst of her self-reproach Onogoro was compelled to laugh, and it was on this high note that the party, conceding that it was now the Second Quarter of the Watch of the Hare, regretfully took their leave of the Lady Izumi and dispersed into the chilly dawn.

Riding the Tiger

❧

Onogoro had requested an appointment to take counsel on the subject of her distressing dream, and on the following day the Master of Divination was announced at her apartments. Through her curtain-of-state she could see the silhouette of the Master as she listened apprehensively to his pronouncement. In a gruff voice interspersed by bouts of throat-clearing the Diviner enjoined her to avoid water in all its forms for a period of several days, to eat no fruit of the sea, and to abstain from sexual intercourse. She must not stroll by the streams and fountains of the Palace gardens, nor might she walk abroad, for this would oblige her to cross at least one of the hundred moated streets of the Capital.

We can imagine Onogoro's dismay, therefore, when, before this taboo period had elapsed, a *katatagae* was pronounced upon all the occupants of the north-east wing of the Palace, owing to the unlucky position of the Tiger Deity, whom the seasonal winds had empowered to a degree considered dangerous.

As the other Ladies-in-Waiting and their maids decamped to the safer houses of relatives and acquaintances, Onogoro, finding herself between the devil and the deep blue sea, sent Tokiden to the Bureau of Divination to consult the Master about her bewildering predicament. Being informed that the Master himself was not available, Tokiden begged advice of one clerk after another. How, she asked, could the Lady Onogoro observe the *katatagae* and remove herself to safety when she was forbidden by taboo to cross water? Could not the period of the taboo be cut short, or the taboo itself overruled? But the clerks, being of low rank and negligible expertise, could not agree among themselves about the protocol, and could not locate anyone with sufficient authority to give a dispensation of the kind her mistress required. His Excellency the Master was not expected back until the Watch of the Monkey, they told the maid haughtily, but as soon as he arrived they would advise him of the lady's situation.

Hour by hour the north-east wind was rising, making a desolate rattling sound in the dry bamboo canes outside the Almond Blossom Chamber, while inside mistress and maid waited anxiously for the Master. The Imperial Apartments were by now almost empty, the Emperor and his retinue having moved for the duration to the Seiryō Palace in the First Ward. At last, in the Second Quarter of the Watch of the Cock, when darkness was already thick over the Palace, the Master arrived with many complaints about the lateness and inconvenience of the hour.

Having consulted the lady's horoscope at length, the Diviner declared, his final assessment was that the threat posed by the Tiger Deity was rather less than the risk entailed in crossing water. The lady should therefore confine herself to her apartments, he concluded, and, giving Onogoro a charm made of willow-wood, he instructed her to keep it about her person as a precaution against the Tiger Demon.

Temperaments as storm-tossed and untranquil as Onogoro's are, as we know, ever prone to possession; little wonder, then, if in her grave dilemma Onogoro yearned for the stolid strength and practised sword of the General. Accordingly, after the Master had taken his leave, she sent Tokiden out into the howling night to carry word to her lover that his presence was sorely needed.

> The seasons of love
> Are so deceptive:
> Are these white almond blossom
> Petals on the wind,
> Or snowflakes?

'Please come,' she wrote. 'I am in danger, yet cannot leave the house.'

The General had given Onogoro a set of twelve *inro*, one for each month of the year, and each fashioned to a seasonal design. For the first month, in honour of the New Year festivities, the *inro* was in the form of a spinning-top; for the second month, a clever rendering of a lantern in beaten bronze mimicked the paper lanterns at the Festival of Inari; for the fourth month, when the silk thread is first drawn from the cocoons, the *inro* was engraved with a pattern of silk-moths, and so on. Since the first month was not yet over, the spinning-top *inro* still dangled from its cord on Onogoro's waist, containing a herbal tincture for her headaches and a sheet or two of paper tissue. It was into this container that she now tucked the willow-wood charm, and snapped the lid shut. Then she sat down to wait for her lover's reply.

Before long Tokiden hurried into the room, her hair ensnarled with dead leaves and her eyes reddened by dust-flurries. Reading the hastily composed letter, Onogoro's heart turned to ice. The General begged her to accept his apologies, explaining that since it was the anniversary of his mother's death, he himself wore the taboo tag and might not venture out of the house for several days.

The thought of her lover shuttered in the safe bosom of his family filled Onogoro with despair, but the hour of the *katatagae* was approaching and, aware of her responsibility to Tokiden, she told the girl that she must go to her aunt's house in the Third Ward and remain there until the danger period was past.

Tokiden dried her tears and fled gratefully into the night, and Onogoro was left alone in the echoing Palace, where hardly a dog or cat remained. Wrapping herself in her over-robe, she clasped the spinning-top *inro* tightly in her hand and sat down at her writing table to wait for whatever was to come.

Now, if every society known to man has its shadow-spirit which by posing an ever-present threat to the integrity of the nation serves the cause of conservatism as effectively as any Imperial army, so the perfumed and exquisite rulers of our land need their Tiger Deity to give substance to the claim that their continued existence is necessary to ensure the security of the populace. For when the Deity has passed on his commanding way, leaving a trail of destruction in his wake, still the Palace stands stock solid, and the street-moats of the Capital run with water, and dispensations issue daily from the inner sanctum of the Council of State, and the common people, seeing that the basic fabric of things remains intact, go about their humble business with renewed confidence.

But what of the Tiger Deity himself, as he appeared in the mind of the unprotected Onogoro, with his great head parting the bamboo canes, and his straw whiskers, and the ragged stripes of his body, and his great green eye glowing through the palm-leaf lattice? As the wind screamed in the almond trees and set all the blinds billowing, Onogoro threw herself down in front of the small shrine of Fudo and prayed for the mercy of the Tiger God, asking desperately, what was his substance and what his desire? To be put out of his restless misery? To find a mate or a dwelling place? Not to be forced for ever to wander abroad? Not to be exiled? Or not to be caged?

Into the frightened heart of the Lady Onogoro moved, as answer, the form of the Deity himself in all his majesty, in his balance of yellow and black, his spill of shadows, his sparks, his dash from the northern seaboard up the craggy slopes of the mountains, his whipping of the waters of Lake Biwa, his sinking of boats and tearing of nets, his shattering of the oyster-shell heaps left by the pearl fishers, his flooding of the rice paddies, his fanning of the funeral pyres until the maddened flames engulfed nearby houses. Onogoro's imagination cowered before this demon who snarled so vengefully and would not be placated until he had rent the arms from her shoulders and the head from her neck and carried it away like a prize into the undergrowth to loll among the ghosts of dead and jealous women.

Shuddering in the grip of her possession, Onogoro ran out on to the veranda under the wild wheeling sky, while the *inro* fell unnoticed from its snapped cord and rolled away into the bamboo thicket. Quite distracted with fear, and hardly knowing north from south, the poor girl stumbled across the garden, past the broken almond trees, past capsized hives where the bees swarmed loose and frantic, until at last she reached the sanctuary of the stableyard.

Inside the stables Oyu struggled to calm the terrified horses. Glimpsing the lad in the dimness, Onogoro flew at him thankfully and clambered upon him like a child, all wild and awry, her hands flailing about her. Although Oyu's heart thudded with joy at this sudden and shocking proximity, he could not disregard the fact that something had to be done before the Lady Onogoro frightened to death not only herself but also his high-strung horses.

With fumbling hands he cast around for a rough blanket and threw it over her, wrapping it tightly so that her limbs were swaddled and restrained. Then, laying the lady on a straw pallet, he put his hand to her brow and soothed her with caresses, until the parts which had been severed and rent asunder rested once more in their proper joints and proper places. Onogoro began to weep softly, for all the world like a child whose parent, summoned from some far-flung wing of the house, at long last hurries into the dark nursery to comfort it.

As for the disposition of our young exorcist, who was wiser than his years but no *bonze* for all that, none can provide better intelligence on the question than the horse Izanami, for she who had felt the balm of his hands was also the sole repository of his secrets, and accordingly knew much. Knew, for instance, as she rolled her dark eye at the couple on the pallet – Onogoro tearful and Oyu meek and mild as a wet-nurse – how many times in his seething thoughts the young man had placed Onogoro on the mare's strong back and ridden helter-skelter to the gates of Paradise. Knew, in addition, the nature of the fateful contract that bound the pair, and, even more seditiously, the names of the score or so of gentlewomen who had also benefited from Oyu's tales and who, preferring to draw a veil over their true predilections, had secured solemn pledges from Oyu that he would never reveal his dealings with them. Thus, in a society of thirty-four ranks, from the Senior First Rank of the Prime Minister to the Lesser Initial Rank Lower Grade of the humblest clerk, Oyu alone had neither position nor accreditation but remained, by necessity, clandestine. But this stern anonymity – which might have embittered a horse, let alone a vigorous and gifted young man – served only to amuse Oyu and foster in him a philosophical bent. The blind son of a country schoolmaster, after all, has many opportunities to learn humility.

In any case, as Oyu had explained to Izanami, he was convinced that his tales – of which each was fashioned to suit a particular client, and none told more than once – would lose their mysterious efficacy if held up to the general glare of publicity, like strange and tremulous sea creatures which, thrown up from the darkest depths, are transformed by the drying rays of the sun into unremarkable salt smears on the shore. Moreover, sometimes he could have sworn that the words which tumbled from his mouth, far from being his own, came to him by way of some spontaneous emission which originated in the unhappy client and fumblingly sought a conduit for its expression. Thus, he reasoned, if people marvelled at the aptness of his tales they had only themselves to thank. And if by this fancy of Oyu's we conclude that the young man was too modest by half, we shall only like him the more for it, for there is always a surfeit of those whose sole aim is to elevate their status in life and therefore hurry to claim credit where none is due. How refreshing it is, then, to discover someone who, rather than railing at a fate which withholds fame, conspires with the first to elude the second. Let what comes from the deep return to the deep was a motto Oyu had whispered in the ear of Izanami many times, and Izanami had nodded her sage head in agreement.

At last the Tiger Deity swept on southwards to batter at the shores of Izumi, leaving the plain of Heian behind him. With the wind no longer roaring, but sighing now in the eaves, Onogoro lay empty-headed on her bed of straw, incorporate as only mother-love can make us, her mind once again all of a piece. Was it some spell Oyu wove, she wondered, that gave rise to this peaceful conviction that there was nothing to be striven after, no one to be challenged or defended against, no cause, even, for grievance?

Before long, however, Onogoro's composure gave way to a more familiar impulse, for she was accustomed to think of happiness not as a present but as a far-off thing, and once again her mind grew restless and scurried out of the stable in search of other spoils. She began to fret that it was Oyu, and not the General, who sat beside her bed, for was it not the General who should have been concerned about her plight, and was he not the one who should have flown to her side to succour her? And why had he not done so? The answers came as thick and fast as troubles. What it all boiled down to, she decided, was that she did not please him enough, had not learned how to, was neither beautiful, good, patient, cunning, accomplished, pliant, passionate, nor powerful enough to vanquish the opposition and make him love her. Quite dejected, now, she threw aside the imprisoning blanket and seized the stable lad by the hand. 'You are a good kind magician, Oyu,' she said, thanking him warmly.

'No need, My Lady,' Oyu replied, but a blush spread across his cheeks, and Izanami saw that the good-humoured stoicism which protected the youth from bitterness and envy was no defence against the unsuitable ardour which afflicted him. As Onogoro rose to take her leave, and Oyu made no move to stop her, Izanami, who had the mind of a matchmaker but not the tongue with which to give tart counsel, could do nothing but snort with disgust at such a listless outcome.

A Pyre of Bees

Two days later, with the *katatagae* lifted, the carriages began to roll back into the Imperial Enclosure, and the maids fell to sweeping, and the gardeners to burning the snapped branches of the ornamental trees and caulking the scars on their trunks.

In the afternoon the Princess Saishō arrived back at her apartments and bullied Onogoro out into the gardens to view the bonfires. The excited Princess insisted on gathering bundles of dead twigs and pine needles to throw on the flames, and exclaimed with pity over the dead bees which littered the ground, their wings stiff and glittering from the night's rain, their furred bodies empty and quiet.

'But they must have a funeral pyre!' cried the Princess, and so Onogoro and Saishō scooped up the bees and made their own fire of bamboo leaves, and watched how rapidly the wings flared up and were consumed, and how the fur crisped, and the bodies shrivelled to black nuggets in the heart of the flames.

The air was full of burning, and smelled of sweet pine and camphor, which tickled their nostrils and made their eyes run with water. Except for the south horizon, where tigerish clouds still towered, the sky was clear and bright, and the gardeners ribbed one another as they worked, and the boisterous shouts of the maids echoed from the apartments. It was a happy scene, and Onogoro would have liked to join in the general gaiety, but she felt quite out of sorts, and could not shake off a strange malaise which dulled her mind and dragged at her body.

By and by Onogoro saw Izumi Shikibu strolling towards them. She was accompanied by a high-ranking nobleman of middle years, and wore the cat Omoto balanced precariously on her shoulder. 'Oh no, not that boring old woman again,' said the Princess rudely and, skittish as ever, ran off into the blown leaves.

Surmising that Shikibu's companion must be either Prince Tametaka or his brother Prince Atsumichi, who were both her lovers, Onogoro hid her face decorously behind her fan. Shikibu, however, would allow no one to stand on ceremony, and, brushing Onogoro's fan aside, presented her cheek for a kiss. 'Now don't be so retiring, Onogoro. I've told the Prince so much about you he feels you're already part of his family. Don't you, Atsumichi?'

Onogoro blushed as the prominent black eyes of the Prince looked her over. Atsumichi made a deep bow, his elegant forelock swinging forward over his shaven temples. 'Indeed I do. In fact, Shikibu and I were just trying to complete that old poem by the hermit Mêng Hao-Jan, and I said, did I not, Shikibu, the Lady Onogoro will surely recall the ending. Now, how does it go . . .?

> 'On this spring morning I wake light-hearted,
> Surrounded by birdsong . . .'

Atsumichi had quoted in the original Chinese. Realising that she was being tested, Onogoro rose to the challenge and furnished the final couplet, not too stumblingly, in the same tongue:

> 'Until I remember the night, the storm,
> And I wonder how many blossoms were broken.'

'Excellent!' cried the Prince, clapping his hands.

'You see?' Shikibu's proud glance commended Onogoro who, embarrassed by too easy a triumph, stretched out a hand to stroke the Lady Omoto. But the cat, which was draped gracefully around Shikibu's shoulders, glared at her without recognition. 'So my brave girl has diced with the Great Commander who routs even Generals,' said Shikibu, for she had heard word of Onogoro's lonely vigil on the Night of the Tiger. She shivered in commiseration. 'Can you imagine anything more terrible, Atsumichi? Even in my safe bed in the Third Ward I pulled the covers over my head and trembled like a leaf!'

'No wonder the Lady Onogoro looks so pale,' the Prince observed, 'after such an ordeal.'

'I am not quite recovered,' Onogoro admitted, quailing a little before the penetrating gaze of the Prince. And indeed it was true. All the joints of her body had begun to ache, her ribs felt crowded and quarrelsome, and her head was so heavy that she carried it gingerly, as if it might roll off her shoulders at any moment.

Just then the Lady Omoto, who had been staring at Onogoro quite fixedly, rose up and sprang without warning at her breast. Onogoro staggered and would have fallen had not the Prince reached out to support her. 'What a she-devil!' scolded Shikibu, grabbing at the heavy body of the cat and extricating its Imperial claws from Onogoro's robe. The Prince, meanwhile, plucked swiftly at the folds of silk at her neck, his hand brushing her skin as he did so. Mortified by this casual intimacy, Onogoro flushed scarlet. The Prince held up the furred body of a bee and looked at it with satisfaction.

'Quite dead, fortunately. Our Lady Omoto grows short-sighted in her old age. Unlike some of us.' His gaze rested appraisingly on Onogoro, and for a moment she was horror-struck. Only if Atsumichi considered her a woman of dubious reputation would he feel entitled to take such liberties, she thought wretchedly. Surely Shikibu had not betrayed her by repeating the tale of Yü Hsüan-chi for her lover's amusement!

Her suspicions were short-lived, however, and dissipated entirely when Shikibu, shooing the cat away, put an arm round her waist and fussed over her possessively, declaring that she would see to it that Onogoro was put straight to bed and remained there until she recovered. 'Leave us, Atsumichi,' she ordered, and Onogoro saw with surprise that the grand nobleman, far from taking offence at such a summary dismissal, complied with a shrug and a good-humoured bow.

'My salutations to His Excellency Taira no Motosuke,' he smirked. 'Such a fine swordsman!'

Onogoro greeted this piece of impudence with a chilly nod, but Shikibu tapped Atsumichi's wrist smartly with her fan. 'Enough, Atsumichi!'

'Old wounds, old wounds,' laughed the Prince, placing a hand over his heart and wincing ruefully.

Shaking an admonishing fist at her lover, Shikibu led Onogoro away. 'Atsumichi is incorrigible,' she sighed. 'All breeding and no manners.' Onogoro was disturbed, however, and begged Shikibu to tell her what was implied by the Prince's pantomime.

'If you must know, not that it's important, there was a time when the Prince took it into his head to pay court to the Lady Ochibu. Now, in my opinion, if the lady found his attentions so unwelcome she should have dealt with it herself like any level-headed person. But instead she panicked like a schoolgirl and told her husband – who of course had no choice but to send the Prince packing.' Shikibu patted Onogoro's hand. 'A silly business altogether. Best forget about it. As Atsumichi would, if he didn't thrive on small grudges.'

Onogoro's head swam with the effort of climbing the steps to the veranda, and she leaned gratefully on Shikibu. Once indoors, her friend cried for green tea to be brought, and soup of water chestnuts. Propped up on her couch and swaddled to the neck in the quilted bedcovers, Onogoro drank thirstily, and fell fast asleep in broad daylight with her head on Shikibu's ample shoulder.

The Rash

The heat of the bonfires stole into Onogoro's dreams as she tossed and turned in her sweat-soaked coverings. When morning came, however, she found herself in bed, clad in a fresh lawn gown, and feeling decidedly better. The Lady Izumi, Tokiden informed her, had insisted on staying all night, and had bathed her head and limbs with lime blossom water until the fever abated. 'Not that it was necessary,' she added with an injured look, 'I told her I could manage perfectly well.'

Onogoro's heart filled with gratitude. 'How kind of her,' she exclaimed. 'Did she leave a note? I must go and thank her today.' She eased herself out of bed and found with relief that her legs, if a little feeble, supported her. Protesting at first at her mistress's resolve to be up and about, Tokiden eventually gave in, and, fetching mirror and combs, set about dressing Onogoro's disordered hair. Now that she had had her way, Onogoro gave herself over to Tokiden's attentions, and even allowed herself to be bullied a little. She bent her head forward obediently as the maid scooped up the long strands from her nape and clucked with dissatisfaction at the snarled ends.

'But what's this, My Lady?' said Tokiden suspiciously, her comb poised in mid stroke.

'What is it, Tokiden?'

'On your shoulder, My Lady. Looks like writing to me.' The maid soaked the sponge and would have washed the offending marks away entirely if Onogoro had not stayed her.

'But what does it say, Tokiden?' Tokiden shrugged furiously, and Onogoro cursed herself, for she had forgotten that the girl could not read. Taking the mirror from the maid she twisted it at an angle and saw that indeed there was writing, several columns of it, in neat characters, written in dark brown ink on her pale skin. In the mirror the characters were reversed, however, and quite indecipherable. Onogoro thought immediately of Shikibu and chuckled with delight. What a witty way to send a good-bye letter, she thought. But since I can't decipher it, the author must read it to me herself!

Tokiden shook her head, perplexed. Of all the ways to send a next-morning letter, she thought, it isn't like the General at all. Then, remembering that the General was still under taboo and had not called for several days, she looked at her mistress with alarm. Next-morning letters were exchanged only between lovers, or her name was Empress Sadako. But between Lady Izumi and the Lady Onogoro? Really, there was no end to the licence of these Court ladies!

Dressed in an azalea-coloured kimono lined with dove-grey silk, with her face freshly powdered but her teeth unblackened, for tooth-blackening was a fashion she had never found attractive, Onogoro went light-footed along the corridors to the Plum Blossom Apartments. Shikibu, however, was distressed to see her friend up and about so soon, and complained: 'I thought I told that maid of yours to keep you in bed at least until tomorrow!'

'But I would really feel quite well,' said Onogoro with a

mischievous smile, 'if it weren't for this nasty rash on my shoulder.'

'Darling,' said Shikibu, her face stricken, 'you don't mean scarlet fever?'

Shikibu's concern seemed so sincere that Onogoro was astonished. Slipping her robe off her shoulder, she displayed the strange eruption. 'But who could have written it, if not you?' she asked in dismay.

'How very odd!' said Shikibu, taking her magnifying glass to the tiny characters. 'It almost looks like a poem. Let me see . . .

> 'Was it your gaze that followed me
> All the way to the mountain's fastness?
> No, it was only the moon,
> Peering over my shoulder.'

'It *was* you,' Onogoro accused. 'Why don't you admit it?'

Shikibu burst out laughing. 'I swear it was not! I think you have a clandestine lover, my dear. And not a bad poet at that!'

'So clandestine that I'm not aware of him myself!' Onogoro retorted, her mind in a turmoil. If Shikibu was telling the truth, where was she to search for the culprit? Was she to believe that some stranger had stolen into her bedchamber with intent to embarrass her?

Shikibu gazed at her wide-eyed. 'What a mystery! We must get to the bottom of it. We shall ask Saishō's Ladies-in-Waiting, one by one. Perhaps someone saw an intruder . . .'

'No!' cried Onogoro, aghast, 'they're such dreadful gossips! Please help me remove the marks immediately.'

Shikibu shrugged. 'As you wish, darling.' Before she set to with sponge and pumice-stone, however, she insisted on copying out the poem, in case the identity of the author should one day come to light. 'We must have proof in order to confront him.' she said sensibly. Then she scrubbed at the characters, but to little avail. The ink appeared to be well nigh indelible, and several treatments with salt and pumice succeeded in blurring the writing only at the cost of irritating Onogoro's skin unbearably. At last Shikibu refused to go on with the harsh ablutions, and instead rubbed salve into the now livid shoulder, and if privately she felt that Onogoro was making a mountain out of a molehill, she did her best to reassure her that the writing would in all probability fade of itself in a day or two.

Next morning Onogoro anxiously examined the scandalous shoulder, and found the inscription flagrant as before. When the General sent word, therefore, that his taboo period was over, and that he wished to call at the Almond Blossom Pavilion on the following day, Onogoro despatched Tokiden with a note begging him to postpone his visit until the night of the full moon, which was four days hence, on account of her fever.

On the morning of the appointed day Onogoro woke early and lay for a while recalling the strangely peaceful dreams that the moon in its burgeoning quarter often inspired in her. How friendly she was, that high-sailing moon which stroked the mountain peaks with cool blue light, and guided the feet of pilgrims over improbable snow-bridges! But then, with a shrinking heart, she remembered the dishonourable stigmata, and rising hurriedly she bade Tokiden fetch the aloe leaves and lemon skins which had been applied each day with little effect. She loosened her robe to bare her shoulder, fully expecting to see the ink stain brazen and unaltered, but when she held up her mirror she exclaimed in astonishment. On her creamy skin there was neither blur nor blemish, and every last character had utterly vanished!

'Well, thanks be,' said Tokiden, who disliked enigmas and had had more than enough of this one. 'Now you'll be good as new for His Excellency.'

Now it happens, none too seldom, that a lady who feels neglected by her lover will, on his arrival at her chamber, be seized by a perverse excitement of which a large component is unacknowledged rage, and with her unstable heart hammering and her febrile tongue chattering, will become quite heedless in her happiness, and throw all caution to the winds. Thus it was that Onogoro, in her eagerness to relate as many entertaining events as possible in the short time at her disposal, quite forgot what was prudent and what was not, and in her anxiety to conceal the bizarre disease which had afflicted her, rashly let slip her conversation with Prince Atsumichi.

The General, whose wife had set off on a pilgrimage to give thanks at the shrine of Ise, and who had looked forward to spending the entire night with his mistress, was cut to the quick. The long knife of jealousy, sheathed for so many years, dug into his vitals anew, and the sensation – this softness, these pulsating innards, the pathos of this unarmoured and cavernous interior – was so unbearable that, pushing it immediately aside, he sought a safe redoubt from which to parry the unanticipated attack. Convincing himself that a scolding would only be for her own good, he fixed Onogoro with a forbidding look. 'Prince Atsumichi is a reprobate,' he declared, 'and not at all the sort of person you should be associating with!' When Onogoro opened her mouth to reply he held up a firm and final hand. 'Enough, my dear. Let it rest there. I hope you'll allow that I know best in some matters.'

Seeing her mistake, Onogoro bowed her head meekly, and was rewarded by the ardent touch of the General's lips, first on her nape, and then on the curve of her breast, until finally, with a sigh more passionate than ever before, the General scooped her up and carried her to the bed.

Listening in his hiding place, Oyu was caught between laughter and dismay. It was amusing, he reflected, how the smallest spark of rivalry invariably set a dull man on fire. How much better for Onogoro, then, if recognising this, she could have turned it to her own advantage. Yet the lessons Oyu had learned behind the *tsuitate* screens of the Capital lay heavy on his heart, for although he did not condemn the desperate and duplicitous stratagems his clients employed in their quest for power over their lovers, nor could he admire them, and he did not relish an Onogoro grown skilful in these matters, far preferring Onogoro as she was: haphazard, mercurial, and, if not entirely guileless, markedly lacking in the sustained cunning which serious intrigue requires.

The Phosphorescence of Ise

'Once on the southern coast of Ise a band of musicians on their way to a festival became inebriated in a village inn, and took it into their heads to delay their onward journey in order to spend the summer evening diving with the pearl fishers.

'Casting off their clothes on the sparkling shore, they frolicked in the waves until the sun sank below the western horizon and the moon rose up to light the phosphorescent seas. Then, refreshed by the salt air, they floundered out of the foam and made ready to return to the inn to satisfy appetites which their exercise had restored.

'All but young Yoshito the *samisen* player, that is, who was called other-worldly on account of his faraway look and the plaintive chords he wrung from his lute, and who now expressed a wish to linger awhile and watch the play of the moonlight on the waters. Laughingly his companions accused him of having an assignation with one of the leathery-skinned fisherwomen, who swam mother-naked like their menfolk and looked with frank-eyed interest at the pale bodies of the musicians. But Yoshito, who had suffered their badinage all the way from Yamato and had quite lost patience with them, merely turned his back and dove, so that the waves shut out every last ribaldry, and he had only the quiet crabs and the corals for company.

'High above him the moon wavered through the water, casting shadows of fish on the floor of the sea. Yoshito swam peacefully in the shallows, observing the spiny sea-urchins and whorled shells, and so silent was he that a shoal of silver herrings, taking him for one of them, enclosed him in a soft momentary caress. Enchanted, young Yoshito held his breath and floated, while the fish slid past him like a field of barley combed by the wind.

'He discovered also that if he dove underwater and thrust his hand above the surface his skin glowed with phosphorescence, and so he lay beneath the waves, turning his hand dreamily this way and that way so that the moonlight glimmered on his fingers, making believe that he was the creature of some better element, and that the hand belonged not to his mortal body but to some luminous aquatic spirit.

'Meanwhile, from the shore, this phenomenon did not go unobserved. It had fallen to the lot of the Lady Okimi to be Vestal at the shrine of Ise that year, and in order to escape from the incessant burden of ceremonial she had taken to wandering the shores at midnight, when her attendants believed her to be asleep.

'Seeing the spirit-hand hovering above the waters, Okimi was at first terrified, and let out a shriek. When, consequently, the head and shoulders of the demon appeared all glimmering from the waves, she fell near-fainting on the sand.

'Standing up in the shallows, Yoshito saw that she was no fisherwoman but a lady of rank, and called out to her, "Don't be afraid, My Lady. What you see is no ghost but a humble musician, whose lute lies beside you on the sand."

'Hearing his human voice, and seeing not only the *samisen* but also the young man's garments piled on a boulder near the water's edge, the Lady Omiki recovered herself.

'Now although Omiki was devout, her temperament did not suit her for celibacy, and she sorely missed her lover in the Capital. And so as Yoshito waded towards her through the shallow water, she raised her fan and

97

from behind its folds observed the ghostly torso that emerged from the sea with a decidedly earthly interest.

'Eager to reassure the lady further, Yoshito pressed on towards the shore, disregarding the sea-urchin spines which pricked at his feet and the cockle shells which stubbed his toes. But suddenly his foot slipped down into a crevice and was pinned there, and try as he might he could not free himself. Peering down into the water he discerned the mighty lips of a giant shell, which had sprung shut and which now gripped his leg like a vice just below the knee.

'On the shore the Lady Omiki, who had lowered her fan for a moment to exhibit her moonlit features, saw the young man stop in his tracks, and wondered in dismay whether her long year of abstinence had robbed her not only of the art of flirtation, but of her looks as well.

' "My Lady," called the hapless Yoshito, "I am trapped by a clam and beg your assistance."

'Her pique turning rapidly to pity, Omiki looked at the stretch of water between them and made her decision. Stripping off her over-robe she laid it on the boulder where the young man's garments were piled, only to see with a chill of realisation that the tidal wavelets now lapped hungrily at the very base of the stone. Omiki's underdress billowed sluggishly around her as she waded deeper and deeper, but she drove herself bravely on.

'At last she reached the trapped youth, who had grasped his leg in both hands and was tugging impotently at it. Omiki saw immediately that she would gain purchase on the shell only by diving under the surface, but each time she attempted to do so her voluminous underdress filled with air and buoyed her up, rendering her powerless.

'Since the situation was by now too urgent for modesty, she turned her back on the young captive and, divesting herself of every last impeding garment, dove mother-naked like the fisherwomen, except that her skin was milk-white, and her prize was not pearls but Yoshito's very life. Again and again Omiki dove down to wrestle with the shell, while her garments floated all unheeded out to sea. She wrenched at the tight-clamped lips of the monster, tearing her hands on the barnacles that rimmed them, and each time she surfaced the waters were a little higher.

'At last Yoshito, who had defended himself by frantic activity from his impending fate, bowed his head and acknowledged the import of the rising tide. "Leave me, good lady", he begged. "Else we two shall perish together."

'Clasping Yoshito's hand in hers, Omiki wept with frustration. Then, hoping that in the course of her service as Vestal some small measure of divinity had adhered like the phosphorescence which now gleamed on her skin, she muttered a fervent prayer to Our Lord Amida, and, as added insurance, went on to invoke the ancient gods, calling on Izanagi, Lord of the Foaming Brine, to intervene.

'No answer came, however, to the two who stood evanescent in the encircling sea, at least none that was ecclesiastical. By now the waves had reached Yoshito's chin and despair had come hand in hand with acceptance.

'Yet even as Yoshito's mind conceded that his fate was imminent, his youthful body rebelled and, cleaving with a savage tenderness to the life that is universal in us, he felt all his senses stir in perfect awakening. His nostrils flared to take in the sweet essence of the salt air, and his skin swooned to the waves' caress, and in his ears echoed the melancholy piping of the leviathans of the deep.

'How lovely she is, he thought, feasting his eyes on the glittering Vestal. How lovely the first and last woman. And as the waters rose, so did Yoshito's member which, loth to relinquish an animal destiny compelling as the phases of the moon or the tug of the tides, staked its ardent claim on the future.

' "Rise up on me, My Lady," he begged, "and take my lips." The waters bore the obedient Vestal graciously up, and weeping she straddled him, the tears making channels in the phosphorescence of her cheeks, and fixed her mouth on his to seal it safely from the brine. Meanwhile her nether lips, having slithered down to enclose his member, now locked around it as tightly as the shell had clamped around his limb.

'Bracing her feet against the serrated lips of the clam, Omiki cupped her hands under Yoshito's chin to hold his head above the waters, while with her whole heart she bore down on him. For a vision of death had risen like a phoenix to set her mind on fire, and what had stemmed from pity and started as sacrifice was now muscular and rolled like thunder in her tormented vitals. For whenever the mind, in extremity, apprehends that it is life itself which dies with every fleeting moment, and that those discarded moments lie heaped behind us like empty oyster shells upon the shore, this knowledge leaves us naked to the urgent winds of the universe, which shriek both joy and destruction. And it was this instantaneous joy which bellowed in her body now, the joy which, as child and mother of annihilation, both acknowledges and celebrates it.

'Enclosing Yoshito in her luminous thighs, the Vestal bucked and leapt like a glittering salmon who races pell-mell up the waterfalls to the source of the river for spawning. Her spine thrashed the water, and in the coupling the doomed Yoshito found such fierce shelter that the waves which lapped at his nostrils seemed as mere ripples on the swell of that fearless love which, wishing only to expend itself, surges up to drown us in its insistent rhythms.

'But as the love-song soared in him, and his mouth

flew free of Omiki's to cry out its final cadenza, the waiting sea rushed in to claim his gasps of ecstasy as its own due, and sent luminescent bubbles to the surface in their place.

'In the new blue cave that was his being, Yoshito felt his consciousness ebb away, yet at the same time all that was bone and blood and music in him filled his member with a boundless and ineffable joy which, in one final elemental thrust, carried the swimmer to his last and farthest shore.

'Omiki gave forth a roar and exploded in the gentle moonlight as Yoshito's face sank beneath the waters, and his being shuddered out triumphantly into her, until all that marked his passing was a circular and slowly spreading ripple in the sea of her, and the lute which, gleaming and phosphorescent, floated away on the tide like some lovely offering for the gods.'

The Spying Eye

Oyu, who had fallen asleep behind the *tsuitate* screen, startled himself awake with a snore, and for a moment held his breath, convinced that an eye was piercing the shadows. The airless room smelled heavily of incense and lovemaking, and soon drowsiness threatened to overtake him once more, but he dared not give in to it, in case another inadvertent sound brought the General to his senses and the General's blade to his throat. The moon, he knew, was at its fullest, but in the overheated chamber he could not sense on his skin the frost or damp which might have told him whether the night was cloudy or clear, and what slats of light might therefore illuminate him as he emerged from the shelter of the screen.

He lay drained after the effort of story-telling, and his limbs grew stiff with frustration, and his belly grumbled, and his love came out of the night like fear and clutched at his throat. Tears ran suddenly from his eyes at the fate of poor trapped Yoshito, and not even the whip of pride could master the flow and bring it under control. For Oyu, who could accept all human weaknesses in others, was less tolerant of his own failings, and of the gamut of affections self-pity was the one he most abominated. Yet here it was, the very animal, crouched and abject, night-blinded yet visible to any passing predator. And he who had rescued Onogoro from the tiger-wrath lay powerless in the grip of it, as the long watches of the night followed one on the other.

At last, when the first birds signalled the advent of dawn, the General's breathing grew deep and sonorous and, judging that the coast was clear, Oyu crept out through the side screen door that led by way of a corridor to Shune's domain in the kitchens. In this way, all unwittingly, he escaped detection not only by the General, but also by the Regent's spy who, encamped below the veranda, waited to resume his surveillance.

The Knee

When morning came Onogoro rolled over to find the General at her side. Never before had she seen her lover's limbs sprawled so carelessly, nor his face so vulnerable and childlike. His hair, she noticed, was grizzled, and his mouth lay expectantly open, like a babe waiting to suckle. Smothering a laugh, she leant over the dreaming face and pushed her nipple between the proferred lips, which pouted and pursed and smacked themselves together in sleep.

At once the General's eyes flew open and regarded the sweet intruder with momentary fright, for in his drowsy vacancy the horizon that rose before him was a vast globe which filled the future and pulsated in the depths of the past. Realising that he had been caught off guard, he seized Onogoro and pinned her down. 'Close your eyes,' he commanded, 'so that I may spy on you in my turn.' Onogoro did as she was told, and felt the General's body withdraw from her, and the General's eyes regard her like the sun from a far distance. His fingers, meanwhile, skimmed her skin, alighting briefly at the ports of breasts and belly on their southward voyage towards the toes.

Onogoro lay in ecstatic compliance, savouring these novel attentions, and the Lady Omoto herself could have been no happier. When the heat of her lover's hand paused a hairsbreadth above her knee, her skin tingled towards his fingers like a flame drawn upwards by the log which it will presently consume. But then the General stiffened. Flexing her knee, he peered, and let out an angry grunt. 'I suppose you're able to account for this?'

Onogoro opened her eyes in dismay. The General stabbed his finger at the place where the back of her thigh met the hollow behind her knee. 'If you had told me that you were short of writing materials,' he said in a voice of bitter sarcasm, 'I could perhaps have remedied the matter.'

Panic gripped Onogoro. She straightened her leg and twisted it this way and that, but could make out only the outer periphery of what she knew in her bones was a poem. 'You don't understand!' she cried.

'Indeed I don't,' said the General with asperity. 'But bearing in mind that you're no contortionist, I can draw my own conclusions!'

'Believe me, I know nothing of the matter! The poems appear of their own accord. Ask the Lady Izumi, I beg you, she will be my witness!' Under the hostile gaze of her lover Onogoro's voice faltered and faded into silence. If her good friend Shikibu had suspected her, how could she convince a man like the General of the mysterious origin of the poems? When all the damning evidence pointed to a secret liaison with some impudent scribe who preferred skin to scrolls!

'Of course you're quite at liberty to take other lovers,' said the General, turning his back on her and coldly gathering up his scattered garments. 'Odd, really, how one persists in believing one has a right to know.'

'Don't go, I implore you,' cried Onogoro, quite distraught. 'I swear there's no other.' But the more wounded the General, the steelier he became, and all Onogoro's pleas fell on deaf ears, until at last she hung her head in despair. 'Please read the inscription to me,' she begged, with the numb heart of a man going to his execution.

The General gazed at her rancorously, for although he was much tempted to believe in her innocence, he was at heart a plain man who hated to appear credulous, and he had no guarantee that this latest plea was not another subterfuge. Jealous curiosity, however, got the better of scruple and, swiftly turning the lady over, he examined the words on the back of her knee.

'Humble, like the evening primrose,
I hide until sundown.
Not in daylight
But in darkness
Do I know myself.'

What riddle is this? he wondered, his suspicions inflamed
anew. Who else but secret suitors hide themselves until
sundown and prattle on about humility? With a snort of
disbelief the General tightened the sash of his trouser-
skirt, flung on his over-robe, and stormed out in high
dudgeon. As his carriage conveyed him back to a house
with no wife in it, pride wrestled with fury and, finding
it childish and demeaning, declared it insupportable, and
engaged his mind instead in the cooler frenzy of strategy.
If the Lady Onogoro was disingenuous, so would he be
in his turn. Nothing could be simpler, after all, than to
delegate one of the Bodyguard to observe the lady's com-
ings and goings, and daily bring him intelligence of her
visitors. With or without the help of the Lady Onogoro,
he would assuredly get to the bottom of the matter!

Left alone, Onogoro lay bemused on the bed. For an
agonised moment she thought that the boy who had
spent the night secreted in the chamber was plainly the
culprit, but common sense banished this suspicion as
quickly as summer sun burns off the morning mists. Since
Oyu could neither see nor write, he could not possibly
be held responsible. She thought of the useless scrubbing
and bleaching; she thought of the anonymous author
who had insinuated his words on to her skin, and rage
welled up in her. How unfair it was! Just as her willing
feet flew forward on the path to happiness, misfortune
clung to her hem like a pestering orphan and tugged her
back into the mire! She dealt the blameless knee a vindic-

tive slap. What must she do to be rid of it? Must she cut out the part entirely, like the wasp-eaten heart of a pear?

The Tough Guy

~✦~

Onogoro slunk along the Palace corridors like a whipped dog, bearing the unwanted brand of the poem on the back of her knee and the unwanted sting of the General's rejection in her heart. Indeed she was fated, she thought, and indeed her fate was a miserable one. Accordingly it was a surly and disconsolate face which greeted Shikibu when she opened the sliding door to admit her friend.

No sooner had the two women embraced than Onogoro hoisted her robe and, stabbing accusingly at the poem, poured out the whole unhappy story. 'This suitor of yours certainly has a strange way of begging for attention,' said Shikibu, feeling quite antagonistic to the rascal who had caused her friend such distress. 'He must be timid as a mouse!'

'Timid?' cried Onogoro. 'He's a tormentor!'

'Tiger or mouse, we'll tread on his tail soon enough. In the meantime it will do the General no harm to feel a little jealous. He'll come running back, you'll see.' Shikibu banished the cat to the corridor – for her pet lizard Boku had just wakened from his winter sleep and taken up residence on the dividing beam, not quite out of reach of the ageing but resourceful Omoto – and asked Ben to bring lime blossom tea. When the two women were seated in comfortable intimacy, she said gently, 'Come now, be calm, and tell me about your work.'

Onogoro's face crumpled like a paper lantern in an autumn cloudburst. 'Not good enough!' she cried. 'Is that not the constant refrain of the poet? Are we not like children, doomed to try endlessly to prove our worth to an unloving parent? And are we not doomed to fail in this endeavour, even if we succeed in seducing the whole world with our work?'

From the dividing beam Boku, the Tough Guy, rotated his left eye through 180 degrees and saw a convex room and two curved ladies on the arc of the couch: the one who had fed him and named him, and another, a strange red-robed one. A sheet of water flooded down the red lady's face, and this made Boku's tail twitch with apprehension, dryness being his element. 'Not good enough.' These were words beyond his comprehension, which lent itself more readily to constructions like good-to-eat, sleep-now, or warm-sun-coming. He wondered if the lady had eaten something bad, something which disagreed with her. His belly rippled in a painful corrugation of memory, and his colour changed from a neutral bamboo to a bright worried brown. Reversing his position so that his head pointed to the ceiling, he retreated behind his eyelids and tried to regain his equanimity.

Shikibu was mystified by Onogoro's outburst. 'However misguided the motive,' she ventured, 'surely it may spur us on to produce great work?'

Ignoring her, Onogoro threw up her hands and shook her fists at the heavens. 'Where are the mothers? And where are the mothers of the gods? All women are orphans!' she cried. 'All women are denied!'

Shikibu gazed at her reckless friend. 'But did you not

deny your own mother, by styling yourself the self-curd-ling lady?'

'My mother hated me,' Onogoro declared with a bitter twist of the mouth. 'Sometimes I think she would have followed the Chinese way if the law had allowed it.'

'But darling,' said Shikibu, much disturbed, 'how could she have hated her own little girl?'

Onogoro began to weep even more piteously. 'Because the girl wasn't good enough! Because the girl was bad!'

On the dividing beam Boku's tongue fluttered convul-sively as he tried to spit out the bad worm that the lady had swallowed. Since the lady's robes were the red and purple colours which meant rage or rutting, he crawled up the beam a little to preserve a safe distance.

Taking a sheet of paper tissue, Shikibu tried to wipe the tears from her friend's ravaged face. Was this mother of Onogoro's such a monster as to starve her own daughter, or beat her into submission? Certainly she had heard tell of such cruelty. Often enough she had seen the lost and demented wandering the market-place and, hearing the interminable circularity of their ravings, in which com-plaint followed self-reproach like a dog chasing its tail, she had wondered whether in fact it was not evil spirits that possessed them but rather the memory of some ill deed suffered at the hands of those who ought to have inspired only love and trust. But Onogoro's mother? No, she could not believe it. 'The girl *is* good enough, dar-ling,' she said staunchly. 'And until you believe it, you will always be at odds with yourself.'

Good-to-eat? thought Boku the Tough Guy: the red lady

is going to eat her, then? Puffing up his cheeks pugnaciously, he turned bright orange against the dull beam, so that Shikibu would heed his warning.

'I wish I had been born a man,' Onogoro muttered sulkily, plucking at the long fringe of her *obi*.

'However you were not,' Shikibu retorted, exasperated, 'and nor was I, and short of a miracle we will stay the sex we are.' Human beings, she thought, were so full of impossible longings, and poets, more than most, insisted on torturing themselves. But to wish to exile one's emotions like this was painful indeed. One might as well wish to shed human skin and become quick and dry and cold-blooded as a lizard!

The Night of the Monkey

Once in every sixty days, when the Sign of the Elder Brother of Metal coincides with the Sign of the Monkey, the Bureau of Divination strongly advises our citizens to spend the whole night awake in order to protect themselves from the many 'corpse-worms' which might otherwise penetrate the orifices of their sleeping bodies, causing them great harm.

So it happened that when *Kōshin* night came round once more, Shikibu, Onogoro and the other ladies gathered together to while away the sleepless hours with word-games and story-telling. The first to suggest a game was the hostess herself, who was clad informally in a loose white robe lined with cherry-coloured silk, with satin slippers to match. Shikibu had hung the apartment with red and gold lanterns, and now she produced a monkey mask worked in dyed and woven palm leaves, proposing that whoever told a story must first don the Mask of Mischief and Wisdom.

'Oh, please let us play the Game of Five Strokes,' cried Umo, a rather eccentric lady who dressed invariably in green whatever the season.

'Later, Umo,' retorted Shōnagon's cousin, who was nick-named Hime, the Princess. 'First we should have a competition, and the winner will be she who devises the most suitable death for a faithless lover.' Without more ado Hime seized the mask and, tying its ribbons behind her head, launched into her tale.

Death By Perfume

'Once there was a faithless courtier who deceived his mistress with three different women in one night. One of the women, being the lady's maidservant, tearfully confessed to her, and the lady, who had had quite enough of her lover's nonsense, conceived a plot to dispose of him.

'On the courtier's next visit she affected a sweet and trusting demeanour, and begged him to accompany her to the perfume-mixing chamber, on the pretext of con-cocting a new scent which would be theirs alone. The courtier, who fancied himself a connoisseur of the per-fumer's art, eagerly followed his mistress to the marble chamber where mixing vats steamed, and angelica leaves hung drying in long strings, and evening primrose petals yielded their oils to the pressure of great iron mangles.

'Never had the courtier smelt such a confluence of scents, and his nostrils thrilled to the harmony of pea-flower and violet, of honeysuckle and lemon balm and wild hyacinth. Passing the grinding slab he pinched powder of nutmeg and cloves between his finger and thumb, and crushed the white crystals which come from the bark of the camphor tree, quoting, as he did so, snippets of poems he thought relevant, for snippets, it must be said, were all he could remember.

'Hiding her scorn at such self-satisfaction, the lady embraced her lover passionately and promised him an entirely novel sensation. Intrigued, the courtier was easily persuaded to remove his garments and lie down on the robe which his mistress had spread on the floor.

'The lady began with dabs of iris and cloves on her lover's temples, and proceeded to the soft hollow at the base of the throat, which received the potent essence of marigold. Under each armpit she dabbed yarrow and gentian, and continued with her tender ministrations until she had distributed the scents across her lover's entire enraptured body.

'But what the lady knew was that, just as an excess of yin transforms itself into the opposite yang principle, so, in certain dosages, the otherwise healing and stimulating flower essences can be induced to take on a negative aspect.

'Once again she plied her vials above the courtier's body, and the mustard plunged her lover into that deep gloom which has no origin, and the mimulus filled him with the fear of illness and its consequences, and the larch convinced him of failure, and the holly pricked his heart with envious vexation, and the honeysuckle brought tears of homesickness to his eyes.

'The heather, added in a certain secret proportion, made mountains out of molehills, and the gorse discouraged him, and the clematis bemused him, and the elm overwhelmed him with inadequacies, and the crab apple convinced him that he was unclean. The chestnut-bud caused him to replay compulsively the memory of his many mistakes, and the willow made him begrudge the good fortune of his fellow men, and the aspen made him sweat and tremble with vague apprehensions, and the cherry plum convinced him that his mind would give way, and the wild rose resigned him to apathy, so that he did not care whether he lived or died but would have preferred, on balance, the latter.

'Satisfied that she had thus brought him to a point of preparedness, the lady administered two more dabs of crab apple to his temples, to exacerbate self-hatred. In a swoon of self-disgust her lover begged her to deal him a fatal dose, so that he might pay the price for all his crimes against her. The lady, seeing the courtier powerless in her arms, took pity on his torment, and delivered a drop of aconite to his waiting tongue. And so died the faithless lover, all naked and relieved, and not since the death of the Shining Prince himself was there ever a corpse so fragrant at its funeral.'

The Dragon Bath

The reference to Prince Genji of Murasaki's tale was considered most witty and urbane, and the stylish demise of the courtier most appropriate to the scale of his deception. Yomiko now begged to take possession of the monkey mask, and launched into the tale of a doctor who not only half-ruined his family by the flower-fees he expended on his visits to the pleasure-district of the town, but when rebuked, responded by abusing his wife for the frequency of her monthly obstacle.

'Now in fact the lady's *tsuki no sawari* occurred no more often than is common among healthy women, but it did flow more copiously. As a doctor, her husband might have been expected to look sympathetically on this complaint, but instead he met her requests for treatment with obdurate refusal, invoking the Shinto taboo on impurity, and entirely washing his hands of the matter.

'Meanwhile, thanks to his sojourns in the pleasure-houses of the town, the doctor had not escaped that particular form of contamination we call *Karyubo*, the flower-and-willow sickness, and it was when it became obvious that this disease had passed from his dissolute body into her own that rage rose up in his wife like bile, and she hatched a plot to be rid of him.

'To expedite her plan, the lady visited all her sisters and cousins and aunts, of whom there were many, and begged them to save for her the product of their monthly obstacle, explaining to some that the fluid provided the best fixing agent for dyeing, and confiding in others that it was the secret ingredient which fertilised the miraculous chrysanthemums which grew in her garden.

'The gentlewomen were a little shocked at first, but since the doctor's wife was a kind woman who bestowed more favours than she begged, they eventually acceded to her request.

'Every month for a year the lady called at the houses of her female relatives, and carried away the fluids in a wooden bowl covered with a silk cloth. Every month she added her own copious flow, preserving the precious hoard in an oak cask which in more prosperous times had stored sake, and adding as a thinning agent a few drops of *anise* tincture stolen from her husband's pharmacy.

'At the year's end the good woman had succeeded in filling the great cask to the brim, and on the eve of the New Year she sat down to her supper solitary but

contented, her husband having elected as usual to celebrate the Festival at his favourite flower-house.

'When the doctor stumbled back from his drunken
debauches, he was no sooner in the door than he let out
his customary bellow of Food! Bath! Bed! Without a
word of complaint, his wife served him a supper of roast
pork and spiced dumplings. The doctor washed down
the heavy meal with draughts of rice wine, and then fell
into a torpor with his head slumped upon the table.

'Meanwhile, in the washing alcove, the water was heat-
ing. "Let me lead you to the bath, dear sir," the lady
begged.

'Outside the sky was red with fireworks as the lady
steered her unsteady spouse to the washing alcove and
dutifully disrobed him. For a moment the inebriated
doctor, seeing the rust-coloured water, thought that the
ruddy light had given it its livid hue. But when he lowered
himself into the steaming liquid he cried in dismay:
"What kind of trick is this?"

' "Calm yourself, husband," said his lady wife, taking
up the sponge as if to begin the ablutions. "I have merely
added some drops of cochineal, to ward off ill fortune.
In my home province of Higo men entering their unlucky
forty-second year must always bathe in crimson water as
a precaution. It is called the Dragon Bath."

'In the dim recesses of his mind the doctor remembered
that he was indeed on the threshold of that inauspicious
age and, falling into a gloomy reverie on the theme of
passing time and fading prowess, he slipped deeper into
the enervating heat of the waters. Yet in his drink-fuddled
brain the colour of the lucky bath struck soothing chords
in him, for the first hue of his infant memory was the
crimson of his mother's underwear. Tears welled up in
his eyes as he recalled the perfect kindness of this long-
lost lady, and for a moment he imagined that it was her
slender fingers which massaged soap-suds into his hair,

and not the clumsy broad hands of his wife. "Gently, woman," he pleaded, in his mood of self-pity, but the hands only kneaded and prodded all the more determinedly, until the doctor's chin was submerged under the waters.

'The doctor felt quite stunned by heat and steam, and could protest only feebly at the rough treatment being meted out to him. "Is this all I deserve?" he spluttered, as the red water licked saltily at his lips.

'The moment of realisation that followed, if horrible, was at least brief. Like Izanagi, who, when he went to lie with his wife Izanami in Hades, ran screaming from the river of maggots which streamed from her body, the doctor recoiled in horror from the disgusting effluvia of his own wife. Unlike the god, however, he was paralysed by the wine in his veins and the soporific vapours of the bath, and could not stir his limbs for flight.

'With a shriek which released the pent-up rage of years, the lady thrust the doctor's head under the ruddy surface and held it there until she was satisfied that his worthless life was utterly extinguished.

'And so the hapless doctor set off for the shores of Jōdō on a river of women's blood, and if it was unlikely that, thus contaminated, he would ever reach the Western Paradise, we can be perfectly sure that his lady wife cared not one single jot.'

Slow-worms

Yomiko ended her tale with an insouciant grin, and the assembled ladies, who had listened in stunned silence, began one by one to applaud. But now Shikibu, with a merry look at Onogoro, launched into a humorous saga in which a lady hired a gang of street urchins to trail her pompous military lover, and instructed them to laugh uproariously at his most dignified moments, thereby humiliating the poor man to death. However, the consensus was that no more dreadful or ingenious death could be conceived of than the one meted out to the doctor, and accordingly Yomiko was voted the outright winner, and the company turned their thoughts to other amusements.

Reminded of her hurt, Onogoro retreated behind her fan and lost all appetite for playing. She had heard no word from the General since their quarrel, and thought it cruel of Shikibu to make fun of him. If by doing so she had intended to banish love and replace it with scorn, then her tale had had quite the opposite effect and, far from being a cure for heartsickness, merely exacerbated Onogoro's hopeless yearning.

'Don't take on so, Onogoro,' Shikibu murmured, drawing her out of the throng and leading her on to the veranda. 'He'll be back, you mark my words.'

The red and gold lanterns swung in the equinoctial breeze as, inside the apartments, the ladies embarked with noisy enthusiasm on the Game of Five Strokes. Onogoro gazed miserably across the gardens towards the stables, where no light burned, for Oyu was a commoner and no corpse-worm on earth could have kept him from his sleep. 'Sometimes I don't think you understand how much I love the General!' she retorted, quite unaware that hidden in the boughs of the wistaria bush below the veranda the General's aide was attending to every word.

The aide, who was a Junior Captain of the Bodyguard specially trained in surveillance, had been there since nightfall, and the shock of hearing such bloodthirsty tales from the mouths of well-bred ladies had raised the hairs on the back of his neck. Now, crouched in the damp branches, chilled by the breeze and startled by the rustle of dead seed-pods, he wished that he had not heard a word. The tales had penetrated his brain like very corpse-worms, and at this moment he could not afford to dwell on such creatures, all unprotected as he was among the snaking dark branches. He could not, in fact, afford to think of any of his bodily orifices, not his mouth – which was closed in a tight seam – nor his ears – which he would have stopped up with paper tissue had they not been the organs of his profession – nor his nostrils – which he needed to breathe through – nor his itching anus – for so much sitting about in the damp and cold meant that piles were an occupational hazard.

Yet the more he suppressed the unwelcome thoughts, the more surely did the armies of the insect world advance across the gardens of his imagination in invisible platoons – first the humble earthworms, forming the infantry, then the creeping armoured millipedes, flanked by the glow-worms with their green lanterns surreptitiously dimmed. On the left flank rippled a tide of white maggots fresh from the corpse of a cormorant, and behind them the sly slow-worms slithered, while last of all came the vipers with their heads held high as ceremonial horses and their venomous fangs poised to strike.

From the interior of the Almond Blossom Chamber the voices of the ladies insinuated themselves into the Captain's unwilling ears. 'The First Stroke,' cried one, 'would be on the inside of the elbow. The Second – on the sole of the foot. The Third – on the eyelids. The Fourth – on the bridge of the nose. And the Fifth – all the way down the spine.' Another voice broke in pertly. 'I would have all five on my *shiofuki*, of course! My spraying-surf clam! And then I'd make sure to ask for fifty more . . .'

Just then a spider dropped from a branch above and scuttled over the Captain's hand, but fortunately his stifled shriek was quite drowned out by the vulgar laughter from the interior. Despite his agitation, he noted – for he was still a professional – that the two ladies on the balcony did not join in with the infernal merriment, but conversed in sombre tones, until the lady he had been employed to observe covered her face with her hands and swore that she would humble herself in any way, if only the General would come back to her. The aide shrank back under a shower of droplets which fell cold and wormlike on his forehead. But then pity took the place of fright, for the drops which drenched him, he realised, were none other than the lady's sincere and salty tears.

Meanwhile the Regent's spy, who had spent as uncomfortable a night under the General's veranda, hurried home to prepare his report for Atsumichi. 'The General seemed distracted,' he wrote, with the many flourishes and curlicues which he believed showed good breeding. 'Hardly spoke to his wife on her return from her retreat. Went often to window as if watching for someone.' 'At dawn received person who passed on to him a written communication. Appeared even more agitated.' 'Servants unable to inform me as to said person's identity. Suggest further surveillance with ref. to possible conspiracy.'

Matsutake Mushrooms

When the General received the young Captain's report he went to the window and stared out at the gleam of the morning sun on the distant waters of Lake Biwa. So deeply engaged was he in pondering the question of Onogoro that he lost all sense of time, and was startled by the gong which signalled the Watch of the Snake. This coincided with the arrival of Onogoro's maid, who had brought a letter from her mistress entreating him to visit, and also a poem.

> On the frail snow bridge
> Which joins the topmost branches
> Of our love
> This humble pilgrim
> Must tread lightly.

Asking Tokiden to wait in the antechamber, the General sat down and attempted to compose a reply-poem. His aide had recounted Onogoro's heartfelt words, and he had a mind to be convinced of her innocence. On the other hand, whenever his brush met the page a strange image rose before him, causing him to tremble in mid stroke and miserably bungle his characters.

Last autumn, he recalled, on a maple-viewing trip to Mount Ogura, he had passed a country vendor carrying her precious hoard of *matsutake* mushrooms strung on a stem of *susuki* grass. Since his passion for Onogoro had but recently burst into bloom, he had purchased several of the delicacies and sent them to her wrapped in a fine gauze scarf. But now in his strange vision it was this very mushroom-string which haunted him, for on it the fungi were crimped and shrunken like ancient heads, and it was the Lady Onogoro herself who swung the *susuki* stem so jauntily from her wrist.

Losing patience with his stillborn poem, the General dispensed with etiquette and wrote a brief reply advising Onogoro that he would pay her a visit on the following afternoon. What he would not dispense with, however, until he had secured some certain guarantee of the lady's probity, was the surveillance he had earlier ordered. But in this the General was no different from his ancestors before him, for, as we know, suspicion runs in the blood of the Taira: after all, in the ancient tale, was it not Lord Taira no Koremachi who, confronted by a beautiful temptress, unmasked her as a baleful demon and forcefully subdued her?

Honey-Trouble

The General's aide, meanwhile, pursued his duties with an agitated heart. Not only did he find it demeaning to keep the Lady Onogoro under observation – a commission as vulgar, in his opinion, as that of the honey-spy who reports to jealous wives on their husbands' visits to the flower-district – but ever since the lady's tears had rained down on his forehead he had been assailed by an uncomfortable conviction that she was innocent. However, he was under orders from his superior, and accordingly returned to his post in the Almond Blossom Gardens.

Shortly before the General was due to arrive for his assignation the aide was startled by the appearance of the Lady Onogoro on her veranda. He saw with alarm that she had descended the steps and was hurrying across the garden towards him. Hiding himself as best he could behind a beehive, the aide reached for the only disguise that was to hand – this being the beekeeper's broad-brimmed hat with its concealing gauze veil. The lady hurried past with a vague nod of acknowledgement, and disappeared through the arched gate which led to the stables, only to reappear shortly afterwards with a young stablehand, with whom she conversed in intimate murmurs. Turning his back on the approaching pair, the young Captain peered and prodded at the hive, from which issued the lively music of the labouring inmates.

As to the nature of these labours, let us take time to explain their substance and division, since there are many who remain in sorry ignorance of the age-old art of apiculture and the life processes it so profitably exploits. Due to an unseasonably warm spell in the third month, the busy workers had already sallied forth to collect the various ingredients needed for their honey-making: the sweet nectar from the first blossoms, the honeydew extracted from plant-sucking insects, the dusty pollen from the anthers of early spring flowers, and the resinous propolis secreted by the buds of the chestnut. On this rich mixture fed the eggs which the Queen had laid in the six-sided cells constructed by her workers from beeswax secreted in tiny flakes on the undersides of their bellies. Since a plentiful supply of honey had accelerated the development of the eggs, two new virgin queens were at this very moment about to emerge from their broodnest and engage in deadly combat over the succession. (After the contest the victor would soar off on her mating flight, drain the sperm from as many drones as she encountered, and leave them to fall dying to the ground, but that is another story which, fascinating as it is, need not concern us here.) This year, however, the rhythms of the hive were all topsy-turvy, for a new virgin cannot fittingly emerge until the old Queen has, as it were, abdicated, and led the swarm off to search for a new domicile.

It was at this explosive juncture, then, that the young Captain, by dint of his inexpert intervention, succeeded not only in plunging his fingers into the sweet oozing cells of a honeycomb, but also dislodged the sluggish dowager who, finding herself evicted, swarmed angrily out of the hive with 10,000 worker bees in her royal wake.

Now, although undernourished bees will rob honey from a neighbouring hive, one should not therefore conclude that they allow reciprocal rights to those who prey on their own larder. Accordingly, as the expelled insects rose up like a geyser under the nose of the intruder, filling his veil until it billowed with noise and bodies, there were some thousand militants who took it upon themselves to retrieve the stolen honey from his fingers. Luckily for the aide, whose vision was occluded by the buzzing host, he could not see the scavengers which clung to his fingers and which, jostling and sucking, created the horrid illusion that his hands were encased in gloves of brown and restless velvet. Lucky also – for we must be thankful on his behalf for small mercies – that a well-fed bee is not generally inclined to sting, but rather goes about its business with single-minded alacrity, unless of course some danger threatens, in which case it will undoubtedly retaliate. And so, as the Captain tore off the beekeeper's hat and flailed it at the swarm around his head, few were the bees which spent themselves in stinging, for even the horde on his hands preferred to carry off the honey they had salvaged to the storehouse of their new palace.

But if, other than a few bee-stings, no great harm came to the Captain from this escapade, the gentleman did sustain injuries to his dignity and peace of mind. His temperament, which already erred on the side of impressionability, became quite phobic, to the extent that even the sight of sticky fingers on his tiny daughter caused him to break into a sweat and vacate the nursery immediately. As to the long-term effects of this pathology on his marital duties, however, we have no details beyond those which our imagination affords us.

A Deaf Ear

In the Lady Onogoro's chamber a small incense-burner on a red lacquer tray sent up spirals of fragrant smoke. His mistress, the General thought, had never looked lovelier, dressed as she was in an under-robe patterned with flowering pinks, and an over-kimono on which was painted the most gorgeous design of swimming carp. All the same, as she sat before him with her eyes downcast and the tears still fresh on her cheeks, the General scanned her face as closely as any roadside physiognomist in his search for signs of perfidy. The lady had sworn her innocence, she had sworn her love, she had kindled his passion – now with its dark admixture of conflict – as never before. And yet, as he removed his outer garments and hurried his mistress to the bed dais, the General's senses quivered with an anxious alertness. He glanced nervously towards the lattices, assailed by the irrational suspicion that an alien eye was upon him, an eye which, stripping him bare, would record his deeds and later hold him to account. As we have by now realised, however, like a tyrant who ignores the urgent pleas of the masses, it was the General's habit to turn a deaf ear to his own multitudinous perceptions. Accordingly he told himself that, since his aide had strict orders to vacate his post once he was safely ensconced in the Almond Blossom Chamber, his privacy was assured, and his qualms were without base or substance.

Meanwhile, on the Lady Onogoro's outer-robe, which hung now from the *tsuitate* screen, the carp with their whiskered mouths gorged on embroidered waterweed, and their lithe tails brushed the head of the hidden Oyu, who had overheard Onogoro's heartfelt and humble protestations.

Onogoro had thrown her arms back over her head, and her hands lay open in surrender, and under the lower edge of the screen her fingers carelessly brushed his mouth, so that he could as easily have used his lips to kiss or suckle, had not love made him timid and rage reined him in. For the General distracted by jealousy was a prospect Oyu could meet with equanimity, even satisfaction, but that Onogoro could prostrate herself before a man so patently unworthy of her was more than self-discipline could bear!

As his breath warmed Onogoro's fingers, Oyu's speaking lips stuttered, and his heart lamented that she should love herself so little. If only she would lavish on herself half the solicitude she squanders on the General, he thought morosely, then we'd see how long she would put up with the wretched fellow! He knew, of course, that in all his clients the lust for pain was ingrained as a bee's thirst for nectar or a bullock's hunger for sweet hay.

Their pursuit of pleasure, regrettably, was only equalled by a wish for punishment, which rose from them like a dense miasma and was without form until Oyu – and this, he now reflected bitterly, was his burden – put words to it.

Yet if Oyu deceived himself in one matter, it was, perhaps, in supposing himself immune from the same configuration which enslaved Onogoro. And so, as he marshalled his horses in all their strength, and lined up the bright cavalry of his love behind her, we cannot help but ponder on his own preference for languishing in the shackles of unrequited love, and wonder why the one who aided others in wooing was never himself the wooer.

The Cold Fish

'Once at the Court of the late Emperor there lived a pair of ill-matched lovers. In her childhood the Lady Hanako had been a harum-scarum girl, much given to climbing trees, damming brooks, and the like, and her mother, despairing of the child's torn garments and snarled hair, had comforted herself with the hope that maturity would cure her of her rash untidiness.

'In her grown womanhood, however, the Lady Hanako was scarcely more ladylike. If she penned a letter to a lover you could be sure that enthusiasm would get the better of craft, and that ink would blot the page or drip unnoticed on her gown. If she tarried at the lily pond to feed the fish, it was a foregone conclusion that her hem would trail in the mud and her long layered sleeves be stained green with waterweed.

'By contrast, Hanako's lover was a man meticulous in

mind and habit, as befitted a Controller in the Bureau of Central Affairs with Special Responsibility for the Imperial Wardrobe. If a loose thread hung from his mistress's gown he would scrupulously pluck it out, and if a speck or two of rice-powder dusted her shoulders – for Hanako's toilet was often slapdash – he would immediately brush it off. The Controller brought the same fastidiousness to the business of lovemaking, approaching his mistress's *iso-ginchaku* with the merest tips of his fingers, and never, to Hanako's dismay, with his lips.

'There came a hot and handsome evening in the Seventh Month when the swallows roistered in the eaves and the apricots glowed fatly on their trees like a thousand infant daughters of the sun. Unable to bear the tedium of her indoor duties, Hanako escaped to the lily pond in the Palace gardens to feed her favourite carp.

'She had called this imposing specimen Yugure, because it was at twilight that he preferred to come to the surface of the pond to graze on waterweed and lily flowers, but also because of his venerable age, which was now approaching forty years. Yet there was nothing of the dotard in this great fish, who was as long as a young deer from nose to tail, and of a boisterous and manly bearing.

'Stirring the water with her fingers, Hanako hummed a song and waited for Yugure to rise from the mud of the bottom and swim up to greet her. After a few moments the great pouting mouth with its four fleshy barbels broke the surface, followed by the green-gold head, the lustrous eyes, and the diamond-patterned scales of the back. Hanako had brought with her boiled peas and grains from the kitchens, and now she offered a little of the mixture to the waiting lips, which closed with pulsating voluptuousness around the delicacy, sucking and smacking at her fingers with a greedy abandon which made her chuckle with delight.

'After passing a peaceful hour in communion with her friend, with a heavy heart Hanako informed him that she must return to her apartments to receive the Controller, who was invariably prompt to the second and brooked no unpunctuality in others. With a flick of his tail Yugure showed her his silvery sides, and swivelled his golden eye and watched her go, worrying a little over the mud stains on her underdress, and the fluff of dandelion seeds in her hair, for he was well aware of her lover's perfectionism.

'When Hanako greeted her lover she was dismayed to receive not one word of affection, but instead a positive tirade of criticism. Throwing her mud-stained clothes in a heap, the Controller instructed the maid to dispose of them. Then he ordered Hanako immediately into the bath, and insisted on supervising her toilet himself. Every orifice must be scrubbed, he commanded, every last hair tweezed out, every flake of dry skin buffed away with the pumice-stone. A final inspection, however, revealed a residue of fish food under Hanako's fingernails, and those the Controller cleaned out himself, with a special bamboo implement and with much fussing and scolding.

'Afterwards Hanako, who positively ached with cleanliness, climbed resignedly into bed and thought longingly of the liquid tickle of the carp, who relished mud and had never turned from her in disdain. Her trials, however, were not over, for, before approaching her *hoto*, the Controller first drew on a pair of cotton gloves, and only then began his hygienic caresses.

'As soon as her lover had concluded his scrupulous congress and lay sleeping, Hanako crept out of bed and, carelessly throwing on an outer-robe, ran to the fish pond for solace.

'Moonlit apricots fell from their branches with a plop and floated on the water as the lady lay all abject on the muddy bank. Meanwhile, Yugure, the giant of twilight, called up from the depths by the sad sound of weeping, rose to the surface in all his kindly majesty.

'Spying Hanako's white hand upon the water, Yugure opened his muscular lips and sucked sympathetically at her fingers, which shed their sadness under his touch and opened out like jasmine flowers.

'Under the bridge of the night sky with the air smelling of apricots the great carp scented out another delicacy, and this was the lady's small bare foot which dangled, abandoned, in the sultry water. The small morsels of her toes filled his ardent mouth, and each one he worshipped separately, until Hanako's eyelids drooped with contentment and her long sigh rippled the surface like a balmy wind.

'With a spiralling dive Yugure swept his silver belly lightly along the curved sole of her foot, and resurfaced to nudge her splendid calf, which glimmered in the moonlight. All thought of her scrupulous lover was banished now, as Hanako rolled on to her back and, luxuriating in the slickness of the mud, stretched her legs out in the shallows until her robe floated up around her like a giant water-lily.

'Yugure circled the lady amorously, for on the table of the waters the feast had been laid for him, and he wished for nothing more than to taste her pleasure.

'Hanako, for her part, felt the golden head butt gently between her thighs, and she clasped her legs eagerly round his broad girth, for his slippery scales were far less chilly to the touch than the pallid skin of her lover. Her small breasts bobbed like apricots on the water as the great lips closed on the kernel of her, and she cried O O O, and hid her face in her tumbling hair, feeling the four tender barbels stroke her with a touch lighter than lark's breath.

'With exquisite consideration, Yugure scooped up water and blew it in spouting fountains upon Hanako's tenderest places, so that when his lips swam back to nibble her they found the lady anchored unflinchingly to her own pleasure, and swelling up to meet them. And if Yugure's heart swelled also, then so might a gardener feel who has watered his pea-flowers lovingly throughout the spring and now admires them in their glorious unfolding.

'With his tickling barbels teasing at her outer crevices, the giant fish enclosed both pea and pod within his noble lips. And there were moments when he sucked, and moments when he blew, and moments when the delicate morsel rolled in his mouth as if it would detach itself from its moorings. The lady's juices flowed saltily, and her limbs quivered, and her belly arched, and he knew that before too long he would be rewarded by the lovely wash and thrash of her.

'At last, with her excellent gate open as never before, Hanako cried out in the velvet night and fed her pleasure to him inch by streaming inch, and Yugure drank down her very good essence and held it hotly in the thrill of his fins and the diamond patterns of his belly, for what better accompaniment is there to the lavish feast of love than the intoxicating wine of the soul?

'And afterwards she laid her mud-slicked hand on his accommodating head, and both carp and lady lolled back in the sultry shallows, she heavy-lidded and content, he with his lidless eyes unwavering under the curious scrutiny of the stars.'

Teeth and Nails

~≥

The eye of the Regent's spy, which had withdrawn from its observation post at the window lattice only to watch the surprising flight of the beekeeper with his trail of veils, followed the occurrences in the dim chamber with detachment.

Immediately the General left, however, the Agent, with a thrill of interest that was purely professional, saw a figure emerge from the shadows behind the lady's bed. As to the meaning of this ménage, the Agent could advance only two hypotheses – first, that it was the lady's lover who, taken by surprise, had secreted himself behind the screen. Or else – and this he considered more likely – under the sentimental guise of a love-assignation the General had cleverly contrived to rendezvous with a cohort. Accordingly it was the second explanation which he presented to Prince Atsumichi, who carried the intelligence immediately to the Regent.

Yorimichi, who was already late for an important meeting with the Chancellor, was less than grateful for the news. 'A love-assignation?' he bellowed, as Osamu struggled to secure his black lacquered head-dress. 'Why are you bothering me with this tittle-tattle, Atsumichi?'

'With respect, Your Excellency, clandestinity is the surest proof of guilt. Realising that he is under suspicion, our man has become cunning.'

'We're talking about our best military commander here,' snapped Yorimichi. 'So don't come to me again unless you have solid proof!'

Atsumichi was outraged. Michinaga, Yorimichi's father, would have sent in the Guards at the first hint of a Taira conspiracy. But then, he reflected bitterly, his had been an administration with teeth and nails, in the form of the matchless Minamoto captains, Yorimitsu and Yorinobu.

Whereas it was becoming glaringly obvious that Yorimi-chi had turned his back on the alliances negotiated by his father and was intent on currying favour with the Taira.

Concealing his animosity, the Prince bowed deeply and took his leave. No sooner was he outside the door, how-ever, than an idea occurred to him, and, like a snake which sloughs off its desiccated skin to be revealed moments later in a new and glossy raiment, he prinked his forelock, smoothed his Court cloak, and hurried towards the apartments of Izumi Shikibu.

The Sword of Jade

That night on his straw pallet in the stables Oyu drowned his discontents in wine and fell into a sullen sleep rife with dreaming. Proud on Izanami's back, he led a regi-ment into battle, in his hand a sword of translucent jade with a blade thin and green as an iris leaf and razor-edged. On the battlefield he sliced manfully to left and to right, contriving, as he scythed the air around him, to behead soldiers and sunflowers alike. Green sap oozed from the thick necks of the fallen enemy, and red blood from the stems of the sunflowers. When the shout of victory went up, however, he cried out to his regiment that he could not see and could not therefore be held responsible for this blind reaping.

Then in the dream Onogoro came to him all vengeful through the field of corpses, her white arms reaching for him. In a fright he spurred his horse, yet still she came after; in a fury he brandished his great jade sword, but the lady flew upon it, impaling herself on the lovely blade. And now her belly was a pumpkin which grew great and filled with children, and even as his sword scored golden gashes in it, these offspring sprang out to encircle him, with their bows at the ready and their hundred arrows aimed at his eyes . . .

Oyu woke with a head thick from rice wine and found himself astride Izanami, with his hands laced tightly in her chestnut mane and his cheek hot and moist against her neck. Murmuring a shocked apology, he sank down on the curry-stool with his head in his hands and alarm in his heart.

Dreams, however, are like coquettes, in that they seek to conceal while at the same time revealing. Dressing our wishes in a different garb, they present them as persecutors, so that as we tremble with fear or disgust we need not admit to ourselves the acts we long to perpetrate. The more critical the mass of pent-up feelings, the more demonic a guise do they adopt, and the more victimised do we then believe ourselves. Thus we evade, for as long as possible, recognising the true alignment of our fate, preferring to languish in disconsolate fantasies rather than take the vital initiative which might thrust us on to a new path. And so it was a dejected Oyu, rather than an Oyu fired decisively with passion, who met the eyes of Shune the kitchen servant when he arrived bearing the stablehand's morning rice.

'Lovesick again!' snorted Shune, who was ancient enough to have little patience with procrastinators. 'Between you and me, my boy, you're at her beck and call too much. What you need to do is show a bit of backbone. Give her an ultimatum. Straight down the line. You or the General.'

Oyu scooped the rice miserably into his mouth and said nothing. If the old man still insisted on believing that he was Onogoro's lover, how could he even begin to convey to him the hopelessness of his position?

'It's not as if she's so high-born, nor you so low,' Shune persisted. 'You can't wriggle out of it like that. I'm telling you, when it comes to the ladies, love conquers all!'

That Shune should harp so optimistically on his prospects inflamed Oyu unbearably. 'In any case, I've decided to leave,' he retorted, waving away the presumptuous old man, 'and that will be the end of it!'

'Well, that'll certainly get you a long way,' said Shune sarcastically. But Oyu, who had only conceived of the idea in the moment that his lips had uttered it, was already well on the way to convincing himself not only that this was the one rational course of action, but also that a visit to his grandmother was long overdue. Tears of nostalgia filled his eyes as he imagined his feet on the tussocked paths of the high mountains, and he smelled the scent of azaleas on the crisp air, and heard the curlew's plaintive call. His head filled with visions of travellers whose rough-woven clothes concealed the nobility of their loneliness. Yes, he decided, seeing himself already kinsman to the itinerant monk with nothing but his begging bowl between him and heaven, or the carefree minstrel who ties his fortune-telling poems to the strings of his bow and goes where the four winds take him; yes, I will leave the Capital tomorrow.

'Oh, have it your own way,' snapped Shune in disgust. 'I don't know what's gone wrong with young folk nowadays!' Collecting the empty rice bowl, he marched off towards the kitchens. Tokiden, however, stopped him in the corridor with a silver platter on which she had heaped the very first cherries of the season. Ordering him to open his mouth, she popped one inside.

'Why so glum, Shune,' she chaffed, 'on such a fine morning?'

'That mistress of yours doesn't know what's good for her,' Shune grumbled. 'She's got that Oyu in a fine pickle, let me tell you. And now he's off to the Eastland and there's no arguing with him.' He spat the cherry stone viciously into the empty rice bowl. 'Giving herself airs and playing with a poor lad's affections – it's not right, no it isn't!'

Tokiden drew herself up. 'Watch your mouth, Shune,' she warned. 'That's my Mistress you're maligning.'

'Oh, begging your pardon, I'm sure,' said Shune, and with an insolent bow, he sauntered off down the corridor.

Tokiden hurried on towards the Almond Blossom Chamber, but on the threshold she stopped dead. Oyu gone! she thought, suppressing a giggle. That'll fairly put the cat among the pigeons! She stuffed two cherries into her mouth and chewed surreptitiously. Then, spitting the pips out of the window, she wiped her mouth on her sleeve and entered the room.

Bitter Cherries

When the General's aide reported to his superior he was a sorry sight. His blisters were greasy with salve, and one of his eyes was quite closed from a swollen sting on the lid. He received the General's condolences with a stony face, and delivered his report in a disapproving monotone. 'Then, shortly before Your Excellency's arrival,' he concluded, 'the lady went to the stables and led a stableboy, with whom she appeared to be on intimate terms, into her apartments.'

'Intimate?' cried the General. 'With a stableboy?' Confident that the report would once again contain nothing which could cast doubt on his mistress's character, he had received the Captain with a light heart, and had even been intending to abort the fellow's distasteful task and wipe the slate clean. Now, however, he was quite beside himself, and raised his hand as if to strike down the bearer of bad tidings. 'I swear you are mistaken!'

The Captain flinched, not only from the continuing pain of the stings, but also at this insult to his professionalism. 'I fear I am not, Your Excellency,' he replied stubbornly, for a truth gained through such suffering as he had endured is not speedily relinquished, however unpalatable it may be.

Dismissing the aide abruptly, the General began to pace the room. Jealousy clawed at his heart and soured his soul, for after all he was no casual lover who must make his way secretly through the dews of dawn, but had shared with Onogoro the ceremony of the Three Nights, and had eaten the Sacred Rice Cakes, thus entering into an open and formal liaison. By making her his secondary consort, he had done his best by her, but, far from displaying gratitude or respect, the unfortunate woman treated him as if he were some fly-by-night!

To and fro he paced, for hour after hour, until the image

of the unknown stableboy was a sword which swung at him from the shadows and separated his head from his body, and the Lady Onogoro strung it, shrunken, on her stem of *susuki* grass and swung it treacherously from her white insouciant wrist.

> Observing our love,
> Even the grave moon
> Lets down her hair
> And dances in the gay skirts
> Of the cherry blossoms.

Onogoro, meanwhile, sat in a happy daze at her writing table, and her thoughts were more tender than barbarous. The General's passion, so keen and sweet, had convinced her that her trial was over, and that she had been found blameless. And so her mind swooned on, dreaming its dreams of moon-terraces and that joyful day when each and every one of her hungers would be assuaged at the bounteous breast of the General.

When Tokiden entered, Onogoro exclaimed at the sight of the polished fruit. She bit into a cherry with greedy delight, but Tokiden's worried face gave her pause. 'What is it, Tokiden?' she asked. 'Out with it.'

Tokiden hung her head and observed Onogoro through her lashes. 'Shune said Oyu's leaving, My Lady. He's going back to the Eastland.'

Her mistress let out a startled laugh. 'But that's impossible! He's said nothing of it to me.'

'Maybe his grandmother's taken bad,' suggested Tokiden, who couldn't resist embroidering a little. 'Though Shune did say . . .' She hesitated, relishing the effect on her mistress. 'No, I shouldn't repeat his nonsense.'

'Come now,' urged Onogoro, 'you can speak frankly.'

'Well, he said Oyu was upset, My Lady. He said you had hurt his feelings.'

Onogoro's smile faded. '*I* had hurt his feelings?'

'Or some such rubbish,' said the maid slyly. 'I wouldn't believe a word of it.'

Onogoro's mind raced. What possible injury could she have done to her good friend Oyu? For a few moments she was quite dumbfounded. But then, with a sudden jolt of recognition, she looked her guilt in the eye. Indeed she had done him ill; moreover, she had almost succeeded in obliterating it from her memory! To enhance her standing among the Court Ladies she had stolen Oyu's tales and passed them off as her own; in fact her reputation as sophisticate rested entirely upon his talents. Certainly, Oyu had every right to be angry at such perfidy! 'Thank you, Tokiden,' she muttered, 'you've done me a service. But now, if you'll please make my excuses to anyone who calls. Tell them I'm unwell and can't be disturbed.'

Tokiden eyed her mistress's downcast face with a curiosity not unmixed with satisfaction. 'As you wish, My Lady.'

Gossip

After making love Shikibu and Atsumichi lounged for a while behind the curtains-of-state. Shikibu had interrupted her work to receive the Prince, and was rather inclined to return to her writing table, but her lover, she saw, was intent on distracting her. And after all the sky was blue and the day was hot, and it was pleasant enough to nibble on melon and radishes and divert oneself with political gossip.

The Governor of Echizen, Atsumichi reported gleefully, had scored an amusing victory. Owing to a famine in his province, he had been unable to provide the Fifth Company of the Imperial Guard with their regular rice ration, and the Guardsmen, incensed by this, had besieged the Governor's mansion in the Capital. Atsumichi bit into a crisp radish and chewed as he spoke. 'They set down their campstools in the courtyard, and blocked all the gates, so that no one could enter or leave. Finally the Governor, who, as you know, has a tongue as smooth as silk, came out to address them, bringing with him a huge tub of sake, which his servants distributed amongst the men. For some hours the Governor spoke of his distress at the unfortunate situation, winding apologies around them like swaddling bands. But then, one by one, the gallant Guardsmen turned pale, and rose from their campstools to flee the courtyard. . . .' Atsumichi smiled slyly. 'However, there were those who, overtaken by their importunate innards, did not make it to the latrines . . .'

Shikibu was shocked. 'A purgative?'

Atsumichi threw back his head and guffawed. 'They say the courtyard was a sight to be seen!'

Shikibu let out a horrified chuckle, and was immediately annoyed with herself. Rogues many of the Guardsmen might be, and much given to drinking and brawling, but fair was fair, and the fact remained that they had just cause for protest.

'Of course they were laughed off every street in the Capital,' said the Prince with satisfaction. 'And that, as you can imagine, was the end of the dispute!'

'How terribly clever of the Governor,' said Shikibu acidly, balking at the expectation that she would automatically take Atsumichi's side. She would have relished an argument, but the Prince deflected her with a languid wave of his hand.

'It's far too hot to fight, my dear,' he admonished. 'In the meantime, let's pity our poor General, who has to lick these roughnecks into shape.'

Shikibu looked sharply at her lover. Sympathy for the General was hardly a regular feature of his repertoire! She had the distinct impression that a plot was hatching, and waited in resigned irritation for Atsumichi's true intent to reveal itself.

'The poor fellow does seem to have fallen under an unlucky star recently,' mused the Prince, fanning himself lazily, 'what with the Lady Onogoro and her odd goings-on.'

Shikibu tensed. 'What goings-on?' she demanded.

The Prince's eyes widened in a pantomime of surprise. 'But the whole Palace is talking about it. Don't tell me you didn't know?'

Shikibu was chagrined. Evidently, despite her own discretion, news of Onogoro's affliction had leaked out, and the business of the poems was common knowledge. 'You shouldn't listen to gossip,' she retorted. 'The poems appear on her body quite mysteriously, like a rash. I think you could take my word for that!'

Atsumichi pricked up his ears, filing away this fascinating snippet for future reference. 'Poems?' he said delicately. 'I meant, of course, the lover our good lady hides behind her *tsuitate* screen. The little cuckoo in the General's nest.'

Shikibu was affronted. 'What nonsense!' she cried, as the ground shifted a little under her feet. 'Secret lover indeed! Onogoro is devoted to the General, more's the pity!'

Atsumichi examined his nails with rapt attention. 'Then she did not tell you his name?'

Shikibu snapped her fan shut and sat up abruptly. 'That's quite enough, Atsumichi! There is no lover, take it from me.' Wrapping her robe around her, she added curtly: 'And now, if you'll forgive me, I have work to do!'

'Well, Onogoro's a sly one, isn't she?' said Atsumichi as he took his leave. Then he sauntered out of the door, satisfied that the seed had been planted, and the crop would be harvested in due course. Shikibu, he was certain, would not rest until she had discovered the identity of the fellow; the poems, moreover, were an unexpected

bonus, and one which promised much fruitful speculation.

Shikibu went out on to the veranda and breathed in
deeply, as if the fresh air would dispel the miasma of
Atsumichi's insinuations. If hurtful things were ranked in
order of severity, she brooded, high on the list would be
taking a woman at her word and finding oneself duped.

Destiny

~❧~

Onogoro left the apartments by the balcony steps and
set out across the gardens. She had wronged Oyu,
and melancholy and remorse filled her. For although she
was resolved to ask him to stay, in her mind's eye he had
already left, and she was powerless to stop him. She saw
him trudging the highways with his bundle on his back;
she saw the darkness fall on him and the moon shine
coldly on his blind eyes. She saw the crows rise cawing
as he moved through the rice fields, only to settle again
in a black sheet behind him.

A great feeling of desolation overtook her then, and she
imagined herself piteously as a poor house with thin
thatch, a rickety house for crows, perched high and perilous. Tears ran from her eyes as she envisioned the young
birds with their shouting beaks and their red gullets and
their hunger. I cannot bear him to leave me, she thought
– but of course I deserve it! I cannot bear anyone to leave
me, she thought – how craven I am! Oh to be a man
and stand strong and indefatigable, rather than a weak
dependent woman, who clings not to one man but to
two!

Thus Onogoro berated herself, lashing herself into a fury of self-loathing as she walked, her brow furrowed and her feet dragging, towards the stable gate. Yet if it had been a man who had contrived to have one lover at the head of the bed and another at the foot, we might ask ourselves whether, having followed his fantasies and secured his desires, he would then have wasted time in self-scrutiny. No, rather he would have congratulated himself on his good management, and looked on it as further proof that the male possesses the mobility of a bee, whereas the female is like a flower rooted in the house.

Thus do society's tenets live all unknown to us in our hearts, and regulate the gaze we cast upon our actions, so that the same conjuncture may take on quite the opposite complexion according to which sex views it. For when the bouncing boy, from the moment of his arrival on this earth, is encouraged to expect an approving audience for his every bellow, it need not surprise us if in later life he aligns himself with these hearty spectators and awards himself plaudits. The girl, on the other hand, must as often as not be content with a more subdued reception, and can expect to be rewarded rather for modest manners and renunciation. And so all too often she runs out to her terrace and gives her power to the moon, and is forever wanting a keeper, one more powerful than she, who will bestow blessings. And if this perfect moon, far from granting her wishes, bears down upon her with unfriendly messages, she grips her balcony rail as tightly as if it were her own body and, bowing her head, concludes that her unhappiness stems from the fact that she has not observed fasts and penances with sufficient rigour, or else must be accepted as part of her inescapable destiny, determined from former lives.

And if the mother did not come, or the child screamed in hunger, or the mother reined in the daughter's pleasures or measured out her love in bribes, rather than letting it flow, as love should, in an unceasing fountain, and if the child shadowed her mother with guilty hopes and pleas and was spurned, let us not be surprised if in later life the daughter clings to a cold and obdurate lover rather than strike out in search of better prospects, for she has learned very well how to wait wretched at the door, but not how to open it when love knocks!

Even for a young woman of spirit – which Onogoro, for all her breast-beating, undoubtedly was – the roads to her desires are long and winding, and pass through hazards of self-doubt and thickets of self-blame, and she travels them in shoes that now pinch her feet, now trip her up, while all the time her ears ring with the pleas and curses of those of her sex who have fallen by the wayside.

The Apology

At the stable gate Onogoro saw Oyu running round the dusty yard, leading a filly on a rope halter. She called his name over the din of trotting hooves, but he did not seem to hear her, and urged the horse into a lively canter. She saw that in order to capture his attention she must run alongside, and this she did, while Oyu's pace now slowed, now quickened, but never once stopped, and his voice cried brusque commands to the filly. Round and round they went, the boy and the horse and the silk-clad lady, she shouting breathless apologies in his ear and he not understanding a word of them, nor knowing for what misdemeanour his forgiveness was sought.

Growing hotter and hotter from her exertions, Onogoro cast off layer after layer, and the discarded underdresses lay like filmy dragonflies' wings in the dust. At last she could run no longer and, hauling at the bridle, succeeded in bringing the lathering horse to a halt.

'My Lady,' Oyu protested, his face set and his chest heaving, 'the equestrian trials are tomorrow! The horse must be trained and ready.'

Onogoro remembered that indeed the next day was the Iris Festival, when races and dressage contests were held in front of the Emperor. 'But I must talk to you,' she implored, 'just for a little while.'

'Very well,' said Oyu, turning aside to lay a quieting hand on the filly's straining withers.

In the stable stall he rubbed the filly down while Onogoro tried to regain her composure. Now that they were face to face embarrassment flooded her, and she regretted having importuned him so passionately. 'I hear you're deserting me!' she said, with a cool little laugh, although it was no laughing matter.

'I am, My Lady,' said Oyu evenly, neither begging her pardon nor allowing himself any expression of regret, for fear of faltering in his resolve.

This recalcitrance stung Onogoro's eyes with startled tears. 'Of course you have every right to be angry,' she said hastily.

'Angry, My Lady?' said Oyu, rubbing furiously at the mare's sleek flanks to disguise the hope which hammered in his heart. For, in recognising his rage, did she not also elevate his rank and appoint him legitimate rival for her affections?

'It was inexcusable to do what I did! I can only plead the weakness of one who has always been too hungry for approval.' Taking Oyu's hand, which smelled of liniment, she held it to her cheek, so that the dampness of her tears might persuade him of her contrition. 'I have been disloyal, Oyu. I have given to others what was rightfully yours. Can you forgive me?'

In the neighbouring stall Izanami pricked up her ears and stamped an eager hoof. As for Oyu himself, the boy could hardly breathe, for surely it was her ardent love she spoke of! Wishing above all to crush her to his breast and plunge his mouth into her clove-scented hair, he hesitated still on the brink of happiness. Ravaged by sweet expectations, he murmured, 'There is nothing to forgive, My Lady.'

'You're too generous, Oyu!' cried Onogoro. 'To think that I passed your stories off as mine, yet you do not reproach me!'

'Stories?' said Oyu, as the marrow froze in him.

'Why yes,' said Onogoro penitently, 'I told them to the Court Ladies as if they were my own.'

Oyu was desolate as realisation dawned on him. Onogoro had said one thing, but his ravening ears had contrived to hear another. How close he had come to believing what his treacherous heart had told him, and to making a towering fool of himself! Numbly, he said, 'The stories are your own. I was no more than the mouthpiece.' His voice came from far off, like the pale cry of a gull on a winter's morning. But as the words echoed in his mind he saw suddenly the muscular mouth of the carp, and desire rose up in him illicit and glittering, and he turned from it in despair.

Onogoro clasped his hands in hers. 'Then you won't go after all!' she cried in relief. For was he not her music and her mainstay, her lullaby and her swaddling bands? And if he did not blame her, it was inconceivable that he should now leave her. Such is the fevered reasoning of those who, viewing events through the blinkers of infancy, cannot believe that their partial understanding is not the universal one. Imagine the consternation of the lady, therefore, when Oyu withdrew from her embrace and stood separate and obdurate beside the steaming horse, with the bared muscles of his forearms tensed and his lip jutting stubbornly.

'I will surely go, My Lady.'

Cut to the quick, Onogoro cried out, 'I knew you had not forgiven me!' In a frenzy of mistaken logic she sank to her knees and, grasping Oyu's calves like the very clam shell of the story, gave vent to sobs of remorse and pleas for mercy.

Blood on the Straw

~

But what of the General, meanwhile, with his heart inflamed by the unwelcome intelligence he had received from the Captain? Having decided at last to go to the lady and have it out with her, he had been told by Tokiden that her mistress was indisposed and could see no one.

For some time he had paced the Palace corridors in a turmoil of frustration, until his feet, as if of their own accord, led him out across the gardens in search of his mysterious rival. In the stableyard the sight of the scattered underdresses assailed his eyes, and a bitter satisfaction filled his heart. Here at last was irrefutable proof that his mistress was faithless and dissembling, and that grave insult had been done to him! Muttering a prayer, he put his hand upon his sword, for did not retribution follow injury as naturally as night followed day?

Hearing his footstep in the yard, Izanami let out a warning whinny, but to no avail. For now the General's shadow filled the doorway, and the General's eyes absorbed the scene in an instant, and his mind as quickly leapt to its own conclusions. There was the unscrupulous Onogoro, not ill at all but amorous on the straw-strewn floor, and there was the wretched fellow bending over her as if to draw her into an embrace. His mind like triumphant cavalry stampeded on ahead of him while his heart dragged unwillingly after, sober in its pain and raw-footed as the meanest infantry. For in his ferment the General had quite forgotten the principal tenet of military management, which is that an army moves at the pace of its slowest man, and ignores his grumblings at its peril. So now, after jousting too long with phantoms, he greeted the appearance of the enemy with a reckless gladness, and lustily sounded the charge. Both caution and chivalry flew from his mind and, without waiting for the stablelad to defend himself, he unsheathed his sword and ran at him.

Hearing the General's battlecry, and seeing him now in his warlike aspect, with his lips curled back in a snarl and his eyes redder than Hachimon's, Onogoro let out a shriek of terror and flung herself at his feet in an attempt to protect the helpless Oyu. But her maddened lover thrust her aside, and the stablelad was left exposed and uncomprehending, for the inner eye which dreamed immaterially of jade weapons and heads which fell like sunflowers was no match for the onrush of the General and his solid blade. The rats shrank back in their odorous nests of hay, and the high-strung horses shivered in their stalls, and the birds flew up in fright from the roof-gable and rose in a squabbling whirlwind above the stableyard. The gregarious starlings, whose own call is a high bright whistle, mimicked the darker human cries, and the doves set up a worried murmuring, and the crows flapped like black flags in the air until, anticipating carrion, they swooped down to sit single-minded at the stable door.

'For pity's sake!' cried Onogoro, as the sword flew up and, poising above Oyu's unsuspecting head, fell again like a white sheet of water. But in the long instant when after and before were as one, there came a commotion at the door, and the scattering shadows of crows, and a sudden cry of 'Murder!' A body hurtled across the stable, and, striking the General in the small of the back, threw him off balance and deflected his aim. Indeed the blade fell, and indeed it struck the unarmed Oyu, but instead of delivering the *coup de grâce* it dealt him a swingeing blow on the shoulder. Blood gushed from the wound as, without a sound, Oyu toppled and fell senseless at Onogoro's feet.

'Disarm him!' cried the Regent's spy to the assiduous Guardsman who had thwarted the attack. The officer, however, belatedly recognising his Supreme Commander, turned pale with fright.

'Your Excellency,' he gasped, snapping himself to attention.

'Fool!' bellowed the General from the towering height of his rage. 'On whose authority do you meddle in private affairs?'

The Regent's spy stepped forward. 'On the authority of His Excellency the Regent,' he said suavely. Turning to the trembling Guard, he barked, 'Arrest this man! He is relieved of his command.'

The General, however, thrust the Guardsman away. 'Spare me the indignity of bonds,' he said witheringly. 'I will have this out with Yorimichi myself!'

At Ongoro's feet the straw was red and the story-teller lay unconscious, felled by the General's jealous assault. 'Send for a doctor!' she begged, trying impotently to staunch the flow of blood with the long sleeve of her robe. In her agony of mind she perceived that the General had discovered her subterfuge, yet it was not she who had paid the price, but the blameless Oyu.

Thus does reason fumblingly attempt to fit form to experience, like a tailor who, lacking a vital dimension of his client, relies on guesswork and surmise to cut his pattern. For we humans cannot abide the thought that the gods may sometimes turn their eyes away from us to attend to their own concerns, and that mistakes may enter the fabric of things, and that the vicious may go scot-free while dreadful accidents befall the innocent.

Clinging to cause and effect, then, Onogoro sought justice where there was none, and, imagining that punishment is to transgression as needle is to thread, she burst into bitter tears. 'Why didn't you smite *me* down?' she cried, as the General was escorted away. 'The boy has not wronged you!'

Izanami rolled her eyes in distress at the smell of blood and confusion: the one spilled by the General's sword, and the other a force which rent the air and set up a wriggling disturbance in her belly. For she had served as the General's mount more than once, and could invariably tell what sentiments her rider denied in order to maintain the illusion of being a man firmly in charge. As he rode upright with his props of bow and quiver, she alone knew the tremble of his dark bowels, his skittish infancy, his weak dreams and his disobedience. Neither perceiving the mare's sentient nature, nor hearing the dark languages that passed between the wild world and his own heart, the General cast out the half of him and weighed her down doubly with dumbness, making of her a mere vehicle to be spurred on or reined in. Oyu, by contrast, both listened and spoke to her, but what he denied was his masterly nature, so that when he rode her the mare was seized with an energy which he had outlawed to his own detriment, and when she flared her nostrils and snorted it was with his joy as well as her own, and his commanding vitality which set her flying straight as an arrow across fences and dykes. It was the man of action which Oyu repudiated, in such deep unknowing that Izanami had found no way of communicating with him what he ought rightly to reclaim.

Meanwhile Onogoro was seized by a strange conviction that she had seen all this before – the jealous fury of the sword, the arm raised impotently to ward it off, the flowers of blood on the straw – and she reeled back both from the scene itself and from the inner template which so eerily and vividly prefigured it.

Is the sword the friend of the woman? she asked herself, half-swooning in the straw. Will the doctor come? Why does the smell of blood inflame my senses? The moon condemns such a cowardly attack, but the red-eyed god demands that the weak must be crushed and cast out. The thoughts flew fast and contradictory as she knelt beside the stricken Oyu. For the General had staked his claim with one sweep of his blade, and she feared the sudden energy that surged in her, that blind desire to ride with the masters, no matter how malevolent, and trample on tenderness and remorse.

Thus, it must be admitted, do the bloody and capricious deeds of the legendary heroes satisfy our atavism, and Kwannon the goddess of forgiveness in all her goodness is no match for one of these. The sword of the hero makes a clean sweep, and the child who is still primitive in us, having punished, as it were, by proxy, is released from the coils of vengeance and can once more assume its idealising and fantastic love. Long might Kwannon rend her garments in despair at the war-fervour which supersedes her more benign authority, but the fact remains that as long as gentlewomen wear the cloak of ineffectual melancholy, even the gentlest of them will thrill vicariously to the power of soldier or statesman, for the flagrancy of his actions allows her to abandon herself immoderately to her own furtive angers and excitements!

It shall not escape us, then, that it was Oyu who in his intuition had discerned these forces in Onogoro, and had mirrored them faithfully in his tales of cruelty and delight. Did she, while agitating for equality, yearn secretly for tyrants? Then he would provide them. While wishing only to melt under the caresses of her lover, did she seethe with fearsome rage? Then he would provide a safe conduit for it, down which love could also flow.

Let us also record, at this juncture, that a greedy wish for pleasure does not necessarily beget the capacity for surrender, just as a hunger for love does not imply a wholehearted acceptance of the love when it is given, since far too often the hunger arises in the first place from a conviction that the love is not deserved and that, paradoxically, one is safer being ill-used than satisfied.

If the Regent's doctor was surprised to find himself in attendance on a stableboy, he gave no sign of it. He arrived expeditiously with two attendants, and tended the wound with cleansing tinctures, and wadded it with cotton stuffs to staunch the blood. Giving Onogoro ointments of arnica to stave off infection, he warned her to watch the patient carefully for signs of fever. On Onogoro's instruction the attendants carried the senseless youth to the Almond Blossom Pavilion, where a tight-lipped Tokiden made up a bed for him in an antechamber already decked with iris flowers and herbal balls in antici-pation of the Festival.

For most of the night Onogoro kept an anxious vigil at Oyu's bedside, until, in the Hour of the Hare, Tokiden shooed away her white-faced mistress and took her place. The exhausted Onogoro noticed with a pang that her maid had placed an iris and a sprig of mugwort on her pillow, to promote good health and ward off bad luck. If the irises had hung earlier from the eaves of the stable, she thought fleetingly, before falling, fully dressed, into a stunned sleep, would they have protected poor Oyu from disaster?

The Lady of Fashion

With the arrest of Taira no Motosuke on his mind, Regent Yorimichi had spent a restless night. Towards dawn he had fallen asleep, and had dreamed of the Iris Festival, where lines of carriages were drawn up to watch the horse races. In the line reserved for ladies of the Third Rank and above, one particularly elegant carriage drew his attention. As was proper, the face of the occupant was invisible behind the bamboo slats of the blinds, but the stylish sleeves of her robe, many-layered, and graded in length so that the patterning of each could be shown to best advantage, hung almost to the wheels of the carriage, rippling like a waterfall on the morning breeze. The longest was of blue-green silk patterned with clouds, while the next sleeve, of plain white beaten silk, shimmered through the one above – a subtle violet shade he had not seen before – and was ravishingly offset by a shorter, wing-shaped sleeve of richest iris-blue. Above that came a foxglove shade, and then palest oyster with a border of cranes in flight, and the whole was topped by a *karaginu* of silver floating-thread brocade. A small hand white as a cockle shell glimmered among the subtle harmonies.

Dazzled, the Regent made up his mind to discover the identity of the sophisticate without delay, even if it meant throwing protocol to the winds. Ordering his coachman to drive alongside the carriage, he leaned out and whispered through the slatted blind: 'Let me see your face, I beg you, and you shall win the love of a Regent.'

No reply came, but the Regent's nostrils flared to savour the curious and subtle scent of the stranger. He whispered again: 'Only let me see your nape, and you will be the consort of a Regent.'

Once again the mysterious lady uttered no response, but her white hand quivered in its nest of sleeves like a frightened bird, further inflaming his senses. 'Let me feast my eyes upon your brow,' he pleaded, 'and you shall be the First Wife of a Regent and bear daughters who will marry Emperors!'

At this the blind moved slightly aside, and although his eyes could not penetrate the darkness of the interior, his imagination burned with a vision of unearthly beauty. But now the little hand tremulously beckoned. 'Enter,' said a lutelike voice.

All on fire, the Regent stepped down from his carriage and slipped inside. The occupant, however, had concealed herself behind the fan of twenty-five folds reserved for those of the very highest rank. 'Reveal yourself, I beg you,' he pleaded, clasping her hand in his, while the unaccustomed scent teased at him unbearably. What could it be? he wondered, for he was quite unable to place it.

The white hand lay cold and still in his. The fluting voice spoke. 'Only if you make me a promise,' it said.

'Anything!' cried the Regent, utterly besotted.

'Promise me that I will be not the First Wife, but the Last . . .'

'Dear lady, your wish is my command,' said the Regent, although in his opinion the request was somewhat unorthodox.

The stranger drew down the gorgeous fan with its pattern of dragons. At first his eyes, unaccustomed to the dimness, could make out nothing. But then he saw the white blur of her face float towards him, a face not painted and powdered but skinless and baneful, the eyes socketed, the teeth bared, the jaw bleached bone.

'You Last Wife welcomes you,' said the mouth with a hideous grin. The Regent, his nostrils belatedly recognising the scent of corruption, let out a shriek and awoke in his tangled bed.

'Oh Lord Buddha preserve me,' he moaned to his pillow, for he knew beyond a doubt that he had seen Death herself. Shivering with fright, he gave thanks that it was only a dream, if a dream horrible enough to keep him in the safety of his apartments on this Festival day. Now that it was the Fifth Month the gloomy predictions of the Diviners resounded in his mind, and, pulling the covers over his head, he reflected in darkness that, despite his qualms, it had been a wise move to place the General under arrest. For the first time he was grateful that he had inherited from his father's administration the prudent and far-sighted Atsumichi. After a dream like that, he thought, one simply can't be too careful!

Artifice

Onogoro opened her eyes on a blue morning and lay for a moment in blank contentment before memory returned, bringing with it a tumult of emotions. Hurrying to Oyu's bedside she found the invalid flushed, but breathing regularly, and she was much relieved to see that there were no signs of further bleeding from the wound. Loth to disturb her maid, who had fallen asleep on the *tatami* mat and was snoring gently, she fetched her own washing water and carried it back to the bedchamber. But, like the moon reflected in the pail of the fishergirl in the ancient story, images of the General's sword seemed to glimmer up at her from the bowl, and her heart shrank back from its cutting edge, and she did not know what to do. Should she go to her lover's house, and enquire of the Lady Ochibu where he had been taken? Or should she take the bit in her teeth and beg an audience with the Regent himself?

She sponged herself hastily, and at first her clouded mind paid no particular attention to the brownish stain on her upper thigh. Dully she looked again, and recognised with a sensation of doom the nature of the marks beside the curling hairs of her *hisho*. Craning, she read:

> My modest house
> Is thatched with rushes.
> Only look within,
> And you will find
> The lotus of eternity.

The words twanged in her mind like the bowstrings of the archers who frighten away the evil spirits from the Palace at dusk. The sponge fell into the bowl with a slap as she sank to her knees. Was there no end to the burdens she had to bear? Her lover was apprehended, her friend gravely wounded, yet still the unscrupulous villain contrived to inscribe his vulgarities on her most secret places. It was as if Fate, seeing her already embattled, had decided to set an extra demon on her for good measure.

Demonic or not, once again the poems with their autonomous pleasure flowered on her skin, and once again were angrily repudiated. And although we may begin to suspect a degree of blindness on Onogoro's part, let us be content for the moment with guessing at what manner of message they carried and whether their anonymous author was wise or wilful!

In the garden the young half brother of Princess Saishō piped his calling-cry to summon his pet hawk, and deep in the bamboo thickets the *higuroshi* struck up their scratchy carol to the sun. At last Onogoro picked herself up and numbly began to put on the garments Tokiden had laid out in honour of the Festival. So rapt in wretchedness was she that she hardly noticed the eight-fold *uchigi* of transparent silks in graded chrysanthemum shades, or the over-robe appliquéd with a breaking-wave motif, and certainly gained no pleasure from them.

Now that her hands had unwittingly dressed her, her feet took her out of the apartments and along the corridor, where the sun made light rectangular patches on the floor-tiles, so that for a second she imagined that someone had strewn letters there for her to read, letters which bore better tidings.

Shikibu had moved her writing things out on to the balcony and, brush in hand, was watching the gardener rake the white sand smooth over the darker earth. When Onogoro was shown in she turned, a frown knitting her brows. 'I was thinking of artifice,' she said coldly, 'and how one thing conceals its opposite . . .' Seeing that Onogoro, although dressed in formal grandeur, was pale and trembling, she restrained the biting comment that was on her lips and took her by the hand. 'Whatever is the matter now?' she sighed.

Onogoro poured out her tale, now in helpless tears, now tearing distractedly at her lovely clothes, and when she had finished Shikibu's mind was reeling. What scandal and intrigue the girl had attracted to herself! As for the General, she would hardly have supposed him so impetuous. 'But why didn't you tell me the truth?' she asked in bewilderment. 'It was Atsumichi who informed me about this secret lover of yours. I, meanwhile, who trusted you, was the last to know!'

'Atsumichi told you?' cried Onogoro, feeling that there was no end to the web of deceit. 'But why does he spread lies about me?'

'Then what *is* the stableboy to you?' Shikibu demanded in exasperation, 'that the General should go mad with jealousy?'

Trapped, Onogoro hid her face in her hands. To reveal Oyu's true role in the affair would be to strip herself naked before Shikibu and feel the lash of her scorn. At the thought of her scathing words Onogoro shrank back in shame. No, she could not bear it. Rather she would have faced the Tiger Demon ten times over. 'Please believe me,' she said wildly, 'Oyu has never been my lover!'

The shrewd Shikibu was not convinced that the whole truth had been divulged, but what preoccupied her more urgently were morose speculations about the part her own lover had played in the tragic debacle. If the Regent's men had apprehended the General, there was no doubt that Atsumichi had been involved in the arrest. She had known that the Prince was up to something, but now she began to suspect that his motives went far beyond mere spite.

Onogoro had begun to cry softly. 'Please tell me how to save the General,' she pleaded.

Shikibu put a finger to her lips. 'Be still. We must think carefully, or your position could be undermined even further.' It might not be wise, she reflected, for Onogoro to remain connected to a lover who, if her instincts did not deceive her, was bound for exile, if not imprisonment. Far better if it appeared that the girl had already terminated the relationship, and the General's outburst had been that of a jilted lover. An expedient solution, perhaps. On the other hand, if too much scandal attached to a woman of Onogoro's relatively low rank it would not be easy for her to find another protector. And since, short of martyring herself, she could not share in the General's misfortune, why then should she share in his disgrace?

But while her brain coded and catalogued the ramifications, Shikibu's heart was full of wrath towards her devious lover. However selfish and impulsive the Atsumichi of her youth, he had been a man of infectious enthusiasm and generous ideals, a man one could not fail to love. What had corrupted him? she wondered bitterly. Was it simply middle age, or the fall from favour of the swashbuckling Minamoto heroes he so venerated? She thought for an anguished moment of the passionate love that had bound them, and the ambiguous circumstances which had soured their union. If I had remained in the Palace as his consort, she asked herself, would he have turned out differently?

Speculation of this sort was too painful to pursue, and with an effort Shikibu focused her thoughts on the more pressing dilemmas of the present. 'You, my dear, must do nothing. Go back to your apartments and see no one until I send for you. I will go to Prince Atsumichi and find out where the General is being held.'

Greatly relieved that the resourceful Shikibu had taken the burden on her own shoulders, Onogoro embraced her tearfully, and counted herself the luckiest woman in the world, to have a friend who was so much wiser and truer than she was.

A Cockade of Iris-root

From her vantage point in Atsumichi's carriage Shikibu paid scant attention to the performance of the Butterfly Dance – exceedingly graceful, to be sure – or to the pantomime about a Chinese general who was so handsome that he had to wear a mask in battle so as not to distract his soldiers. She herself had distractions of her own, and the most troublesome was represented by the complacent profile of the Prince, whose head-dress wore a jaunty cockade of iris-root, and who clapped his hands delightedly at each new entertainment, despite having seen every one of them fifty times before. 'But what will happen to the General now?' she persisted.

'Let's leave that to the Council of Ministers, shall we?' said the Prince benignly. 'Exile, perhaps? Our Lord Yorimichi, being squeamish, is against imprisonment. But I imagine he may be persuaded. After all, people must learn that they can't get away with trying to murder the servants of the Emperor, mustn't they. No matter how lowly.'

Anger filled her, but she dared not show it, for Onogoro's sake. Instead, she must apply cool reason. If, as Atsumichi implied, the unfortunate General posed a serious threat to the security of the State, simple logic dictated that banishing him to some lawless province where his cohorts could rally round him was hardly the most sagacious course of action! Therefore, she reflected, if Yorimichi is arguing for exile, it can only mean that his main aim is to minimise the scandal and forestall an irreparable rift with his Taira allies. For a banished nobleman could always be recalled from the provinces and reinstated in the Capital, whereas a jailed one would be publicly stripped of his rank and rice lands and doomed to perpetual disgrace – an insult which would never be tolerated by the General's powerful kinsmen.

She spread her fan and studied the Prince covertly, observing how age had succeeded in intensifying, as if by parody, the boyishness of his features, the wayward pout of his mouth. Yet while mischief could be condoned in a powerless child, it was corrosive in the adult, where, strengthened by will and tempered by cunning, it took the form of full-fledged malice. Nothing would give him more pleasure, she realised, than to have the General imprisoned, thereby sparking off a Taira revolt which his old Minamoto allies could decisively rout!

As the carriages left the enclosure and followed the

Emperor's palanquin towards the Hōgaku-den, Shikibu clenched her fists in frustration. Such are the men of reason who preside over the machinery of government, she thought grimly. Yet what course of action was open to her? She could not lobby the Council of Ministers, or otherwise cast the light of publicity on Atsumichi's motives. Had she been a man, she would immediately have sought audience with the Regent himself; a woman, however, though she had the selfsame heart and brain and was every bit as able, was allowed no more influence on the affairs of state than was the meanest sparrow.

History

꩜

Meanwhile, in the gardens of the Palace, the gardeners were hard at work repairing the nocturnal damage of the moles. These blind creatures, who, we are assured, are as trustworthy and single-minded as the porcupine, had burrowed far from their grass-lined nests in search of worms and grubs, and at intervals had thrown up dark hillocks to subvert the smooth perfection of the sand. Unbeknown to the servants of the Emperor, moreover, they had already excavated a vast network of tunnels which stretched from the north wing of the Palace to the south, and from the east wing to the west, so that the foundations rested on earth as airy and insubstantial as rice wafers. Not without cause did the famed historian Cho-Iyu take the humble mole as his emblem, for he wished to remind us that a wise man will honour the power of persistence, whose dogged snout and shovelling feet have undermined the stability of more Empires than any impatient uprising!

But let us leave aside our speculations on history and return to the present day, which was long and hot and dragged past as slowly as a woodcart hauled by a feeble old bullock. Onogoro had lit purifying fires of poppy seeds at the four corners of Oyu's bed; she had sponged the invalid's forehead with lime blossom water and offered prayers for his recovery at her corner shrine, and since there was nothing more to be done for him in the meantime, she took out the maxims of Lao-Tzu and attempted to calm her mind by perusing them.

> Those who flow as life flows
> Need no other force
> They feel neither wear nor tear
> Need neither repair nor mending.

If only Shikibu would bring news of the General, she thought; if only I could write to him and tell him that, although he was very wrong to attack Oyu, I am able to forgive him; if only I could share in his misfortune and through loyalty lighten the days of his disgrace! These obsessive thoughts brought her nothing but torment, however, and once again she tried to concentrate on the text before her, this time forcing herself to read aloud.

> 'Yield and you need not break
> Bent you can straighten
> Emptied you can hold.'

Far from comforting her, the words of the Master pricked her brain and roused her to fury. What wisdom was this? Was she not already bent double under the weight of her burdens? Having lost everything, was she not already emptier than a bowl on fast day? And who now would fill her up? Absorbed once more in brooding on her calamity, she hardly heard the faint voice behind her, which intoned weakly:

> 'Torn you can mend
> And as want can reward you
> So wealth can bewilder.'

Oyu's eyes were open, and his fingers fluttered up to feel his bandaged shoulder. Onogoro flew to tell Tokiden to fetch iced water and sherbet, and returned to his bedside to tend to him. 'Where am I?' he asked haltingly, licking his dry lips.

'Safe in my apartments,' Onogoro replied, 'where Tokiden and I will look after you until you're quite recovered.'

Oyu started up, a look of terror on his face. 'The sword,' he muttered, his hand searching restlessly across the bed-covers, 'where is the sword?'

Onogoro was alarmed, and tried to settle the boy back against the pillow she had fashioned from a padded kimono. 'It's all over,' she soothed, 'you're safe now.'

'You were wounded by the General,' said Tokiden, holding a spoonful of ice water to his lips. 'Drink up.'

Tears filled Onogoro's eyes at this callous mention of her lover. She looked reproachfully at Tokiden, who shrugged and straightened the bedcovers in a businesslike fashion. 'He should sleep now,' the maid said flatly. 'The doctor said sleep's the best medicine.'

But although Oyu's eyes were closed and his body motionless, he was hardly asleep. Believing that he was once more behind the *tsuitate* screen in Onogoro's bedchamber, his poor confused brain sought and found its customary role, and his lips began to frame a story.

The Doll Festival

~&

Once in the shadows of Mount Yudono in Echigo province lived a smith-priest who was so devout that he tempered the blades of his swords with holy water, which he carried down daily to his village smithy from the small temple in the foothills where he held devotions.

'The smith, whose name was Jokō, led a life so blameless that the older villagers were in awe of him, feeling that he must be an incarnation of the Buddha himself. A stream of village girls rippled daily past his door, popping their heads into the smithy to greet him, and indeed to glimpse the swelling chest which gleamed with sweat in the fierce heat of the forge, and although some were lovely as mimosa flowers, and succulent as a full field of clover, their charms never once tempted the priest from the strait path Our Lord Amida had set for him.

'Their vanity slighted, the girls tossed their heads and told each other scornfully, Why, he is too holy by half! Perhaps he was a eunuch, the vulgar ones surmised. Perhaps too keen a blade had slipped one day, excising his vital parts.

'But the priest's conscientious service was so widely respected that the girls did not dare to slander him within earshot of their parents. Year after year Jokō presided at funerals, blessed births, and cured possessions, and there was not a single festival of the calendar that he did not celebrate in his mountain chapel.

When the Third Month came round once more, the *Hina-Matsuri*, or traditional Girl's Festival, was held in the village. After the feasting and games were over, dolls of Imperial proportions were carried on gilded litters up the winding path to the chapel and posted in tiers on the altar, there to remain for safe-keeping until the month was over.

'Every skill of potter and weaver, dyer and lacemaker, had been employed to ensure a lifelike effect, and for a poor village no expense had been spared. The many-layered gowns of the effigies billowed like banked clouds at sunset, and the silver thread of their *obi*s glittered in the shafts of sunlight which peeped through the tiny window. Real hair made up their lustrous wigs, real tortoiseshell their combs, and their shining eyes were ground from chips of black jet. Each finger and toe was lovingly rendered and finished to an eggshell perfection, and each pair of carmine lips was parted to reveal teeth of finest mother of pearl.

'The contrast between the austerity of the chapel and its sumptuous congregation of dolls could not have been more extreme. The scent of their hair drowned out the ordinary sandalwood of the incense, and their skirts gave the dizzying impression of a cherry orchard in full bloom. The petals of these flowers did not close at nightfall, however, but held themselves immodestly open to sun and moon alike, entirely obscuring, moreover, the sober stone statue of the Buddha.

'Kneeling before the altar in his rough robe and straw sandals, the ascetic Jokō tried to suppress the repulsion such excesses inspired in him. The villagers, after all, had charged him with responsibility for the dolls, and who was he to stand in judgement on their age-old practices? The scrupulous priest peered through the small window to the clean line of the mountains beyond, and with a sigh returned his gaze to the claustrophobic interior. He had examined his conscience and his conscience had admonished him, saying that spiritual pride was indeed a sin which only strict penance could atone for. He resolved, therefore, to set aside his distaste and treat his unwelcome guests with punctilious courtesy for the duration of their stay.

'Jokō prostrated himself before the altar and gave thanks for guidance, and when he raised his head a score of dusty faces regarded him. Immediately the young priest was ashamed of himself. How dingy the dolls had become, through his neglect! Reproaching himself, he filled a bowl with water and set to with a rag, scrubbing fervently at the grimy cheeks.

'Jokō was obliged to climb on to the altar to reach the topmost tier, and could not help noticing in passing that the doll at the end of the line was taller than the others, and more lissom. The curve of her eyebrows, moreover, was as fine as the arc of the new moon, and the sideways tilt of her lips was pure mischief.

'When it came to the task of foot-washing, the priest found that he must go on hands and knees and nose among the scented hems, and despite his sternest intentions his imagination was assailed by lascivious thoughts. He could not rid his mind of the image of a dog which, thrusting its snout under the dresses of unwary girls, causes its victims to utter all manner of alarming shrieks.

'He had come once again to the end of the line, and noticed with surprise that the feet of the tall mannequin were as muddy as urchins'. Just at that moment he heard a sound which distinctly resembled a giggle, and he spun round, startled. How embarrassing if he were to be discovered at such a task, no matter how stainless the motive behind it! Yet there was no sign of a visitor, neither in the gloom of the interior nor in the sunny yard outside. Concluding that the struggle with his conscience had been too strenuous and had stretched his nerves, the priest hurried to sponge the mud from the feet of the mannequin. Then, with some relief, he closed the door of the chapel behind him and set out down the path to the village.

'After a good night's sleep and a day of honest labour at the forge, Jokō felt much strengthened, and returned to the chapel that evening full of resolve to serve his parishioners humbly, no matter how galling the tasks demanded of him.

'After reciting the daily *sutras* he examined his charges one by one, here smoothing the fold of a robe, there brushing a cobweb from an elegant head-dress. What now? he asked himself, standing to attention with his washrag at the ready and his brows knitted dutifully together.

'Just then he glanced at the doll at the end of the line and saw that her skirt had somehow contrived to hook itself above the knee, revealing two perfectly fashioned, but exceedingly dirty calves. How could he have overlooked this before? Castigating himself for such laxness, Jokō mounted the altar and set to scrubbing. Once again his undignified scramble among the skirts summoned up the unseemly spectre of the dog, and the agitated priest broke into a feverish sweat. To suppress the vision he scrubbed even harder, and angry words rose to his lips. Whatever have you been up to? he scolded. Anyone would think you had spent the night in a foxhole! For truly, the mannequins were so lifelike that one could easily imagine how they might giggle behind one's back or, if left unsupervised, hoist their skirts above their haunches and indulge in any number of midnight vices.

'At that moment a few drops of moisture fell on the priest's tonsured pate, and he dropped his washrag in alarm, hardly daring to look up at the china face above him, in case he might see real tears. However, the cheeks were smooth and dry, and the jet eyes stared vacantly. Reprimanding himself for giving in to superstition, Jokō forced himself to complete the task he had begun. Then, satisfied that strict self-discipline had triumphed, he prostrated himself before the altar and gave thanks.

'However, as anyone knows with half a wit in his head, the more tightly the sheaves are bound, the more snug will be the nest of the wily muskrat within. And so, as the rice boats carry the tithes downriver to the counting-houses of the noble manors, the stowaway nibbles secretly at the cargo, and when the sheaves are untied for thrashing, many is the Lord who finds his offerings despoiled.

'Flat on the cold floor, then, with the bouquets of skirts foaming above him, Jokō saw that he had forgotten to unhook the tallest doll's hem and smooth her skirt down properly over her ankles. As he attended to this oversight, however, a thought entered his mind. If previously he had not noticed that the calves were soiled, what guarantee was there that the thighs did not also require his attentions? If a thing is to be done, said his craftsman's heart, let it be done thoroughly! Do I stint on the scrollwork in the dark interior of the scabbard, he asked himself, simply because it will not see the light of day? Accordingly he tweaked up the hem of the skirt to reveal the doll's translucent thighs, and found them subtle in their sweep and marvellously wrought, and, as far as he could see, every bit as pristine as moonrise.

'But what was this? Holding his breath, Jokō hoisted the hem a little higher, and peered at a glistening drop on the inside of her thigh. Was it glue, perhaps, leaking from the seam of the mannequin? The drop rolled downwards and, reaching the knee, fell with a plop on the altar. Jokō stared at it as if it had been a fish with wings, or a beetle with a bird's beak, or some chimera from the pages of the *Kojiki*. Another drop appeared now on the upper reaches of the thigh of the doll and, following the selfsame course as its predecessor, fell between her feet.

'Unable to detect what seam the fluid sprang from, Jokō threw the silken skirt over the mannequin's head, and was confronted by the sight of a set of red lawn underdrawers, as lovingly stitched as any bride's trousseau, and open-gusseted to boot, a practical fact which Jokō, in the course of his celibate life, had never had occasion to discover, and which therefore shocked him unduly. Why, any vagrant might enter here, he thought, like the fox who scents out the hole in the chicken run, and raids it at his pleasure! From the slit in the scarlet cloth, moreover, several black and lifelike hairs protruded. How admirable is the craftsman, he told himself, transfixed, who spares no effort in his attempts to achieve perfection! Just then a drop of clear fluid slithered from one of the black hairs and fell at Jokō's feet. Here, then, was the imperfect seam, the spilt glue, the source of the leak!

'Trembling, the priest drew aside the soft red cloth and tested the place meticulously, until he located the fatal flaw. A warm wetness enclosed his finger, and he put it to his lips like a child, unthinkingly, to taste if it was salt or sweet. This is no glue! he cried, springing back in shock. He glared at the doll, who stood so brazenly on the altar with her skirt over her head and her *hisho* peeping like devil's mischief through the open gusset of her drawers, and once again he could have sworn that a shiver of amusement stirred the still air of the chapel.

'Someone has had his way with you! he cried, furiously restoring the doll's clothing to a semblance of decency. You are nothing but harlots, the lot of you!

'Then he fled down the path to the village with a trill of girlish laughter echoing in his ears. That night on his pallet in the smithy he tossed and turned, his mind an enemy to him, and his body its brutish cohort. With morning came the return of sanity, however, and once again he reproached himself, for had he not been as negligent in his duty towards his charges as a father who fails to protect the honour of his daughters?

'Leaving the forge unlit and the smithy unmanned, the priest snatched up his keenest sword and hastened to the chapel, resolved to stand guard at the door and put paid to any rapacious intruder.

'All day he sat cross-legged before the altar, his back firmly turned to the audience of dolls, his eye on the door, and his sword at the ready. Behind him the skirts of his charges rustled like mice in the draught, and their scent assailed his susceptible nostrils. Late in the afternoon, stiff-limbed and drowsy as an autumn wasp, he went out for a breath of air. He scanned the hillside with an eagle eye, but no traveller moved on the winding path, and the bleak moors were a red desert in the setting sun. Leaving his sword by the door, he quickly relieved himself over the low wall which surrounded the yard.

'As he fumbled to refasten his robe, however, his eye fell on the spot where the stream had landed, and his hand rested for a moment on his member, and he stood uncomprehending. For was there not a footprint on the muddy bank below, and was there not another beside it – indeed, here were two sets of tracks, the one coming and the one going, which, if followed, would surely lead him to the lair of the intruder. And his member rose up all unbidden and, stiff as a sword, scented the trail and pointed the way. Furious with blushes, the priest thrust it back into his robes with a chastening hand, and, taking up his weapon, rushed off into the gloaming.

'Now he followed the tracks across rushing streams, and now hacked a path through thorny spinifex; ardent in pursuit, the warrior would not be foiled, even if he must crawl on his hands and knees with his nose to the ground.

'But what in the world is this? The fanatical priest stopped dead and stared at the ground. The moon had scarcely risen, and it was far too early for dew. But there, between the footprints, a dewy trail was visible, a spoor of shameful drops which glistened like tears.

'Since the prints were those which pointed towards the chapel, rather than those which led away from it, an abhorrent vision rose before the priest. On his way to despoil the innocents the reprobate cannot contain his lust! he thought, and, clutching his sword in righteous fury, he spurred himself on through the growing dusk.

'At last he came to a halt in a high gully flanked by outcrops of quartz-flecked rock. Here he was astonished to see that the footprints ended at the mouth of a good-sized hole in a muddy bank.

'Jokō's mind reeled. What manner of demon was it that could live in a hole in the ground and sally forth from the Underworld in human form? Trembling with fear, he concealed himself behind a boulder and steeled himself to fight the good fight, whether his adversary appear in the abominable guise of fanged wolf, or tusked boar, or long-clawed bear.

'For some hours the priest crouched behind the rock with his hand on his sword, his body numbed by the mountain cold, and his brain alive with apparitions. To steel his resolve and keep himself alert, he summoned up an image of his defenceless charges, all ranked upon the chapel altar, and began to catalogue each face and feature like an anxious goatherd who makes an inventory of his flock. He counted from right to left along the rows, at first finding all present and correct. At the end of the topmost line, however, his eye paused and his heart beat faster, for a shadowy gap marked the place where the tall and lissom doll had stood!

'Just then the clouds drew back from the moon, and, as if in a dream, the very effigy herself appeared on the threshold of the gully, gorgeously garbed, and raven-haired, and muddy-footed as an urchin.

'In a swoon of disbelief the priest watched the girl move gracefully over the rough ground to the very mouth of the demon's den, where she bent down and emitted a low whistle. Out of the dark hole a red muzzle appeared, and then the entire long body of a fox slithered into the moonlight and circled her on padding feet, the low plume of his tail brushing the ground behind him.

'Jokō clutched eagerly at his sword, and would have rushed to rescue the helpless girl, but all of a sudden his limbs were unaccountably leaden, and his mind moved as if through a muddy swamp. What sorcery is this that glues me to the ground? thought the young *bonze* in terror. The demon will surely tear her into a thousand pieces, and I can do nothing to save her. What a wretched caretaker I am!

'For now the circles grew smaller, and the muzzle scented hungrily at the hem of the flowerlike gown. And yet the victim did not appear in the least alarmed by this; rather she seemed to be entranced, and giggled behind her hand, and flirted her skirts this way and that to tease the monster.

'The fox backed away and sat on its haunches, patiently observing her. Now her hands twitched her hem above her knees, and now she let it drop with a vulgar laugh. Now she pirouetted, flicking her skirt to the waist; now she bent to exhibit the red flag of her underwear, and now drew open the slit to show the white flesh of her buttocks.

'At last, her dance concluded, she stood silent before the waiting animal. The fox slunk towards her with a growl, and raised her hem with its prurient snout. With a sigh she spread her legs apart, while, encouraged, the demon thrust his head entirely under her skirt, his tail alert and bushy now with excitement.

'Taking a corner of her gown in her teeth, the innocent chewed at it lasciviously, at the same time parting her underwear to reveal the spreading lips beneath. The long pink tongue of the fox fell to licking, and before long ardent moans issued from his victim. Suddenly she fell to her knees, presenting urgent white buttocks to her lusty familiar.

'Appalled beyond measure, the young priest saw that the demon was well equipped to take advantage of this shameless offer. Out from its belly grew a member more slender than that of the human male, but longer, and crowned with a nub of impressive proportions. The fox lost no time in mounting its wanton mate, and in a few moments the gully echoed with their wolfish howls as both doll and demon shuddered to their moonlit zenith.

'Then, without more ado, the immodest girl jumped up, smoothed down her gown, and hurried out of the gully, leaving behind her a tell-tale trail of glistening drops.

'Spasms of disgust shook the young priest, releasing him from his paralysis, and he leapt out of his hiding place. The fox turned its head towards him and fixed him with its yellow eye, but showed no fear. Assuredly it is a demon, Jokō thought, who rests secure in the knowledge that one may take one's sword to him and kill him, but he will rise intact and ravish again another day! Nevertheless he raised his sword and, uttering a rapid *nembutsu* to the Buddha, severed the beast's head from its body.

'There, he said to himself. It is done. Now I will deal with the girl. And righteousness rushed through him like a wind, and bore him back to the chapel on its triumphant wings.

'On the altar the oil-lamp burned brightly, and the dolls stood prim and straight and lifeless. With the point of his sword he accused the tall one at the end of the line. Step down, he commanded, and show your feet! However, the disobedient hussy did not move, and the priest jumped up on to the altar with the firm intention of exposing her once and for all, and thereby making an example of her. For one rotten apple in a barrel, as everyone knows, will very soon spoil its unblemished companions.

'The priest threw up the hem of the gorgeous skirt, fully expecting to uncover the muddy evidence of her guilt, but the words of condemnation died on his lips. Lo and behold, the little feet were lily-white and blameless, and the thighs untainted, and the whole of her had no more life in it than a vase of finest china!

'The baffled priest stared at the toes, and the toes taunted him, and through the tiny chapel rustled a sound like girlish laughter. At last he leapt down from the altar with fear twisting at his innards and a hundred eyes upon him. What was it they stared at so gleefully, covering their mouths with their hands? And why did his rough robe rise so lewdly before his belly, as if stretched by some tent-pole within?

'Suffused by terrible blushes, the hapless priest looked down and saw emerging from the folds not the human member he had disciplined so unswervingly, but, to his astonishment, the thrusting muzzle of the fox, and its arrogant yellow eye, and indeed the entire long lascivious head which he had earlier excised.

'And the stern cloak of his vengeance fell from him, and he stood all abject in his fox-lust before the merry eyes of his charges, while the chapel resounded to the deafening echo of their laughter.'

If the senseless Oyu still strove to entertain his beloved, it was as well that he was unaware of his effect on the Lady Onogoro. For what in happier times might have guaranteed her relief, in present circumstances could only act as salt in the wound of her anguish, and she stopped her ears with her hands and fled weeping from the sick-room.

Shikibu's Diary

~❧~

Shikibu came sad-faced from the Festival Feast, and told Onogoro what had transpired. 'The General is under house arrest,' she said. 'The Council of State will pass judgement within a few days.'

Onogoro was distraught. 'But how can I help him?' she cried.

Shikibu shook her head. Weighed down by knowledge, she felt slow and stiff and older than the hills. 'There are forces at work against you which are powerless. Forces that will also sweep you away, if you aren't extremely careful.' She glanced at the curtain which screened the sleeping Oyu. 'Look after your invalid well. It may go better for the General if he makes a quick recovery.'

'But I must write to him immediately!' Onogoro cried.

Shikibu said heavily, 'My dear, from now on it would be far safer not to become involved with the General's affairs.'

Mutinous tears sprang to Onogoro's eyes. 'No one has the right to demand that of me!'

Shikibu took her by the shoulders and would have shaken her like a recalcitrant child, but she stopped herself on the brink. In the face of love's rashness the counsel of experience was as ineffectual as a wattle fence against a tidal wave, but neither was brute force a solution. 'Think of your future,' she implored. 'We women must fend for ourselves as best we can.' Swiftly turning away, she took her leave, and hurried back to her apartments with her fan held up in front of her face to conceal her turmoil.

When she opened the old diary, however, her grief would be held back no longer, and as she read of those long-gone days a fit of violent weeping overtook her. How young they had been, she and Atsumichi, and how fiery their desire! She remembered how loth she had been to move into the South Palace and face his wife's hostility. Already wounded by her refusal, the Prince had heard false gossip about her supposed lovers.

This morning, a terrible letter from the Prince. In it was written: 'I was a fool to believe in you.' There was a poem which cut me to the quick.

> *You are faithless,*
> *yet I will not complain.*
> *Deep as the silent sea*
> *is the hate in my heart.*

Reading it, my limbs trembled unbearably and I fell upon the bed. For hour upon wretched hour I asked myself what I had done to deserve such accusations. Had I spoken too warmly to a courtier? Had I smiled behind my fan at the Chancellor? Or was it because that oaf Yukinari, who makes a nuisance of himself with every lady at Court, tried to slip a note into my sleeve at the Sacred Readings?

There are so many extraordinary rumours about me that I can only suspect that someone in the Prince's household is intent on slander, believing that I am about to yield to his urgent desire and move myself into the Palace. On the other hand, there are nights when the moonlight through the pines turns the white sand to snow, and at those times my heart is high, and I cannot believe that the course of our love will be thwarted by false and trifling rumours. Did the Prince but know it, my heart is so faithful that my confidantes yawn and turn away from me, for I no longer provide them with intrigue or titillation. So faithful that were the glorious Prince Genji himself to strum his lute below my balcony, to my ears it would be no more seductive that the snuffling of an old sow.

All this I wish to tell him, yet I cannot write to him, for it galls me to think that the Prince should be swayed by every gust of gossip, this way and that, like a willow in a storm wind, and that he should believe me capable of such perfidy. Truly a man's heart is a shameful thing, if it is bleak and without trust!

Since I did not explain myself, the Prince wrote again, saying, 'Why do you not answer? I heard something I did not believe, and wrote to you in the ardent hope that you would laugh at my suspicions and banish them from my mind! But this silence pains me beyond bearing. Am I to believe that your heart has changed so swiftly? Take care with me, or else I will be inclined to believe in the rumours.'

Suddenly I wanted to know what he had heard, and I wrote to him: 'If only you could come to me this very instant! I hunger to see you, yet how can I come to your house when I am buried in slander?'

But the Prince was angry with me and accused me of

faintheartedness. He wrote cruel words, piling insult upon injury. Here is the measure of his mistrust: 'I say to myself, I will not suspect, I will not resent, but my heart does not follow my will.'

As if stabbed by the thousand spines of the sea-urchin, I am steeped in poison. It seems that his enmity towards me will never cease.

Shikibu knew that it was foolishness to dwell thus on past history, yet she was compelled to read on.

Today the last leaves fell from the maple tree outside the window. Truly it is winter now, and although the sky is clear and bright, there is no consolation without the Prince beside me.

Wilfully he commands: 'There is no other way than to resolve to come to me.' How selfish men are! He relies on me boundlessly, yet refuses to see that there are grave risks entailed in what he demands of me. Vociferously he doubts my love, yet refuses to grant that I too have grounds for doubt!

Too bitter to write to him, I sent instead an old poem by Ono no Komachi, whose eloquence, unlike mine, never deserted her.

> *Submit to you —*
> *could that be what you're saying?*
> *The way ripples on water*
> *submit to an idling wind?*

Dull moon, narrow days. On bleak nights when the gong sounds for bedtime I lie heaped in goatskins by the cold brazier; no strength to stir the embers, no power to hold back my tears. Yet in each and every dream the Prince gathers me gladly into his arms!

This morning the frost was very white on the ground, and a servant came from the Prince with anxious enquiries about my well-being. There was a fan with a painting of dew on bamboo leaves, and a message which touched me deeply: 'When I sit down to write, my thoughts crumble under the weight of love. I cannot let you out of my heart.'

Out of torment comes truth, unstoppable as spring. To this I have no answer, and all stubbornness falls from me like an outworn cloak. All day I have been tearful and joyful, at the window, at the open door, even as the wind dashed the first snow of winter against my sleeve. If he asks for forgiveness, he is already forgiven.

Wise, unwise – such terms can no longer protect me from my wild longing to see and be seen by him. Truly words serve us ill, by placing false boundaries on the indivisible; one might as well try to fence the shifting sea in strips like rice fields! I say 'he', I say 'I', yet between his heart and mine there is no such distinction.

Shikibu closed the diary and held it in her hands. She had gone, finally, to the Palace, but the unkindness she had met from the lady and her retinue would never be erased from her memory. Brushing aside her protests, the reckless Prince had offended protocol by moving her into the north wing of the house, which should by rights have been reserved for the use of the First Wife, and this lady, in deadly umbrage, had removed herself to the house of her parents, thus setting up a great outcry. Such scandal and opprobrium had fallen on Shikibu's head that she fled both Prince and Palace under cover of the night, and did not set eyes on him again until many years later, by which time she had married the worthy Yasumasa.

Thus she had made her choice and her escape, and although she and Atsumichi had become lovers again after the death of her husband, out of chaos and confusion they had taken their decisive roads, and fate had decreed that their young and headstrong love would not survive the divergence.

The sun was setting. Shikibu dried her tears and sadly lit the lamps. She could do nothing to preserve Onogoro from her passion, indeed perhaps she should not. But at least, finally, she could declare the end of her regard for Prince Atsumichi.

Chinese Opera

～

> O that it was New Year –
> I could sew Heaven and Earth
> Into a silken purse,
> And send it to you for good luck . . .

Please believe that the stableboy is innocent, wrote Onogoro with rapid strokes of her brush. For myself I care nothing and expect no forgiveness. I wish only for your safe release from custody.

Without signing the letter, and without knowing whether her lover would ever receive it, she instructed Tokiden's youngest brother to convey it to his house.

At last the curtains of night draw aside, and here is the

General on his balcony steps, with lavender dawn as his witness. Arms clasped around his knees, he stares unseeing at the mist rising above the artificial lake, and the sailing ducks, and the tortoise's improbable progress along the shore. Like a singer in an old play he sits motionless, eyes narrowed on the horizon and his ruin, as if at any moment he might fill the garden with the soaring notes of some tragic lament. But this singer has no song, and the stillness is broken only by a faint whisper in his mind, a voice which tugs at him and demands his attention. Yet why can he not make out what the voice is saying? Surely it is because the wretched cockerel has begun to crow deafeningly as he struts, flaring with colour, across the dawn garden. His throat arched like a bow and his coxcomb erect as any Imperial head-dress, he inscribes the boundaries of his domains and herds his hens within them, and his drill-sergeant's voice drowns out all subtler discourses.

Onogoro's letter, meanwhile, came into the hands of a Guardsman who was gravely embarrassed by playing the role of custodian to his former commander and who, telling himself that after all he had received no orders regarding correspondence, delivered it with a shamefaced bow. The General ran his eyes briefly over the missive and let it loll on the steps beside him. Again he strained to hear the inner whispering voice, but again the infuriating din of the cock assaulted his senses. Picking up a pebble, he hurled it savagely at the bird, and saw with satisfaction how it leapt squawking into the air and shed a bright stream of shit on the raked white sand of the garden.

When her uncle Yorimichi arrived to see the General, the Lady Ochibu affronted protocol by throwing herself on the Regent's mercy. 'Only promise me that the children will not be separated from us,' she pleaded through her tears. While the Regent conversed with her through the curtains-of-state, her eldest son, a delightful boy of three, played on the *tatami* mat at his feet. Surely the sight of his great-nephew will melt his heart, she thought desperately. Her sobs grew louder. 'I know I have no right to petition Your Excellency, but I am quite beside myself!'

'Dear lady, you have my word,' said Yorimichi, so dismayed that for a moment he managed to convince himself that the decision was his alone. He picked up the little boy, who was dressed most charmingly in a scarlet brocade jacket and aster-coloured trouser-skirt, and took him on his knee. Hearing his mother weeping, however, the impish smile faded from the infant's face, and a tear ran down his plump cheek. Stubbornly he struggled to free himself, as if he would run to protect her. This evidence of manliness in such a tiny fellow moved the Regent deeply. Releasing the boy, he showered assurances on the distraught mother, and took his leave with a leaden heart. Nothing would have pleased him more than to cancel his audience with the General and flee the place immediately, but duty must needs win out over sentiment, and he allowed himself to be escorted to the south wing of the house, where the prisoner awaited him.

Shikibu wrote to Atsumichi:

> The sun in my heart
> Was already low and wintry
> Now it has vanished utterly
> Below the horizon.

Your scheming is despicable and dangerous. I wish to

have nothing more to do with you. Do not communicate with me again.

From the General Onogoro received a note whose cold formality stabbed her to the heart.

> I am told that the Regent's intercession persuaded the Ministers to commute my sentence to exile, and that I have him to thank for my new position as Provisional Governor of Dewa. I and my family are to be removed there on the fifteenth of the month, and therefore bid you farewell and good health.
>
> Taira no Motosuke

The faithful Shikibu, who hardly left Onogoro's side in the desolate days that followed, spoke to her sturdily and told her to be glad for him. For although the post of Provisional Governor with its insultingly low status was a measure of the General's disgrace, how much worse matters could have been! But however hard Onogoro tried to count her blessings, the thought of the long miles to the far north and the yawning distance between her and her lover seared her soul and turned this wise counsel to ashes.

'How quickly everything passes!' she burst out one day in anguish. 'Only two weeks ago the General was held in high esteem, but now he is replaced and his name expunged from the register, as if he had never existed!'

Once again Shikibu reminded her friend that the Council of Ministers had not imposed the maximum sentence. Since she was not without informants she knew, moreover, that even small mercies have their price. Prince Tametaka had told her that in exchange for leniency the Regent had been forced to strike a bargain with Atsumichi and his supporters. The levy they had extracted was no less than the reinstatement of the veteran Minamoto Yorimitsu, whom the General had originally replaced, as Minister of War. But if Shikibu was tempted to give the idealistic young poet a bracing lesson in *realpolitik*, she could see from Onogoro's tear-stained face that this was hardly the time for it, and held her tongue accordingly.

Cormorants

Next day the General's caravan, flanked by a dozen out-riders from the Palace Guard, set out from the Great North Gate of the Capital. After the carriages had passed the barrier which surrounds the Imperial City, the General, glimpsing through his slatted blind the huge wooden Buddha towering above its rude enclosing fence, leaned out of his window to watch the vast face turn through a half-circle of passionless surveillance. At last he let the blind drop and retreated into darkness. We are no more than ants, he thought in unaccustomed humility; for two months we will crawl across the kingdom as it pleases you, O Lord Buddha.

Wrapping his robe around him against the morning chill, he tried once more to concentrate on the faint tantalising voice of fortune. Before him the outriders noisily cleared the roads of foot-travellers, and behind him in her own carriage the Lady Ochibu recited the Lotus *Sutra*. Then came the carriage containing the nurse and the two children, the one suckling at her breast, the other clinging like a burr to her sleeve. In this way the cavalcade passed over Seta Bridge and rolled dustily through the settle-ments of Nadeshima and Chikubushima. At the barrier at Osaka Pass the company alighted for the usual inspection, and glimpsed from their high point the misty and distant islands of Lake Biwa. The road turned south and skirted the shoulder of the mountain high above the lake, which was visible now and again through the green frill of new larch needles. Dark storm clouds hovered as they passed through Imigami, and as they descended towards the shores of the lake a sudden hailstorm scourged the surface of the water, sending the cormorant-fishers scurrying to their huts.

As nature displayed its warlike aspect to his gaze, the General's mind was suddenly quite empty of intention, and his eye became the quiet eye of the traveller, who after all needs neither aim nor strategy, but must only suffer himself to be conveyed from here to there. Hunched in hemp collars which were still attached by cords to the boats of their owners, the captive cormorants bowed their heads against the rain, and the General, watching them, heard the unfamiliar whispering of his heart. Stripped of his dignity, and bedraggled as the unhappy birds, he wondered suddenly what worth there was in the strict code of the parade-ground. He had struck out like any man of action whose honour is impugned, yet what a pretty pass it had brought him to! With an unpleasant sinking sensation he drew Onogoro's letter from the folds of his robe and read it a second time. Had she indeed made a fool of him, or was he the one at fault, for turning a deaf ear to her entreaties? The General's mind creaked like the wheels of a carriage whose oxen strain to free it from the winter mud, for the man who in military strategy was without equal was the merest novice in the deeper dilemmas of the heart.

After a while the General noticed that his wife had also drawn up her carriage blinds and, with one arm round their elder boy, was staring out at the rain. Her closed fan tapped a rhythm on the rim of the door, and her mouth was open in a half-smile. When Ochibu realised that she was under observation she dropped her eyes guiltily, and her face assumed a sombre and dutiful expression. For reasons which he did not understand, the General was pained by this, and shook his head smilingly, hoping in this way to impress on her that a strict adherence to his every sorrow was not required.

Convulsions

While the General travelled eastwards into exile, Oyu too embarked on a journey, although his was one without carriages or outriders or fixed destination. Floating in fever, he lay surrounded by a luxury quite unknown to him, by scented sheets and incense-smoke and the rustling silk of ladies' robes. And as the women moved around him like shadows he sank into the fabulous world of infancy and searched there for his long-dead mother. Had not the hem of her dress made that selfsame slithering sound on the *tatami* mat? he wondered; had not her distant voice reduced itself to that same sibilant music? It was as if at any moment he might reach back behind the barrier of the brain-fever that had blinded him and encounter her once more, quite life-sized and entire. Strain as he might, however, he could glimpse only fragments of the lady: the wide-spaced teeth between smiling lips, the strange pink flush which had stained the palms of her hands.

Yet by and by he found that, if he could not see the lady herself, he could see himself quite clearly through her eyes: a chubby infant, sturdy-limbed and kicking urgently. Now he was crawling along his mother's belly, now she held out her hands towards him, only to fall back exhausted on the bed. As keenly as if it were yesterday, Oyu felt the pain of denial. And now the infant face purpled with rage, and he beat at her with his fists and drummed fiercely with his tiny feet . . . At that moment everything was dark and obliterated, as if the light that was his mother had gone out as a punishment, and there were neither images, nor eyes to see through, nor love to heal. In the fevered facets of Oyu's mind the meaning was crystal clear, and he quaked with fear and cried out, I have killed her! I have killed my mother!

The clove-scented spectre that was Onogoro came fleeing through the night. 'Run for the doctor,' she hissed to the fox-shape who was the other. The doctor came in his black imagination like a bat, and Oyu smelled the rotting seaweed smell of his teeth.

'Watch carefully for convulsions,' the voice cautioned. 'Carry him to the bath-house and immerse him if need be.'

Now he was stripped and squirming, and water ran over him. A hand capped his forehead, and a cool wind flowed over him. 'No, no,' soothed a feminine voice. 'You did not kill her. The wish is not at all the same as the deed.'

Is it so? Can it be true? thought Oyu, as his mind flipped over and over like a counter in the *tagi* game. Was his mother's death, if not her own doing, then her own concern, and none of his? Yet if it was not he who had driven her down into darkness, neither could he retrieve her from it by action or penance. Of her own free will she had abandoned him! He started up, thrusting aside the ministering hands and flailing at them with vengeful fists.

Arms came around him to restrain his fervour, and a heavy body pinned him down. 'Watch out!' came the cry, 'he has sharp teeth!' He tasted the bitterness of tincture in his mouth, and then the sleeping draught towed him out like a boat on the sluggish delta of sadness and cast him adrift there with not even the moon for company.

The Way of the Lady Omoto

Some days later the fever abated a little, and Onogoro reluctantly left Oyu's bedside to accompany Shikibu to a poetry competition between the rival courts of the First and Second Empresses, to whose latter salon both poets belonged. Abandoned by her mistress, the Lady Omoto strolled sullenly through the Palace in search of diversion. Discovering the invalid captive in his silken covers, she sprang on to his stomach and settled into a seductive purring.

The sound stirred Oyu in his delirium, and so it was that a cat bigger than a bullock took up residence in his celestial bedroom and fixed him with its wise and golden stare. The sun struck sparks from the animal's fur, haloing it with radiance, and Oyu was not at all surprised when the numinous visitor launched without preamble into a discourse on the precepts of the Tao Te Ching. 'Worldly morality is as nothing,' the cat pronounced. 'Instead, one must seek accord with the conscience of the Universe.'

The voice was deep and thrummed. With a thrill of recognition, Oyu realised that he was conversing with none other than Lao-Tzu himself. 'And what is the conscience of the Universe,' he ventured eagerly, 'if not energy, its rising and falling, its gathering and dispersion?'

The beast nodded sagaciously. 'The conscience of the Universe and the breath of the Universe are indeed one and the same.'

'Existence itself!' cried Oyu, feeling the word course through his soul like a white breath and fill him with vitality. The radiant vision of the Master rose above him like joy incarnate, and every separate cell of his body ached with enlightenment. How blessed I am, he thought, to know Being without effort and without end! Serenely he lay on his pillows and savoured the enormity of it. How easy, he marvelled, to wish for nothing! For everything comes to those beloved of the Universe, so all I need do is leave matters in Its perfect hands.

Love leaked into him from the all-encompassing heart of the Sage; love ran a thousand *cho* leading his lady by the bridle. Again and again Onogoro flung herself at his feet, and he who had suffered needlessly for love took her by the hand and raised her up into abundance . . .

But now light splintered the happy image like falling water or the downward flash of a sword, and Oyu shielded his eyes in fright. 'Master,' he moaned.

The cat looked at him askance and lashed its lissom tail. 'For some men it is as hard to accept fullness as emptiness, to suffer the flow of the tide as well as its ebb.'

I have displeased him, thought Oyu desperately, as the cat turned a graceful circle and prepared to leave. 'Please stay, Your Honour,' he begged, but the golden eyes looked gravely down at him.

'Just as dream is the intelligence of the body, so action is the intelligence of the will. You must take care with the end as you do with the beginning!' Stretching its elegant legs, the vision retreated behind a sunbeam. 'Beware of spiritual laziness!' the voice enjoined, but Oyu was convinced that the cat, with a parting glance over its shoulder, had winked at him.

The Stone Bridge

When the poem arrived from the General Onogoro held it like a hot coal in the tongs of her fingers.

> Like the cormorants
> On the fisher-boats at Uji
> I am doomed to dive and dive
> Yet never taste the fish.

There was no note. She probed the poem many times but could not certainly decipher its meaning. Perhaps he is lost and bewildered without me, she thought. Yet he says nothing about forgiveness! Once again she travelled many difficult pathways of the heart in search of her love, but she could not catch up with him.

At last, exhausted, she fell into a depression from which neither Shikibu nor Tokiden could rouse her. At first they tried to rally her by reminding her that the boy needed her care, but to no avail. Finally they let her be, and now they had two invalids in the house: the blind one transfixed by visions, and the poet basilisk-faced and speechless.

Yet perhaps it was better that they simply watched over her and left her to heal in darkness. For it is said that En-no-Shokaku, the great magician who could command even deities, once summoned the gods of many mountains to build a stone bridge at Kumé on Mount Katuragi. The goddess of this mountain was very shy and worked only at night, never showing herself before others. The magician grew impatient with her unco-operative attitude and punished her by unveiling her. That, then, was the cause of the failure in the work, for the magician's precious bridge was never completed. The meaning taken from this legend is that the inmost soul works only in the dark, and if one tries to bring it to clear consciousness, the work itself will fail!

The Way of the *Upāsaka*

~℮

In the meantime the General's caravan breasted the pass at Mitsusaka Mountain, traversed the juniper-scented shoulder of Mount Atsumi, and dismounted for inspection at the barrier of Fuha. From the rolling foothills of Mino the company descended to the flat rice-lands of the coast, and crossed to Owari Province by the Kuromata ferry.

On the ferry the General caught sight of two *yama-bushi*, sinewy-legged *bonze*s in rough sandals and dilapidated robes. They sat eating their rice in the merciless glare of the sun, rude-mannered men with weatherbeaten faces and absent eyes. He was struck by the strength he detected in them, and for the first time found himself envying the austere life of the mountaineer-priest. Simple piety combined with harsh and healthy exercise – such a regime would toughen a man as surely as the degeneracy of the Court would weaken him!

He could not resist asking where the priests were travelling to, and in reply the younger of the two pointed north to the high mountains of Hida, whose peaks were snow-white teeth on the midsummer horizon. The sight of such pristine heights first uplifted the General's soul, then plunged him back into the frustration of his predicament. How enviable, indeed, were those who were free to follow the Way of the *Upāsaka*!

When the ferry reached the landing-stage the General said a reluctant farewell to the two *yama-bushi*, and watched them stride off at speed across the salt flats. Alone in his carriage once more, he wrote:

> From the marshes of my heart
> I cannot see the shadows
> Of the cranes
> Passing over the mountain snows.

Consider the poor General, then, who at his late age has felt the restless surge of the spirit, and for the first time finds himself not one plain monolith, but tripartite in the activity of his soul. No scholar of Scripture, it had never been apparent to him that the soul is comprised of several conflicting factions. The mild and happy *nigi-mitama* cares for its owner's prosperity and health, while the rough and raging *ara-mitama* performs adventurous tasks. The *nigi-mitama* is further subdivided, and has as its aspect *kushi-mitama*, the wondrous and mysterious. By this ignorance the General had frozen himself like the mountain snows, and in his self-awareness had progressed as slowly as any glacier. Now, however, thanks to adversity, he was tossed in the turbulent meltwaters, and never knew from one day to the next which was the raft that would save him from drowning.

Consider also, as the white water of poetry tugs at the General's heart, whether any connection can be made between this spontaneous flow and the ebb of Onogoro's embarrassing ailment, which had not recurred since her lover departed. It would not be the strangest thing in the world, after all, if a force which is blocked in the man moved through subterranean channels and, meeting less resistance in the woman, burst from her like a geyser! But this, it must be stressed, is only one hypothesis!

The Retreat

Since the Sixth Month is one in which our citizens commonly undertake ritual purification, Shikibu accompanied the listless Onogoro to the temple on Higoshiyama Mountain, some distance to the east of the Capital. There the two women remained for several days of fasting and prayer, finding the elevated situation of the monastery most conducive to meditation. Each morning they bathed in a clear pool under a waterfall, while around them in the cool woods the deer grazed the new velvet of their horns against the birch trunks, and below them the whole of Heian-Kyo was laid out in all its splendour, misty by day and starred with torches by night.

Onogoro spent many hours contemplating the Capital from her vantage point on the mountain. She saw the moats which bordered the streets glittering like a grid in the sun. She saw the fires which broke out sporadically in the poorer districts, and the dust-trails of grand caravans as the well-to-do sped out of the hot city to picnic at Kamo or sail in the pleasure boats of Lake Biwa.

On the fourth day of the retreat she saw the smoke rise from the pyres at the burial ground on the distant outskirts of the city, and spent much time envisioning her own funeral, with its circle of lady mourners and ceremonial readings of her most famous poems. Detail by detail the picture completed itself: the snow on the parasols, the weeping-willow branches frozen into the icy surface of the lake. A wintry scene, although it was now high summer. Assuredly, she thought, my life is over and my days are ashes. But do I really mean to do away with myself? And if so, when? And how will the deed be done?

But here was the General now in the dark *shiishiba* cloth of deep mourning, prostrate with anguish and remorse, a sight which brought tears of pity to her eyes. And now the ladies grasp his arms and drag him back from the pyre before grief drives him to self-immolation – yet where is the mistress whose corpse he would fling himself upon? Entirely absent from her depiction of the scene was any rendering of herself, other than as onlooker! Sensing the anomaly, Onogoro tried to concentrate on the idea of herself as dead, as the body-which-is-mourned. But in the embrace of the flames she saw her hand not smooth and familiar but black and crisp as the poor burnt bodies of the bees, and she drew back from the vision and trembled under the pine trees, full of that superstitious fear which death quite rightly inspires in us, since without it how many legions of unhappy lovers would throw themselves headfirst and heedlessly into the nether world? Chastened by her experience, Onogoro crept nearer to Shikibu, who lay dreaming on a carpet of pine needles with one plump arm thrown back above her head, and resolved to keep her thoughts henceforth on the land of the living.

On the fifth day she rose early and wrote a poem.

> Forget the febrile perfumes
> Of the Court.
> On the road to Higoshiyama
> The wild garlic wood
> Smells sweeter to the heart.

On the sixth day she woke clear-eyed and told Shikibu solemnly that she should be getting back, for Oyu would need her.

Rivals

Oyu, as it happens, had been very well looked after in Onogoro's absence. Although still very weak, he had survived the worst depredations of the fever, and now passed most of his waking hours in the full light of consciousness. Shune the kitchen servant arrived with a dish of quail's eggs filched from the larder, and regaled him with improbably bawdy stories. The old man congratulated Oyu on his move from stableyard to bedchamber. 'Things have turned out pretty well for you after all,' he said with a ribald laugh. 'Keep in with that good-looking maid, if you want my opinion, and they'll turn out even better!'

Tokiden, meanwhile, had followed the doctor's instructions to the letter. She changed the dressings daily, bathing the wound and applying ointment. She held the spoon while the invalid drank soups and strengthening infusions. She combed his long black hair and washed his long white limbs, setting good sense against his blushes. She even succumbed a little to the sadism which goes hand-in-glove with the role of nurse, but if she teased the boy about his accoutrements it was no worse humiliation than any man helpless in the hands of woman may anticipate.

In the meantime a great many letters had arrived for the invalid, and piled up on his pillow, for Tokiden, of course, could not read them to him. On her daily visits the Lady Omoto batted them aside with a deliberate paw, for she could hear the muffled pleas which leaked from them, and she had become exceedingly jealous of Oyu's attention. Draping herself like a scarf around his throat, she would purr possessively, and would not be ousted.

One day Tokiden saw that the sheets were covered with blue hairs, and scolded her roundly. She would have thrown the animal off the bed, but Oyu protested. Curled in his mind was the great cat who had discoursed on theology, and whom he had believed to be the Master himself in all his dignity. The memory tickled him, and he burst out laughing. 'The rhythms of nature are but part of the conscience of the Universe,' he said, convulsed, 'so you can't blame the Master if his winter coat is moulting!' Tears of mirth ran from his eyes as he tried to tell the maid about his visitation.

Tokiden looked at him perplexed. Had the fever addled his brain? 'I'll get the exorcist to you,' she threatened, but his merriment was so infectious that soon she too was giggling helplessly. And before the pious set up the cry of blasphemy, let them reflect that, since laughter sloughs off the skin of morbidity and lets the spirit soar, the Sage himself was no doubt well content to be the butt of such a joke!

This, then, was the scene that met Onogoro and Shikibu when they returned from their retreat: the cat, the strewn letters, the riot of laughter that filled the four corners of the house. The mood of the place was changed, and changed utterly, and for a moment Onogoro stood affronted, resentful of this assault on her despondency. She fingered the fallen petals of a tulip and saw dust on her writing table. Tokiden, no doubt, had been kept too busy to attend to her housework! But it seemed mean-spirited to insist on melancholy, and with a grateful smile at the pink-faced maid she went to Oyu's bedside. 'How well he looks,' she said, taking his wrist and feeling for the pulse.

'He's improving, My Lady,' said Tokiden with a hasty bow, 'but the doctor says he must eat and eat.'

Onogoro was suddenly seized by a great desire to be busy. Although she herself had had little appetite for weeks, she decided to go to the kitchens and assemble a large supper with which to tempt Oyu.

The effect of the gay pair on Onogoro did not escape Shikibu, and once again she had a sense of secrets undivulged. 'So many letters from well-wishers!' she wryly observed. 'Shall we read them to you?'

The prospect so alarmed Oyu that he sobered immediately. 'Please don't trouble yourself, My Lady,' he begged between hiccups.

'Why, it's no trouble at all,' said Shikibu and, sweeping aside the invalid's objections, the great poet applied herself to the letters. She read:

> Cold as the ashes
> Of the brazier
> Is the bed of the lover
> Who has no words.

O that my prayers would restore you to health!

'No signature,' she added in some puzzlement, but Oyu merely blushed and shrugged. She opened the next letter, which was signed only with an initial.

> Silence is a poor servant,
> When not even the helping hand
> Of the moon
> Can open the bed-curtains.

Wishing you a speedy recovery. S.

When Shikibu had read out all the letters she looked at Oyu curiously. Every last one was the product of a tutored brush, and all were imbued with the same plaintive longing. Could they be from lovers? Did the boy's slight frame conceal gargantuan appetites? Or perhaps he was supplying services of some other kind? Her mind skimmed through many suspicions and discarded most. As Onogoro had pointed out, the blind youth could not write, a fact which severely limited his capacity for mischief. All the same, it would do no harm to probe a little. 'You must be a skilful groom indeed,' she chaffed, 'to make yourself so indispensable!'

Oyu muttered a few words about the immoderate love

of men for their horses and wished that a chasm might open up and swallow him. The lie was transparent, but Oyu's misery was so obvious that Shikibu regretted having embarrassed him. She would have dropped the subject entirely, but at that moment Onogoro and Toki-den entered with laden trays and announced supper, and Oyu tugged at her sleeve and whispered wretchedly: 'I can explain everything! But for the moment say nothing to the Lady Onogoro, I beg you!' Although greatly taken aback, Shikibu assured him of her silence. What a mysterious boy he is! she thought. Yet somehow I am sure there is no harm in him.

On the *tatami* mat Tokiden and Onogoro laid out a dozen bowls. There was a salad of water chestnut and radishes, glazed strips of duckling with oysters, fried squid with sliced ginger, eggplant, green onions, lobster claws, beancurd, persimmons, walnuts, tamarinds, pickled cabbage, poppy-seed tarts, and pears cooked in honey and cinnamon. Having served the meal, Tokiden would have withdrawn from the room, but Onogoro was quite adamant that she stay and eat with them, and so all four set to without ceremony, helping themselves and each other as the fancy took them. Onogoro prised the flesh from a lobster claw and placed the morsels between Oyu's lips, while Shikibu and Tokiden made a game of spearing the most surprising combinations of sweet and sour foods, to tease his palate.

On the sidelines the Lady Omoto waited patiently for her share, as she was far too well bred to beg. Becoming tipsy, the ladies forbade Oyu and Tokiden to address them formally, and declared that rank and precedence were abolished for the duration. The Lady Omoto, how-ever, would have none of their nonsense, and refused to answer to her plain name no matter what inducements were offered.

By this time Tokiden was also drunk enough to forget herself. 'She's just jealous,' cried the maid, snatching up the cat and addressing her boisterously. 'You've had him all to yourself and you don't like rivals, do you?' She tweaked back Oyu's bedcovers and thrust the startled cat inside. 'There,' she said with satisfied malice. 'That's better, isn't it?'

Shikibu burst out laughing at Oyu's droll expression. Propped up on his pillows like a lord, warmed with wine and plied with delicacies, he had the air of a man quite stupefied by his good fortune. Onogoro looked on with a determined little smile. She did not know why Tokiden's forwardness troubled her so. Since the good-humoured girl had had sole charge of Oyu for several days it was hardly remarkable that the two should have become familiar. If their easy affection saddened her, it could only be that it served as a cruel reminder of the simple happiness she herself had longed for and lost!

She began to bustle around the bed, and as she plumped the pillows and piled up the empty bowls she said briskly, 'Now we don't want to tire him out, do we, Tokiden!' Then she flounced off to the kitchen with her tray, leaving Oyu breathless in the wake of her ministrations.

Exhausted by the ambiguity of his position, Oyu lay back and closed his eyes. Shikibu and Tokiden whispered to each other that he was asleep, and stole out of the room. But Oyu's pride was sorely hurt and his mind was racing. In the hectic high spirits of the evening he had scarcely exchanged one word with Onogoro, and now he was utterly convinced that if she made much of him, it was purely to salve her own conscience. Left alone, he sank into angry despair. How can I bear it? he thought. Now that I am rendered more powerless than ever, the lady feels quite free to treat me like a child or a plaything! Would she have me plumb the depths of abjection, knowing that I have need of her? For she no longer needs me in the slightest, now that her precious General is gone.

To make matters worse, his own conscience was far from easy, and the thought of his narrow escape over the letters brought him out in a cold sweat. Never in his life had he felt so wretched, or so trapped. I will not be her sick little bird, he fumed. No one will keep me in such a shameful cage! Suddenly infuriated beyond bearing by all the silk and fur and luxury, he scooped up the cat and threw her violently out of the bed. He thought of Izanami impatient in her stall, he thought of plain food and the sound of bees and the sun on the stableyard. I will make myself well, he vowed. I will set her free of every last obligation!

The Tides of Owari

~❧

On Narumi shore in Owari, the General watched the shallow waters rush in across the sand. His elder son, who wore a green sheet of seaweed wrapped around him like a cloak, waddled through the waves like a tiny Emperor, crying brusque commands at his nurse, while a train of seaweed trailed behind him.

In the shade of the cloth pavilion which the Guardsmen had erected in the dunes, the Lady Ochibu tended the baby. All the General could see of her was an outstretched arm and a pointing finger, and he imagined that she must be cradling the infant in the crook of her shoulder and turning his head towards the sea so that he could watch his capering brother. The General smiled sadly at the comical spectacle on the shore. How sweet the child, yet how bitter his future, he thought, wondering what rank of position the boy could now look forward to. Neither rebuke nor complaint had passed his wife's lips from the beginning, but the responsibility for the downturn in their fortunes weighed on him all the more heavily for her forbearance.

He rose stiffly and threw off his clothes, intending to wash away the dust of the journey in the tide. Yet the sand in the shallows sucked at his feet, and the warm waters did not refresh. He struck out towards the cooler depths and swam strongly, as if violent exercise might put an end to brooding. But his thoughts would not be diverted from their morbid path, and as the shore receded into the distance he began to see himself more certainly as a passenger from one life to another. If death was one's inevitable destination, he mused, could it not also be a solution? A quick death could wipe away disgrace and leave the slate clean. As a Fujiwara, the Lady Ochibu would presently be readmitted to the Court, and before long would procure a suitable protector for herself and her children.

The General was suddenly calm. This, surely, was the answer. He set his eyes on the unbroken line of the south horizon and stilled his soul for sacrifice. He strove downwards with steepled hands and kicking feet, and the water pressed hard on his eyes and ears, but would not have him. Up he came like a cork to the surface, for if the Lord of the Deep is as capricious as a child in what he swallows or refuses, he is also as discriminating, and if there is to be a contest of wills he will certainly be the one to win it.

Gasping, the General gathered himself for another attempt. Faintly from the shore came a thin cry which tugged at him, but he set his heart against it and dove again, only to be summarily ejected. The cries of his son had alerted his wife, who stood now at the water's edge, waving her red sleeves wildly.

He could not do it. Resigned to failure, he swam slowly back to the shore and waded through the shallows to his family. The little boy had soiled himself in his distress, and the nurse was splashing his limbs with sea water. As the General approached, his shrieks grew louder, and he would not be comforted until his father had taken him in his arms. Understanding perfectly what had been his intention, the Lady Ochibu turned her tear-stained face away from him.

The boy was dried and quieted, and the baby returned to the nurse's breast. Meanwhile the General was ashamed, for he saw that despair had dulled his wits. Why had he not realised that the outcome would be this frenzy of sorrow? He followed his wife silently up the beach, while the Guardsmen looked on, impassive, from the dunes.

A Plague of Snails

Onogoro was surprised to find that her timid invalid had become demanding. He called for mounds of rice, for dried fish, for dishes of sweet potato and spinach. He complained that his scar itched, and asked for salt baths to be prepared for him. He insisted that his bed be carried out on to the balcony, so that he could feel the sun on his skin. In her guilt Onogoro gave in to him, and indeed found herself vying with Tokiden to satisfy his whims. 'When they're fretting, they're mending,' said the maid sagely, as she shooed her mistress back to her writing table and ran about his bidding. Onogoro protested, saying that it was a privilege to care for him, but the shrewd maid shrugged and said: 'Begging your pardon, My Lady, but it's not good for a person to be treated like a penance.'

When the vivacious maid asked one morning if she could visit her aunt in the Third Ward, Onogoro gladly said yes. 'Stay for a day or two,' she said. 'See your friends. You really do deserve a rest.' From her closet she took out a robe of mustard beaten silk with a double border of asters. 'The colour really doesn't suit me at all,' she declared, slipping it over Tokiden's shoulders. Perhaps she has someone special, she thought, as the maid admired herself in the mirror. Perhaps even an assignation. She imagined a strong young man with broad shoulders and eyes as black as elderberries, a gardener or a boat-builder, perhaps. They would meet at the corner of the market where the spices rose in scented pyramids: cardamom and cumin, saffron and cinnamon and caraway seeds. They would buy the best bronze pears from the Korean's basket; they would eat rice cakes, and dawdle through the streets talking of marriage, and that night when he knocked lightly on her shutters her aunt would turn a deaf ear to the furtive noises of their love. Yes, thought Onogoro, a girl like Tokiden really ought to have a lover!

On the veranda Oyu had already been awake for some

time, and had heard Tokiden take her leave. Now that he was growing stronger, his member rose and clamoured with the birds at dawn, but he muffled his bitter yearning by plotting his escape. With the support of the balcony rail, he thought, I can already take a few steps. Today, therefore, I will double that, and tomorrow I will walk unaided to the stables. Determined not to allow himself to be humiliated by the poet's all too tender mercies, Oyu called out querulously for his breakfast. Tokiden's care he could accept with good grace, but he would far rather make an active nuisance of himself than feel beholden to Onogoro!

Under the balcony the gardeners were waging war on a plague of snails. In the night the pests had stripped the bamboo shoots, gobbled off the heads of pinks, made portholes in the peony leaves. The raked sand of the garden was netted by their silver trails. The gardeners smashed the shells with spades, or hurled them against the walls, while the starlings fluttered down to peck at the unexpected feast. Loth to intrude on the invalid, Onogoro had been watching the carnage from her window, but now she flew to fetch rice and melon from the kitchen and carried it eagerly out to him.

Oyu received the tray with the shortest of thanks, and began to eat greedily, telling her between mouthfuls that he intended to walk in the gardens that day, and would need her help. 'Fifty paces,' he said challengingly, 'I've set my mind on it!'

'Surely it's too soon!' Onogoro protested. She began to fuss around him, straightening his pillow and plucking blown leaves from his bedcovers. She asked herself how Tokiden would have dealt with such determination, and whether she would have resisted him. 'What if the wound reopens or the fever recurs?' she fretted, feeling herself quite deficient in nursing skills.

'Fifty paces!' Oyu insisted, pushing the tray aside and struggling to his feet. How wilful he is, she thought, watching the moods of mutiny pass across his face. One would be hard put to win a battle with him! Yet the thought was so attractive to her that she found herself returning to it throughout the morning, even as she supported his arm and guided him across the gardens. How wilful he is, she repeated inwardly whenever he missed his footing or stopped to gasp for breath, and the thought of that hidden steel erased from her mind the debility that should properly have concerned her. How wilful men are, she reflected, and smiled with secret pleasure, and preened herself a little.

In the afternoon Onogoro moved her writing table on to the balcony to keep Oyu company while he rested, but after the walk her mind was fine-strung and her thoughts would not settle. Somewhere under the blue skies the General travelled eastwards under guard; his wheels were muddy and his progress slow, and she could find no memory of herself in his carriage. In the garden raked piles of snail shells oozed a pale slime. The sight of such destruction filled her with pity, and she wrote swiftly:

> Surrounded by enemies
> He hauls his house
> Across the land . . .

Before she had time to complete the poem Oyu interrupted her by announcing that he had something important to say. A light wind fluttered her papers, bringing with it the scent of the camphor tree. She turned towards Oyu, who had propped himself up on his elbows and was scowling into space. 'How ominous that sounds,' she said indulgently.

Oyu was mortified by her tone, and spoke with a harshness he had not intended. 'Once, My Lady, you asked forgiveness of me, because you had passed my stories on to others.'

Onogoro was perturbed. 'I can understand, of course, if you feel unable to forgive me,' she said hastily.

'The truth is . . .' Cursing the gods, Oyu threw himself into the breach. 'The truth is, since I have also told them to other ladies, in similar circumstances to your own, there is no need at all to blame yourself.'

Onogoro could hardly believe her ears. 'In similar circumstances?' she repeated. As realisation dawned on her she flushed darkly at the thought of his promiscuity. How intolerable to think that he had not reserved his tales for her ears alone, nor presided solely over her particular excitement! 'So I was not the only one?'

'Far from it, My Lady,' said Oyu brutally. 'I have clients all over the Capital.' A painful silence followed, in which Oyu, like the stoic he was, tried to resign himself to rejection. Miserable wretch, he berated himself: so this is how you repay a lady's kindness! Yet paradoxically, having confessed the worst, he felt the lightness of relief flow into his limbs.

Abandoned to the general run, Onogoro could not have felt more humiliated. Yet with an ungovernable prurience her spying eye insisted on regaling her with all the sights the blind story-teller had not seen. Here was a lady who wrapped her limbs chrysanthemum-like around her lover, here another who opened to him like the trumpet of a convolvulus. Here was a prying finger, a bruised nipple; here a fair imitation of a rutting stag, and here a sow grunting.

Onogoro was silent for so long that Oyu thought she might never speak to him again. At last she said, in a voice barely above a whisper: 'A few moments ago I searched in my heart for the General, and I was shocked. For all I could find was the image of a snail, quite ponderous and slow.' How thin his trail, she thought, and how quickly it fades. She burst into wretched sobs. 'So now you see how faithless I am!' she wailed. Then, rising so forcefully that she overturned her writing table and scattered brushes and poems alike, she fled from the balcony.

Consider Onogoro, then, as she runs across the gardens with her silk robe flying behind her. Will she go to Shikibu and, cleaving to her for comfort, risk the added shame of confessing all? Will she forgive her own disloyal thoughts about the absent General? Like any poet, Onogoro knows that metaphor, springing simultaneously as it does from body, mind and soul, does not lie. By metaphor, then, she has betrayed her lover as surely as if she had consorted with another and, moreover, has dealt a deadly affront to that familiar part of her which is the strict standard-bearer of tragedy. Small hope for Oyu, however, if she cannot relinquish this standard to another player – the General, for example, is already rehearsing for the part – but clings instead to her habitual role as mimic in the theatre of suffering! Better that she should learn as soon as possible that persistence of the will is only a virtue when it accords with deeper rhythms and, bending before the wind and springing up like *susuki* grass after its passing, moves with the breath of the Universe.

The Bat

~~

The sun sets. The din of the *higuroshi* dies down. Glowworms wink in the bamboo thickets. Oyu must find his feet and fetch his own supper from the kitchens, for Onogoro has not returned to her apartments. Instead she circles Shikibu's chamber with her bursting head clutched between her fists, for neither confessions nor infusions can ease her pounding headache.

At last Shikibu persuaded her to lie down on the couch and, bending over her, applied her fingertips to that place between the eyebrows where unshed tears gather. What an enigma the girl is, she thought. So ardent and tormented, yet enterprising enough to hire a story-teller to enhance her pleasure! Thinking of the pillow boy, Shikibu did not know whether to laugh or cry. All over the Capital, it seemed, women of wit were recruiting this talented auxiliary, and stowing him behind their *tsuitate* screens. Atsumichi himself would have admired such duplicity. What mistresses of intrigue we are, she marvelled, and what lengths we will go to to please or flatter our lovers!

Onogoro grimaced with pain under the pressure of Shikibu's fingers, and she let out a strangled gasp. 'But how *could* he?' she cried. Her cheeks were flushed, her temples shiny with sweat. Why, she loves the boy! thought Shikibu in surprise. 'Please let me stay with you tonight,' Onogoro implored, 'I refuse to go back while he is there!'

Shikibu sighed. Now she was quite convinced. She

decided to say nothing, however, but to let the girl come to it in her own time. 'Of course you must stay,' she replied, 'but I really must get ready for the salon.' She no longer cares for the General, she mused, and of course she is punishing herself for it! She went into her dressing room, where Ben had laid out a gauze under-robe and a single over-robe of thinnest silk, owing to the heat of the night. Soon the ladies would be arriving, and she had asked her maid to lay out cushions under the plum trees in the garden, where the air was cooler.

'I'm going,' Shikibu announced, floating into the room with her moth-coloured sleeves spread wide. Bright motes of light flickered before Onogoro's eyes. She nodded feebly, and Shikibu slipped away, leaving a faint scent of lilacs behind her. Left alone, Onogoro flattened her palms across her bursting forehead and fought the feeling that had come over her. She panted in the heat, her silk robe clung damply to her thighs.

In the gardens the fireflies were out and bats sheered silently in the twilight. The shadowy figure of Ben moved across the grass, lighting incense cones to deter mosquitoes. When Shikibu ran down the steps to greet the ladies, they were careful with her, for they had heard of her break with Prince Atsumichi. One after another rested a hand on her shoulder, or placed an arm around her waist, or stroked her cheek lightly with a closed fan. Darkness rustled in the folds of their robes as they sat down on the spread mats and tucked their feet under them.

Shikibu looked round the circle of intimates. How grandly Shōnagon is dressed, she thought, and her hairstyle is really too elaborate for such a sultry night. Young Hime was pregnant and showed off her small bulge proudly, stroking it as if it were a pet cat. 'Hime is grown so lazy, her mind is turned to mud!' jeered Yomiko. 'Who then shall tell us a story?'

Shikibu was pensive, her thoughts preoccupied with Onogoro and her injudicious love. A legend came to her, a strange tale of a people without rank or position. The nurse who had told her the story had sworn it to be true, and although later it had been impressed on her that the lower orders are forever confusing folk-tale with history and filling the ears of babes with sacrilegious notions, at the time she had believed every word. The tale concerned a time before Emperors, when a dark and diffident race inhabited the fertile craters of volcanoes and did not claim descent from Ohmi-Kami, the Heaven-Illumining goddess, or indeed from any god at all. This society admitted neither distinctions of rank nor the supremacy of one sex over another, nor even that hierarchy in which man in his blindness claims sentience for himself alone and lords it over the other animals. The sun-scorched skin of these citizens was the red-gold of partridge feathers; they sniffed sulphurous vapours and sailed the crater-lakes on boats carved from pumice-stone, and men and women alike laboured to build the hanging bridges which spanned the gorges between one summit and another. Mount Ashigara in Sagami, it was said, was the only one of the peaks that remained, for the others had erupted long ago, sweeping away their inhabitants on a sea of boiling lava.

'I have a story,' said Shikibu.

Onogoro's head throbbed unmercifully, her flesh pressed outwards to stretch her skin. The preposterous idea returned to her but she would not have it. I cannot possibly love the boy, she berated herself. She tossed restlessly; she lay on her side, her back, her belly, but no position gave relief. At last, kneeling on the couch, she tucked her head down between her knees and curled into a ball of pain. Like a bat who gives birth hanging upside down from a branch and must thrust her infant upwards against gravity, her red tongue swelling with distress, her ineffably startled eyes staring with the effort, until finally a black blind nightmare creature slithers from her belly and makes a grab with great clawed hands lest it fall to a premature death . . . Such was the coming to light of the intolerable notion – difficult of delivery, dark as a demon, yet fated to cling on until it reached maturity.

In the garden Shikibu's sombre tale came to an end. 'No rank or precedence?' cried Sei Shōnagon. 'Equality of the sexes? I think there would be little sport in it!' She yawned exquisitely. 'But here's the very woman we need!' she exclaimed, catching sight of Onogoro on the balcony. 'Shikibu has given us such a drab time, darling. Won't you come and tell us something amusing?'

Shikibu turned and saw her friend silhouetted against the bright interior, her red gown rimmed with fiery light. 'She isn't well,' she scolded, 'we mustn't bother her.' The ladies fell silent as Onogoro moved across the garden towards them, scandal rippling in every fold of her robe. Some leaned towards one another and whispered the news about the General; others opened their fans and fluttered them casually, as if to deny the very thought of gossip.

'Something amusing?' Onogoro echoed, gazing at the company as if through a mist. 'Would a love-story be suitable?'

'There's no need,' said Shikibu hastily. 'Don't mind Shōnagon.'

'Yes, yes!' cried the ladies in the moonlight, 'a love story!' And their fans flickered in the air like bats as they got ready to concentrate on pleasure.

The Oshidori Couple

❧

'Once in a manor on the coast of Echigo lived a young girl whose mother was both strict and suspicious. The lady constantly scolded her husband for being too lenient with his daughter, and if, to keep the peace, he promised to correct the girl, he generally forgot, for he was far more interested in his horses and orchards than in overseeing the proper discipline of his offspring.

'The girl, whose name was Naishi, took glad advantage of the opportunities afforded by her father's laxity and, having persuaded him to teach her to ride, ran quite wild on hill and sea shore.

'As Naishi entered her teens and began to be subject to her monthly obstacle, her mother's surveillance increased. Every hour the girl spent with her father would rouse the good lady to jealous condemnation, and the increasing curtailment of her freedom meant that even her solitary rides had to be sacrificed. Naishi grew exceedingly sullen, and took to brooding on the lost paradise of her youth. What have I done to deserve such unhappiness? she wondered, and even thought of entering a convent, for it seemed that there was no end to the debts owed to her mother and the incomprehensible amends to be made.

'One day in spring her father set off on a journey to the distant Capital, and Naishi was left to her mother's tender mercies. The girl sat alone in the stables, cleaning her nails with a splinter of wood and agonising over her situation. It was difficult not to resent her mother's severity, and to replace rebellion with filial devotion. She wondered if it was so with other girls and other mothers, but she did not know any, and could not ask, and therefore concluded that her desire for life and freedom must be a dangerous fire indeed, if it required such constant stamping out!

'All at once a horse was brought in by one of her father's outriders, limping badly from an injury to the fetlock. The young stallion went by the odd name of Oshidori – perhaps because his facial markings were reminiscent of the bold white eyebrow of the mandarin duck – and had recently been acquired from a lord in the neighbouring province of Kotsuke. Her father, she knew, was very proud of the fine animal. "We are afraid the bone is broken," said the outrider, "and the horse may have to be destroyed."

' "Never!" cried Naishi, rallying her energies, for in view of the palpable injury sustained by the magnificent horse, her own wounds seemed insignificant. She ordered the man to return to her father's caravan with word that she herself would tend to the stricken horse – her mother, she thought, could hardly raise objections to that! With careful fingers she probed the cannon bone and the pastern, but found no break. A swelling around the fetlock joint indicated that the ligaments were torn, and so she set to with poultices, and bound the limb with supporting bandages, and went to bed that night optimistic about the prospects for the stallion's recovery.

'Day after day she found in the injured animal a focus not only for her pity but also for her pent-up forces. Tending him was a consolation for the crippling boredom of the ladylike duties imposed by her mother, so much so that although she was gratified by her patient's rapid progress, she looked forward apprehensively to the time when he would heal completely and leave her without useful occupation.

'One moon-viewing night in the middle of the month Naishi hurried through her supper and, telling her mother that she had her monthly obstacle and was retiring early, slipped out to the stable to remove the bandages. The swelling had quite disappeared and the stallion, testing the strength of the fetlock, pranced joyfully and tossed his mane in the moonlight.

' "My job is done now," said Naishi, reflecting sadly that since Oshidori was sound and swift once more, she and her skills were no longer needed.

' "Not entirely, My Lady," said a voice from the stable stall.

'Naishi's heart leapt in her breast. "Who's there?" she demanded, peering through the slanting moonrays in an attempt to detect the servant or outrider who had spoken.

' "The horse is well, thank you," said the voice, "but the man is still stricken."

'Realising that it was the stallion himself who had spoken, Naishi quailed with fright and hid trembling behind a straw-filled manger. "This is demon's work!" she cried, and would have fled the stable, had not Oshidori begged in a heartfelt voice:

' "Please stay, Lady Naishi. I have found much solace in your company."

'Naishi calmed a little at this, and peeped at the horse through the wooden bars of the crib. How beautiful he was with the white flashes on his forehead, his neck so arched and his mane so thick, and he a gentle beast without harm or malice, his head held high in the moonlight and the brush of his tail lashing all the evil from the shadows! "But how is it that a stallion can speak?" she asked at last.

' "I am no stallion," Oshidori replied, "but a man enchanted. A *tengu* fastened me in this form through no fault of my own, and there is only one way to release me. For that I beg your help."

' "But I am a mere girl," said Naishi, the surge of her fervent heart belying her modest demeanour, "how can I be of any use to you?"

' "I see no girl, but a woman," Oshidori declared, "and only a woman can help me."

'Naishi felt a shock pass through her, a fearful blush that rooted her to the spot and rushed up to blossom on her cheeks and brow. She had never heard herself so described, except in terms of warning or remonstration and, sensing that any evidence of femininity would be taken by her mother as a rivalrous affront, had suppressed most of the normal fantasies of the growing girl. But now, like a lover who hides in the chilly shadows under the balcony until beckoned into the intimacy of his mistress's chamber, so Naishi's secret desires responded with grateful haste to Oshidori's summons. "Tell me how," she whispered, creeping out from behind the manger.

' "Only set aside your modesty and let me glimpse the moonlight on your white shoulder," begged Oshidori.

'Turning her face away so that the horse could not see her agitation, Naishi drew aside her robe to reveal the shoulder that none but her mother and her nurse had ever laid eyes on. The moon kissed it with adoring lips, and, in claiming it for her own, gave it back to the girl as never before, the skin alert and the flesh enlivened, and the blood hammering up from the heart to empower the muscles.

'The horse thanked her with a happy sigh, and Naishi covered herself. After all, it was not so much to ask! she thought, feeling rather smug and excited.

' "Now humble yourself," begged Oshidori, "and grant me a glimpse of your white knee."

'This request made Naishi feel even more bashful, but the lure of the power invested in her overcame her qualms. She drew up her hem, and the darkness came

217

with it. Moonlight flooded her legs, and she remembered with a childish pang how her mother would scrub and scrub at her knees, bemoaning the dirt ingrained in them. The horse, however, found no such cause for complaint, and once again snorted with contentment. "Are you now released from your predicament?" Naishi asked reluctantly, for a reckless part of her yearned for the game to continue.

' "I realise that it is a great deal to ask," said the stallion gravely, "but only if you show me your *hisho* shall I find release."

'In an attempt to conceal her eagerness, Naishi replied with a brisk nod. She hoisted her skirt in a businesslike fashion, like a shopkeeper who raises his morning blinds with a rattle to reveal his wares. The moon touched them with her practised fingers: the dark entangled thatch, the red bud of the lotus which burgeoned under her appreciative gaze.

'The black eye of the stallion swept the girl with a hundred caresses, and a heat like eternity came into the core of her, so that she felt for the first time the secret source of her rebellious energy. What a blessing, after all, to be a woman! she thought, sinking to her knees in the sweet-smelling straw.

'It was at this ecstatic and forgetful moment that Naishi's mother, with an unerring instinct for interference, swept angrily into the stable. The moonlight fell stark and plain on her daughter's womanly form, and with a shrief of outrage the good lady dragged Naishi to her feet. Taking her by the hair, she marched her back to the house, where she beat her with a willow-wand and thrust her unceremoniously into a cellar below the kitchens.

'Incarcerated like a criminal, Naishi lay stunned for some days, refusing all food, while the cockroaches chattered around her in sociable hordes, speaking of injustice and her mother's infamy.

'When her mother came on the third day to entreat her to take some nourishment, Naishi confronted her coldly, demanding to know why she harboured such hatred towards her. Incensed, the lady flew at her daughter and beat her again, calling her all manner of names, and swearing that she would stay in the cellar until she mended her ways.

' "Don't give in," urged the cockroaches, as they finished up the last morsels of the supper that Naishi had renounced. "Sweet appetite should never be denied." And with a rustle like the wind they hurried to the barred window and began to devour the rotted wood of the frame.

'That night Naishi loosened the window and made her escape across the dark gardens and through the dry bamboo shanks that bordered the estate.

'In the morning the alarm went up, and outriders were despatched in pursuit of the fugitive. Hearing their shouts in the distance, Naishi ran and ran, but at last she could go no further, and climbed into a hollow tree in the hope that her pursuers would pass on by.

'Before long they drew near, and to her horror Naishi heard the leader declare that they would rest there awhile to eat and drink, for the slut was on foot and had no chance of escaping them. Evidently news of her escapade in the stables had leaked out and, imprisoned within the tree, she was obliged to eavesdrop on the most ribald gossip and surmise.

'When the men had eaten their fill and slaked their thirst with wine, the leader of the posse, noticing a knot-hole in the very tree which concealed the girl, taunted his men with lewd encouragements. "Such a pretty *shio-fuki*!" he cried. "But who will be the first to sample it?"

' "I will," cried one of the younger outriders, who was

so tall that he had to stoop down and straddle his legs wide to fit his member into the knothole. Bravo! shouted his companions as he found entry, all unaware that within the tree he had also gained the entrance-arch of another, more fleshly body.

'Intrigued by this strange spoon that stirred in her *hisho*, Naishi could not help recalling the moonlit stable and the ravishing eye of the horse, and, regretting that the sensations had been so prematurely discontinued, she decided that the counsel of the cockroaches was wiser by far than her mother's. How good it feels, she marvelled, clamping a hand over her mouth so that no sound could betray her, but how sad that it is all over so quickly!

'Immediately the first lad had spent himself, a second leapt into the breach, but he too expired after a few rapid thrusts. By now sweet appetite was keenly whetted, and Naishi bit her lips to stifle the groans of her mounting pleasure.

'On and on came the eager outriders, each entrant honour-bound to prove his manhood by reaching the finishing post in a shorter time than any of his predecessors, and thereby ensuring that the invisible Naishi was left unsatisfied. Presently all were spent, and one was crowned with leaves and declared the winner, and with much chaffing and joking they rode off to resume the pursuit, never knowing just how intimate they had been with their quarry.

'You will be wondering, though, whatever happened to the horse Oshidori, and the man trapped within him.

'Naishi's generous exhibition had effectively undone the man's entrancement, and the transformation from horse to human had occurred moments after her mother had dragged the girl away.

'The young lord had remained disconsolate in the environs of the house until the outcry precipitated by Naishi's escape. Then, following the trail of the outriders, he had observed their cavortings from the cover of a blackthorn thicket. Now that the revellers had gone, he crept out of hiding and called Naishi's name, hoping against hope that she had concealed herself in the undergrowth to outwit them.

'From her cage in the hollow tree Naishi recognised the voice of Oshidori, and her heart thundered with excitement. "I am here," she cried, "but I cannot free myself!"

'The young lord was filled with concern, and hurried to the tree, asking solicitously if she was in discomfort.

' "I am indeed," said Naishi truthfully, for her pent-up energies cried out for release..

'At last a handsome face appeared in the branches above her, and a comely arm reached down to help her from her hiding place. The lord, who had been privy to the beastly antics which the tree had hosted, was outraged on Naishi's behalf. "Allow me to succour you as you have succoured me," he begged, and, fetching water from a stream, he tenderly bathed the sweat from her face.

'But Naishi was not so easily soothed, for as her eye explored the man she recalled also the horse in him, the toss of the head and the ardent stamp of the hoof, and her appetite, whetted by the abbreviated foreplay of the outriders, burned forcefully in her. Let he who began it also finish it, she thought. Without more ado she drew him down in the dry leaves, while the sun blinked through the branches in astonishment.

'Released from the corseting tree, her body quickly found the rhythm and the pace of a rider, and since the man who had been the horse was wiser than many, if a little surprised to be so boldly mounted, he was more than gladly ridden!

'Thus sweet appetite was satisfied at length, and together the couple made their happy escape – she from her mother's tyranny, and he from his imprisoning and wilful demon. And years later their passion was still so fresh and fulsome that those who looked upon it called them the Oshidori couple, after the mandarin ducks who paddle in pairs and, as legend has it, once mated, are forever inseparable.'

Plum Blossom

So absorbed was Onogoro in the arcane obsessions of her tale that she had almost forgotten her audience. Her eyes were blank and shining; her hair, raggedly pinned, escaped from its combs.

'Well done!' said Shōnagon, but the applause was uncomfortable, for the least perceptive audience will sense when a story is not told primarily for their benefit, but aims instead at settling private scores. And where, after all, is the entertainment in that?

Hime, who lounged on a cushion with her head in Yomiko's lap, let out a small superior belch. She thought of the sweetheart she carried in her belly, and of the stories she would spin for him – wonderful tales which would bind him to her for ever. Gazing up at the starry sky, she luxuriated in the future. If he is a boy, she mused, he will worship me; if a girl, she will never have the slightest cause for complaint.

Plunged into reverie, the ladies were silent, and around the head of each one of them was a gathering of ghosts, plume-like and flickering in the irregular light of the lanterns. Some thought of what they had lost, others of what had yet to be gained, and more than one wished that in love, as in poetry, she could have courage, cast herself out on the buffeting wind, over the trembling water.

'How melancholy we are tonight,' lamented Shōnagon. 'Even the Lady Omoto has deserted us.'

'Perhaps the *karma* is bad for story-telling,' said Shikibu, who was not one to manufacture gaiety where none existed. Glimpsing the cold blaze of the moon through the plum branches, she shivered. It was said that of all trees the plum stood for courage, for it alone sent forth blossoms when the snow was still on the ground. So why should anyone be surprised, she brooded, if the fruit was sharper than the peach or apricot? She wondered suddenly what her fate would be, and that of her friends. Would they paint a young face on a raddled one, or find an *oshidori* man who would brave ridicule for the sake of fidelity? Would they live as happy dowagers in the bosom of their families, or wander the chattering corridors of the Palace like grey shades? Would they attain fame through their own efforts only to fall from favour and end their days in penury? If only courage mounted up as easily as the years, she mused, it would be there with its strong arms when we needed it most!

The Work Done in the Dark

Onogoro, meanwhile, was struck by a singular coincidence. Leaving the party, she hurried back to the Plum Blossom Apartments in a state of some excitement. Shoulder, knee, *hisho*, she repeated breathlessly, rummaging in the drawer where Shikibu had put the poems for safe keeping. For hadn't these selfsame parts cunningly contrived to exhibit themselves in the story she had just told? Laying the three poems in front of her, she studied them for clues.

The shoulder:

Was it your gaze which followed me
All the way to the mountain fastness?
No, it was only the moon,
Peering over my shoulder.

Whose yearning voice was this, and from what exile did it speak? Onogoro wished to succour it.

The knee:

Humble, like the evening primrose,
I hide until sundown,
For only in darkness
Shall I know myself.

Now patient, now despairing, now finding wisdom: Onogoro's heart was touched.

The *hisho*

My modest house
Is thatched with rushes
Only seek within
And you will find
The lotus of eternity.

Here the energetic intelligence of the body paraded itself for her attention, and sought above all to be admitted.

Exiled, it flaunted its intrinsic worth and demanded reinstatement. Onogoro remembered how sweet it had been to display the young girl's accoutrements to the approving eye of the moonlight. But wasn't it I myself, she thought, who was the author and the audience, the seer and the seen? (And also, we might add, the dragon who punished the daughter for her pleasure, but rather than hurry to draw Onogoro's attention to this oversight, let us keep mum for the moment and savour our privileged viewpoint.)

Onogoro pondered a while, and at last the meaning came to her in all its clarity. Now I see it! she thought. We must cherish the selves that flower in us as lovingly as an author husbands his characters. Be they saints or wastrels, tigers or lizards, we must admit them all the same, rather than keep them in exile! For who else will love them if we do not?

She stood stock still in the centre of the room, and it was as if all the lanterns of her mind flared up and cast a bright light on her. In this instant what she saw was not topsy-turvy at all, but harmonious as a house with strong pillars, and eaves at the proper angles, and lintels in their graceful places, and all the rooms linked and in order. Transfixed, she thought: Why, I am my own keeper!

What an auspicious night it had been!

The Sick Bullock

After crossing the mountain pass of Sayo-no-Nakayama the General's caravan made fair speed through Suruga province and forded the Oi river some distance from the coast. On the lower slopes of Mount Ashigara, however, one of the bullocks which drew the Lady Ochibu's carriage trembled, and rolled its eyes, and died with a white foam at its mouth. The Guardsmen dragged the corpse from its harness and threw it into the ditch, declaring that they would set up camp at the roadside until a replacement could be fetched from the nearest village.

Meanwhile the General's restless feet took him towards the crest of a hill from which he hoped to glimpse the glossy skin of the sea at moonrise. Before he reached this vantage point, however, he entered a grove of birch trees and here stumbled upon the ruined temple of Takesheba-dera. The wooden pillars were eaten away by rot and ants, and *shinobu* grass straggled mournfully from the eaves. The sight encouraged melancholy thoughts of what he had lost, and what had still to be surrendered. With a heart suddenly stricken, he remembered Onogoro, and the love affair that must also be left behind for ever. But he could not bear to dwell for long on the painful period with which the poet was so inextricably linked, and putting his yearnings strictly behind him, he forced himself to consider how he might bring order from disorder and set his life on a new course.

In the forecourt of the temple lay a litter of emerald tiles which wind and weather had dislodged from the roof. The General picked up a broken tile and looked around for the missing piece, his mind absent, his search loose and purposeful as a grazing goat. Soon he held the other fragment in his hand, and by fitting the two halves together was able to reconstitute the whole. He scraped away the moss and lichen, and there in his hands the tile lay good as new and bluer than heaven. I will keep it as a reminder of the impermanence of all things, he said to himself. Then he thought, no, I will give it to the Lady Ochibu, who has always been singularly devout. As he reflected on his wife's piety, a novel idea came to him. Would it not be possible, he wondered, to take her with him to the mountains? The *yama-bushi* were lay priests who set no store by celibacy; indeed, many of them were married. It would be a spartan life, assuredly, but spiritual wealth would more than compensate for the lack of material comforts.

Turning back towards the camp, the General began to make plans for himself and his family. Their escape, he was sure, would occasion little uproar, for the province was too far-flung and his position too lowly. Once delivered into obscurity in Dewa, they could slip away and vanish once and for all behind the high white mists of the mountains!

Thus the General drove away all darker reflections, and with a heart uncommonly light and easy, hurried back towards the pavilions, where the cooking fires already glowed red in the twilight. The Lady Ochibu came through the dusk to meet him, but as she approached her face filled with consternation.

'The boy is not with you?' she cried. 'Then we have lost him!' He had disappeared an hour before, she told her husband tearfully, and since neither she nor the nurse had been able to find him in the vicinity of the camp, they had told themselves that he had accompanied his father.

The General calmed his wife and made her lie down in the pavilion where the nurse was settling the baby for the night. 'He cannot be far away,' he assured her, 'and after all he is a sensible little fellow.' Since darkness was falling fast, he took a lighted brand from the fire and patrolled the line of carriages, peering into each one, and even thrusting the torch underneath in case the boy might be hiding mischievously there. He looked behind the kitchen tent, and scoured the bushes and boulders at the roadside. Concern grew in him, and he resolved to ask the Guardsmen to take lanterns and spread the search further afield. As he turned away from the last carriage his torch illuminated the glossy hide of an animal: it was the carcase of the bullock, discarded and forgotten in the ditch. He moved closer, and the flickering light picked out first the white crescent of a horn, and then a scrap of red material. With a cry of relief he jumped down into the ditch. For there, with his arms wound protectively around the beast's neck, and his tear-stained face pressed close to its dead and staring eye, lay his elder son, quite fast asleep. The General lifted him tenderly up, intending to carry him to the pavilion, but the boy woke with a shudder and struggled to free himself. Stretching his arms towards the bullock, the child began to wail. 'Come now,' said the General, 'the beast is dead.'

'But he's lonely,' said the boy between sobs, 'he has no one to keep him company.'

'The gods will look after him,' said the General, 'and you must keep your mother company, for she is worried about you.' The child appeared to be soothed by this, and allowed himself to be put to bed, on condition that his parents said prayers for the unfortunate animal.

Later the General returned to the ditch and, taking his sword, severed one of the beast's horns. This he placed on his son's pillow to comfort him, but once again the boy's eyes filled with tears. 'You won't ever die, will you, father?' he pleaded.

'Certainly not,' promised the General with a smile.

'Never never never,' the boy intoned, holding hard to the curved white horn.

A Bridge of Magpies

Onogoro lay down on Shikibu's couch but would not let herself sleep, for sleep might bring forgetfulness, and by the morning her brand new self might have vanished with the darkness that had bred it. I have punished myself enough, she decided, reiterating the lofty thoughts that filled her mind. The secret, then, is to know oneself, and to love oneself, whatever happens, for those who treat themselves badly will only encourage others to do the same. How simple it is, she thought, yet how difficult to learn! The General is gone, and all the better, since I see now that it is starvation which whips one to a frenzy, and I do believe I never truly loved the man at all!

Armed with her new weapons, Onogoro cut swathes through her history, and in no scenario was she ill-used, for she would not tolerate it. If I had known then what I know now, she reflected, I would have acted *thus* and *thus*. I have strained to forgive the General, but in the meantime have shown myself no mercy, for guilt and self-pity have imprisoned me in childhood, and I have never learned to trust myself!

It was time, then, to turn her back on the imperfect past, and launch herself forward into her newfound freedom. This was her resolute decision, and from its clear view-point she would henceforth think of the General with pity and affection, but no more. Onogoro sighed and sank back into the pillows, satisfied as any stonemason who has done a good day's work. The roof-tiles are laid, the entrance-pillars cleanly carved; the temple stands solid and complete, and tomorrow the worship can commence. With these uplifting thoughts the poet's eyes closed and her hands fell limp and open on the coverlet.

If only escape from the dragon-mother could be accomplished in life as easily as it was in Onogoro's story!

In the dawn hours Shikibu, who had spent the night with Prince Tametaka, returned to her apartments and tiptoed past the couch where her friend lay asleep. Suddenly Onogoro sat up straight and said clearly: 'Are we fated to love only those who hurt us?' Startled, Shikibu was about to reply, but, noticing that Onogoro's eyes were tight-closed, she realised that the girl had spoken out of a dream and, having framed the question, far from requiring an answer, was perfectly content to resume her slumbers.

Like a cloud of mosquitoes hopes came to torment Oyu. The General a snail! He could hardly believe that Onogoro had expressed such disillusionment about her lover. All night he fretted miserably on his balcony bed under the wry stars, but did not dare go in search of her, for in seeking to free himself from the coils of her pity, he had succeeded only too well, and had undoubtedly wounded her. Yet somehow he could not rid himself of the impression that her feeling towards him was quite other than the repugnance he so manifestly deserved.

What, then, was to be done? For hours he wrestled with

himself, and when the dawn wind came to cool his face he hauled himself weakly from his bed, but still had not reached a decision. In truth, his only clear desire was to be in the presence of Izanami once more, and to feel her white breath flow strongly into him.

With an effort Oyu navigated a path to the stables, where he was greeted with rapturous snorts of welcome. When he addressed the spirit of the horse, however, he found her answers stern.

'So what's your excuse for inaction now?' the mare demanded.

'It is not so easy to stumble from darkness into a world full of light,' Oyu replied sulkily.

The horse was exasperated, and stamped her hoof. 'Such humility is misplaced,' came the tart rejoinder. 'You *are* her world, since love has gripped her.'

Oyu sank down on the grooming stool. 'How can it be?' he breathed, as the darkness dropped from him like a stone.

'Can you not see,' the horse insisted, 'you are the cherry tree round which cluster all the small hungry birds of her love, you the moon she envies from her balcony, the teasing metaphor half-glimpsed while she writes: she cannot let go of you. You the stone bench she would rest on in the cool shade of the camphor tree, you her temple and her pleasure-boat. Yours the eye which burns her with blushes, the lantern which lights her path: she cannot find her way without you. You her cooking-fire and the clear water she bathes in: her world is replete with you. You her very breath and her music – such is the power and the responsibility of love.'

The words were too bright for Oyu and stripped him naked. Meanwhile his limbs were seized by a furious agitation of which wild hope was the largest component. 'Can it really be so?' he cried.

The mare flicked her tail at him like a lash. 'Tonight is the seventh of the Seventh,' she said irritably. 'Have you forgotten?' If he does not act now, she thought, I wash my hands of him. Does he expect me to build him a bridge of heavenly magpies as well?

What Izanami referred to, of course, was the legend of the Herdsman and the Weaver, which has always been a favourite with our citizens. Because of her love for the Herdsman, the story goes, the Weaver neglected her work on the clothes of the gods, while the Herdsman neglected his cattle. As punishment the Emperor of Heaven turned the lovers into two stars, and placed them at opposite extremities of the Milky Way. In mitigation, however, he declared that the stars may meet once a year, on the seventh night of the Seventh Month, when a company of heavenly magpies forms a bridge which the Weaver may cross to join her lover. To celebrate this occasion, leaves are spread in the gardens of the Emperor's residence, and everyone prays for a clear night, since a cloudy one would obscure the heavens and bring bad luck. While his Majesty and his retinue wait and watch anxiously for the meeting of the two stars, Court Poets read aloud poems they have composed in honour of the lovers. In private households various rituals are also observed, and women pray to the Weaver star for skill in the arts of music, weaving and poetry. Needless to say, the night of the Weaver Festival is also an extremely auspicious time for those whose hearts incline towards each other and whose bodies yearn for union!

Maga-tama Beads

Next day Tokiden returned to the Almond Blossom Apartments to find her mistress absent. Nor was there any sign of Oyu, other than a sprawl of bedclothes on the balcony and a slice of melon on which flies feasted in the noon heat. Wrinkling her nose in disapproval, the maid began to tidy energetically. The Lady Onogoro was an indifferent nurse, to be sure, but she was an even worse housekeeper!

Meanwhile, in the Plum Blossom Apartments, Onogoro struggled with the poem she would be expected to present that night at the Festival.

'Hungry breath of his herd . . .' she wrote.

'Love is our heedless fodder . . .' she wrote.

Finally she settled on the following, which she read aloud to Shikibu.

> 'They say I sewed a ragged seam
> And your cattle weakened
> And fell by the wayside.
> This much is certain:
> Love alone was our fodder,
> Our most extravagant cloak.'

Shikibu clapped her hands appreciatively, and replied with her offering.

> 'What does it matter
> If the moon hides her face
> In the rain?
> We will meet the more tenderly,
> Keeping our secrets.'

Onogoro found Shikibu's poem lithe, subtle, and in all ways superior, but instead of feeling downcast and belittling her own effort she felt grateful for the excellence of the work. How privileged I am to be granted such models to aspire to! she thought. Her heart leapt with joyful anticipation at the prospect of all she had yet to learn, for although the path to improvement was no doubt long, at this moment it seemed an eminently pleasurable one. How glorious, she thought, to be apprenticed to art itself, to be led again and again to the secret heart of the lotus!

Shikibu could not but be aware of Onogoro's rapt mood, and her mind, perceiving all too clearly the cause of the transformation, filled with bittersweet reflections. Indeed, she mused, love was the best food for poets, for it opened the heart to each and every gift of nature, until the whole world seemed to surround one with its bounty. In that happy delusion, the birds seemed to sing for one's particular delight, the flowers to follow one with their midsummer faces, and the autumn plums to strain at their very stalks, so eager were they to plummet into one's waiting hands. Oh enviable state! she thought. Oh fortunate Onogoro!

There was much for the two friends to do before evening, however, and the young poet's entrancement must needs be interrupted by a sojourn in the bath-house and a visit to the Soothsayer to consult the all-important horoscopes. Then came the lengthy business of hair-washing, a service Ben was prevailed upon to render to both ladies in tandem, since any suggestion that Onogoro might return to her own apartments to perform her toilet brought her out in furious blushes.

While the amiable Ben presided, Shikibu and Onogoro knelt together at the basin and watched the streams of their long hair mingle in the water, until neither could tell which strands belonged to whom, and they cried out childishly at the shock of the cold rinsing, and shook their wet heads afterwards like otters.

Onogoro scandalised Ben by declaring her intention to go out into the garden with her hair neither dry nor dressed, in order to make offerings to the Weaver star. With the sleek black cloaks of their hair sweeping the pebbles, the two friends festooned the wistaria boughs with strings of tiny beads, and hung blue and white strips of *ni kite* cloth from the plum trees. Shikibu murmured the customary words of supplication; Onogoro, meanwhile, pressed the *maga-tama* beads wordlessly to her cheek, and if we do not know whether she prayed for help in love or in poetry, we can form our own opinion as to where most assistance was needed!

So the afternoon passed swiftly in these pleasant occupations. The ladies' hair drew every last hot ray from the sun, which sank exhausted behind the Palace walls, until at last Ben declared it dry, and dressed it up elaborately in tortoiseshell combs. Then, tucking their scrolls into their sleeves, the two poets set out for the gardens of the Emperor.

The hush of waiting which had fallen over the Court was broken only by a peacock's cry from the darkness beyond the lake. In the heavens Vega and Altair inched shyly towards each other until at last, embracing, they flared in a combined delirium of brightness. Down on earth applause rang out, and the noble guests drank toasts to the lovers in thanks for the luck that was now guaranteed to grace the year to come.

Onogoro watched the sky intently. How sad it was that the two stars were fated to move apart only moments after they had consummated their union, and, each resuming its smaller, independent glow, continued on their separate ways. Cruel gods, she thought, who decree that brief rapture is bought at the cost of such long schism, and who condemn lovers on the one hand to the pain of yearning, or else to the shame of forgetting! And her heart beat in her throat as she took her leave of Shikibu and Prince Tametaka and, spreading her fan before her face, made her way quickly towards the Almond Blossom Gardens.

Secrets

❧

'Is it a cloudy night or clear?' asked Oyu from his exalted seat on Izanami's back.

'A bright night,' said the mare, for the moon was rising.

'Then the lovers have met?'

'Met and parted,' answered Izanami, steering a path

between the dark boughs of the almond trees, which might otherwise have dislodged her rider.

Encouraged by this good omen, Oyu dismounted on the balcony steps and, tethering the horse loosely to the rail, slipped through the screen door and entered the empty apartment.

The Scent of the Cedar

Immediately Onogoro saw the moonlit shape of the horse a thought pierced her breast like a knife. Could it be that the wilful Oyu had revived his intention to leave for the Eastern Mountains? Was she to lose her love in the very moment of finding it?

She ran up the steps and threw the door open. 'Oyu,' she cried to the dark room, but no answer came. She called out for Tokiden, but remembered that the maid was serving at the festivities. Lighting the lantern, she searched each room in turn but, finding no one, she sank down on the bed and gave way to a fit of desolation, for when rioting hopes storm the gates of our heart they also leave us open to disappointment's bleak invasions.

From behind the *tsuitate* screen came a small sound like a scratch. Assuming that the cat was secreted there, and feeling sadly in need of consolation, Onogoro called out to her. 'Come, Omoto.' Instead of the mew of the lordly animal, however, a human voice issued from behind the screen.

'Once in Hida province,' it began, 'there was a schoolteacher who lived in a hill village with his small son, his wife having passed away some years before . . .'

Misery was banished, and happiness flowed in Onogoro like a river which, swollen by spring storms, threatens to burst its banks and carry all before it. She plucked the combs from her hair and shook it free, so that the long strands crept across the bed and stole under the *tsuitate* screen to tease Oyu's fingertips. Trembling, Oyu continued:

'The same brain fever that had carried off the scholar's wife had struck his child blind, and, since he feared for his son's future, he was at great pains to instil in him all the learning that could be transmitted by reading aloud.

'When the scholar in his turn passed on, his son, though barely a youth, was left to provide not only for himself but also for his elderly grandmother. This lady had once been a great poet at Court but, lacking a protector, had fallen on hard times and was now obliged to turn to her family for support. Sorely regretting the fading of her beauty, she bemoaned her fate from morning till night, so that the youth was hard put to persuade her out of her gloom.

'To me you are always beautiful, grandmother, he would assure her, for since he could not see her, what did he have to go on but the descriptions she furnished of her glorious heyday, when her skin was pearl white, and her black hair swept the ground for a league behind her, and she was the envy of a Court well-stocked with ravishing beauties? Mollified, the old lady would stoke up the fire and read him her poems and stories the whole night long, thus feeding his avid hunger for literature in the most edifying manner.

'Eventually the lord on whose manor the pair subsisted saw that the boy, although blind, was able-bodied and good with animals, and accordingly set him to work as a herdsman on the high pastures which surrounded the village. The black cattle were docile, and came willingly to his whistle, and the youth was happy to be thus employed with the amiable beasts. In sun and in rain he ranged the pastures with stories filling his head, and dreamed as he lay in the summer grass of the heavenly beauties his grandmother described, of their perfectly oval faces and their perfectly white feet which peeped from under the peacock hems of their dresses. The fingers of the sun caressed his face and the perfume of the hill azaleas dizzied him, and he pretended to himself that one day he would meet a young lady who, having lost her protector, came to him awash with tears, whereupon he would gallantly succour her.

'In the throes of these fancies the boy would roll over and press his body to the soft ground, or run his fingers over the damp moss of a tree-trunk or the velvet corollas of foxgloves. For by now he was on the threshold of manhood, and might quite properly have married, if he had had family to advise him and act on his behalf. But since his grandmother was fast becoming senile, and the boy could not in his blind state pay court unaided, his vital needs grew wild and untrammelled as the honeysuckle in the woods which bordered the pastures.'

Onogoro reached out and pushed the screen aside. 'Come, Oyu,' she said, drawing him into the bed beside her and begging him to continue. With the assurance of the Lady Omoto, she nudged his shoulder with her own, and aligned her knee with his, and curled in her claws contentedly. And the Master in his feline guise stalked the cardinal points to guard them both from harm, and the breath of the Universe blew out the lanterns, so that the moonlight could shed its white petals over them.

'One hot day while the cattle slept in the shade of the pines, an earth tremor shuddered through the forest, and the youth clutched at a sturdy cedar tree for support. When the tremor had passed and the ground was once more solid beneath his feet, he sniffed the spicy cedar-scent and found it enticing.

'Circling the trunk with his arms, he laid his cheek against the silky fibres of the bark. A pliant quality in the bark aroused him and, making believe that it was the waist of a lovely woman, he crushed his body against it, while the cattle turned their tactful heads away and flicked their sleepy tails.

'Since pleasure is of all explorers the most audacious, by and by his body sought and found a nook or knothole in the trunk which by its size and smoothness offered a high degree of hospitality to his member. Mossy without and sappy within, the cranny was indeed an excellent gate to eternity, and the youth entered it with the thankful fervour of one who has been virgin overlong. With many sighs, and with a surfeit of those groans and gasps which are both the soul's breath and the vestige of the beastly in us, the youth surged out across looming space in a blind somersault, saluted the smiling gods, and sank down warm and shining as a newborn upon the accommodating earth.

'It was then that he heard a grunt issue from the tree. Dumbfounded, he put his ear to the trunk. "It will take more than that to melt me!" said a matter-of-fact voice which was unmistakably female.

'The youth jumped back in fright, for if a demon inhabited the cedar tree he had exposed himself to great danger. Hastily he muttered apologies for having importuned the spirit, and was rewarded with a sigh.

' "Demon I am not, but demon it was that put me here," the voice complained.

'The youth plucked up his courage. "But who are you," he asked, "if not a demon?"

' "I cannot tell you who I am," the voice replied, "but I can tell you my story if you wish to hear it." Without waiting for the youth to answer, she went on bitterly: "Once I was a Lady-in-Waiting at Court, and from no fault of my own but beauty all men looked at me. Being young and lusty, I took many lovers: some three score and ten, as a matter of fact. Eventually my protector grew furiously jealous, and called upon a *tengu* to take revenge on me. This *tengu* was hideous and winged, and with his feather fan he cast a spell which doomed me to be walled up where no man can see me, and so wooden that no man can ever stir my passion."

' "Surely such a spell can be undone," said the youth eagerly, "if one knows how to undo it." Just as he was setting mind and will to the question, a scorpion stung his bare foot, and he leapt cursing into the air, for he, assuredly, was not made of wood, and felt its sting like fire.

'An idea struck him, and he asked: "Is it true that you can feel nothing?"

' "Nothing at all," the voice replied sadly.

'Reaching unerringly to the ground the youth snatched up the scorpion and thrust it into the knothole, where it scurried angrily to and fro, stinging whatever it touched.

' "Ah," said the voice, "now I feel a little something!" '

Onogoro hardly dared to breathe as Oyu's fingers drew back the folds of her robe. Here was the soft moss, and here the sap, and here the sting of passion. She struggled a little, and laughter flew out of her like butterflies. 'Don't be frightened', said Oyu.

'Frightened?' she said defiantly, and hid her face in her sleeve to conceal her sudden blushes, until she realised not only that he could not see her, but that the blind are not so easily hoodwinked.

'At this faint encouragement,' Oyu continued, 'the youth felt his ardour swell again, and he longed to enter the excellent gate once more. But first the scorpion had to be dealt with.

'Picking up some dry rushes, he made a fire of them and threw them into the knothole to incinerate the insect. "I feel a small glow!" said the voice in surprise.'

Eyes wide in the dappled darkness, Onogoro waited for the dreaded touch of his finger, and her heat rose to it all thick and unbidden. The moon was almost full, and high in the Milky Way the Weaver, who had lost her lover and was doomed to journey to the far end of the Universe without him, looked down on her and scowled with envy.

'Hoping to put the fire out, the boy urinated into the knothole, but the flames had taken hold. "Ah, slickness," said the voice in tones of nostalgia. "How the warmth grows in me!"

'Frustrated, the youth dragged a gorse bush up by the roots and beat at the fire in fury, in case the lady might be consumed entirely before he could take her in his arms.

' "Ah sweet punishment," the voice crooned, "won't you pierce me to the core?" '

'Oh!' cried Onogoro in dismay, for the words of the captive lady had stirred an unerring echo in her. It was as if Oyu could read her mind, and no amount of dissembling could conceal from him the clandestine lineaments of her desire.

Oyu had propped himself on one elbow and was looking down on her with a mischievous smile. Onogoro stared wildly back at him. He could not see her, did not know what bird or beast was represented on her dress or mimicked by her gesture, or which role was enacted by her hands, or eyes, or nape, or the fluent curve of her spine. All this was lost on him and fell into the abyss. She let out a groan. How dangerous everything is, she thought, feeling for the first time in plain view and undisguised.

'But what happens now?' she demanded. 'Will the fire burn her up, or will she be released from her prison?'

Sinking his face in her long hair Oyu rose up stealthily and entered her. Onogoro gasped at the risk and stopped talking. 'We'll see,' he said breathlessly, 'we'll see.'

The Fields of Paradise

Let us leave the pair, then, to the short summer night made timeless by love; ignoring both murmured promises and shrieks of delight, let us become like outrunners who go ahead to clear the road, and consider the fate, some days hence, of the luckless General.

With his escape planned, and the future cast in his mind's eye as clearly as a hawk's eye fixes an otter, the General was impatient to arrive in Dewa, and the incomparable orchards of Mushashi passed all too slowly before his carriage window.

But the gods, who are never crueller than when they detect an arrogance of will, hoisted the net of fate to trap the General like a helpless snipe. Lately the Guardsmen had received intelligence that Taira Tadatsune, the Vice-Governor of Kadzusa, had mounted a blood-feud against his Taira kinsmen. Having killed the Governor of Awa, he was now set to overrun Shimosa province. Indeed, when the caravan crossed into Shimosa it was a derelict vista which assailed their eyes, for the rice fields had been torched, the homesteads pillaged, and the livestock senselessly put to the sword.

The Guards quailed under the smoke which blackened the birdless sky, and would not continue, saying that they feared for their lives. With the excuse of seeking safe passage for the caravan, the General persuaded them that he must seek urgent audience with the warlike Tadatsune, who was in fact his mother's cousin and had favoured him since childhood. But his true motive in seeking this conference was statesmanly and honourable in the extreme, for such bloody rivalry was inimical to him, and he intended to plead for a truce, thus laying the foundation stone on which a bridge of trust and reason might be raised between the warring Taira factions.

Leaving his wife and children in the care of the remaining Guardsmen, the General set out with two cohorts for the headquarters of his uncle. As darkness fell they entered the field of sunflowers in which Tadatsune's army was billeted, and were duly escorted to the warlord's pavilion.

The old warrior fell on the General's neck and embraced him most fondly, for he had not laid eyes on his nephew since he had left the provinces to take up his exalted post in the Capital. Food and drink were called for, and Tadatsune would hear every detail of the sorry events which had led to the General's exile. 'A nest of spies and intrigue!' he snorted, running his finger lustily along the sharp blade of his sword. 'Stay with us here,

Motosuke. We are rude enough, but straightforward in our dealings.'

The General declined the offer with many expressions of gratitude, and began to put his case for a peaceful solution to the conflict. As the night and the arguments wore on, however, he saw that Tadatsune would not easily relent, and that he must utilise all the skills of diplomacy which he had formerly held in contempt. Near dawn, when his reserves were all but exhausted and his hopes at their lowest ebb, the old warlord surprised him by agreeing to a compromise. So it happened that as the moon sank below the horizon the two men raised their cups in a toast to the end of dissension, and to the future unity and security of the Taira.

Bleary-eyed but satisfied, the General rose to bid farewell to his uncle, but at that moment a great cacophony of horns and shouts rang out, signalling an enemy attack. Half-dressed, the soldiers scurried to their posts as a rain of arrows fell on the encampment. Throwing a sword to the General, Tadatsune cried angrily: 'You see how our Taira cousins make peace with us?' Then, with a loud war-whoop, he sallied out among the sunflowers.

The General was greatly saddened, but being in his bones a man of action, he had no choice but to defend his kinsmen, and so he hoisted his sword and followed Tadatsune into the field of war.

Unbeknown to both men, however, the aggressors were not Taira at all, but troops under the command of the famed captain Minamoto Yorinobu, who was at that time Governor of Kai. Yorinobu had been commissioned by his brother Yorimitsu – who, we will recall, had now replaced the General as Minister of War – to bring

Tadatsune to order, and in the process to annex as many Taira lands as possible.

Although a veteran of sixty, Yorinobu was still the wiliest of tacticians, and had had Tadatsune's camp surrounded for some hours. Accordingly his troops pressed forward from all points of the compass, repeatedly outflanking those portions of the Taira army which attempted to retreat, and dispatching them without mercy. As for the General, before he had taken thirty steps, a pitiless blow from a Minamoto sword struck him from behind, felling him instantly, and his head, detached from his body, lolled away among the snapped and broken heads of the sunflowers, while his eyes stared open in blind surprise at this view from the edge of paradise.

With the definitive rout of the Taira, and the position of his Minamoto allies once more secured, we might assume that our Lord Atsumichi rejoiced to see the summit of his ambitions gloriously achieved. Shocking to relate, then, that the Prince chose this very zenith to hang himself most suddenly in a woodshed, leaving behind him neither testament nor apologia. The Regent and his Ministers were utterly at a loss to explain the tragedy, and none of the ladies of the Court could understand what fault-line had opened under the great noble and precipitated such a mean and drastic demise – except perhaps the peerless poet, Izumi Shikibu, who of all women knew how to keep her counsel.

And if no more was heard of Onogoro and her lover, we may assume that they found sanctuary in some forgotten hamlet in the Eastern Mountains, where the cattle are lean and black and the smell of wild garlic is sharp in the woods. Let us hope, then, that the gods in their mercy grant the Oshidori couple a robust happiness, and a life long enough to learn from. For are not all things frail and fleeting, and does not the wind blow the years through us like fallen blossoms?